Here's w
the _Holly_

MW00936277

"Gemma Halliday's witty, entertaining writing style shines through in her new book! I look forward to seeing lots more of Tina as this series continues. A fun read!"
—*Fresh Fiction*

"(*HOLLYWOOD SCANDALS*) is a great start to a new series that I will definitely be following as Halliday writes the kind of books that just make you smile and put you in a great mood. They're just so enjoyable and I would without a doubt recommend this book to romance and mystery readers alike."
—*Enchanted By Books*

"(*HOLLYWOOD SCANDALS*) is very well written with smart and funny dialogue. It is a well-paced story that is thoroughly enjoyable with a mystery, a little romance, and a lot of laughs. Readers are sure to enjoy this delightful tale which is highly recommended."
—*Romance Reviews Today*

"The latest in the Hollywood Headlines series is 320 pages of pure fun. Halliday has created yet another laugh-out-loud whodunit. She breathes life into her mystery with a rich cast of vivid, pulp-fiction type characters and a heroine worth rooting for. 4 1/2 stars!"
—*RT Book Reviews*

BOOKS BY GEMMA HALLIDAY

High Heels Mysteries
Spying in High Heels
Killer in High Heels
Undercover in High Heels
Christmas in High Heels
(short story)
Alibi in High Heels
Mayhem in High Heels
Honeymoon in High Heels
(short story)
Sweetheart in High Heels
(short story)
Fearless in High Heels
Danger in High Heels
Homicide in High Heels
Deadly in High Heels
Suspect in High Heels
Peril in High Heels
Jeopardy in High Heels

Wine & Dine Mysteries
A Sip Before Dying
Chocolate Covered Death
Victim in the Vineyard
Marriage, Merlot & Murder
Death in Wine Country
Fashion, Rosé & Foul Play
Witness at the Winery

Hollywood Headlines
Mysteries
Hollywood Scandals
Hollywood Secrets
Hollywood Confessions
Hollywood Holiday
(short story)
Hollywood Deception

Marty Hudson Mysteries
Sherlock Holmes and the Case
of the Brash Blonde
Sherlock Holmes and the Case
of the Disappearing Diva
Sherlock Holmes and the Case
of the Wealthy Widow

Tahoe Tessie Mysteries
Luck Be A Lady
Hey Big Spender
Baby It's Cold Outside
(holiday short story)

Jamie Bond Mysteries
Unbreakable Bond
Secret Bond
Bond Bombshell
(short story)
Lethal Bond
Dangerous Bond
Bond Ambition
(short story)
Fatal Bond
Deadly Bond

Hartley Grace Featherstone
Mysteries
Deadly Cool
Social Suicide
Wicked Games

Other Works
Play Dead
Viva Las Vegas
A High Heels Haunting
Watching You (short story)
Confessions of a Bombshell
Bandit (short story)

HOLLYWOOD HOMICIDE

a Hollywood Headlines mystery

GEMMA HALLIDAY

AND

ANNE MARIE STODDARD

HOLLYWOOD HOMICIDE

CHAPTER ONE

———

"Tina, all I can see is your head," I told the purple-haired woman sitting across the table from me.

Tina Bender, my friend and co-worker at the *L.A. Informer,* ignored me as she happily munched on a shrimp verde taco. "Ohmigod, these things are to die for," she said through a mouthful of food. She swallowed. "Seriously, have you tried them?"

It was a Friday afternoon, and we were seated on the patio outside Jose's Taco Casa, a hole-in-the-wall Mexican restaurant in Encino. I'd specifically requested this table for its location behind a large potted arrangement of cacti. I'd also chosen this exact seat. Thanks to Tina and the plants, I couldn't be seen from the street—but I had a perfect view of the comings and goings of about half the block. That is, when Tina wasn't leaning over and obstructing it. I was tempted to push her backward into one of the thorny cacti if she didn't get out of the way.

Kidding! Mostly...

"Scoot left," I instructed, tilting my body sideways in the chair to aim my camera past her.

"Oh. Sorry," she said, inching to the left. "But I thought this was a lunch date." She looked pointedly down at my full plate. "You haven't even touched your food."

"I'm having dinner with Trace tonight," I replied, putting the camera lens back up to my eye. "I need to reserve my appetite."

Tina snorted. "You won't be satisfying your appetite for *food*, honey."

I lowered the camera, giving her an exaggerated eye roll. "Very funny, Bender." Though, I kinda hoped she was right on some level. "He won't say where we're going," I told her. "But I do know it's someplace swanky. He asked me to wear something nice."

Tina grinned at me. "Of course he did. Do you ever *not* go somewhere swanky?"

I stuck my tongue out. She had a point, though. Trace Brody was one of Hollywood's hottest commodities and a bona fide movie star. How a tabloid paparazzo like me had been lucky enough to grab his attentions, I was still not sure. But thankfully, I had. For the past few months Trace and I had been an item, and last month I'd actually heard him use the words "girl" and "friend" together. Which was a big step in a Hollywood relationship, knowing how the tabloids jumped on words like those. (At least, we did at the *Informer*!)

I set down my camera and grabbed a triangle of my quesadilla, chewing slowly as I savored the melted cheese. After a second bite, I made a show of dabbing at my mouth with a napkin. "There," I said, tossing the crumpled paper ball onto my plate. "I ate something. Better?"

Tina's lips quirked. "Yep." She gestured to my camera. "Carry on."

I refocused the lens of my Nikon and located the shop window once again. A leggy young woman with long black hair stepped into my line of vision. "Bingo."

I'd been trailing Joanie Parker all morning, and I'd finally hit pay dirt. The raven-haired starlet had burst onto the reality TV scene a couple of years ago as a recurring side character on *The Real Co-eds of Beverly Hills*. While she'd kept her backstory as ambiguous as the origin of her plump lips, she'd quickly made a career out of being famous. My favorite sort of celebrity—the kind who needed media attention like most people needed air. However today the tabloid princess was not only sans her usual pound and a half of makeup (Was that an actual pimple I saw? Oh, lucky day!), but she had also shed her designer threads in favor of a pair of baggy pants, a white, grungy (and not in the trendy way) tank top, and a pink camouflage trucker hat. "Must be laundry day at Chateau Parker," I muttered. If Tina and I hadn't been stealthily following her all over LA that morning, I wouldn't have recognized her.

"Maybe she's going for incognito," Tina said, peeking over her shoulder at the dressed-down diva across the street.

"Don't turn around!" I whispered. "I don't want to tip her off that she's being photographed." I snapped away, clicking shot after shot of Joanie bending over in her saggy pants. She scooped up her pooch, a little teacup Pomeranian named Isabelle, and let the fluffy little pup give her a dog slobber facial. It was an adorable moment, though Joanie's expression in the photos wasn't exactly flattering. "I almost feel bad about this," I admitted to Tina, who had turned her attention to the menu.

"Husband with her?" she asked.

Joanie was married to NFL linebacker Antoine Parker, and their relationship was a notoriously tumultuous one. Joanie had even tried to stab him with a stiletto heel last month outside a Malibu restaurant. Unfortunately, I hadn't been following her that night.

I shook my head. "Nope. Just the dog."

"Hold that thought." Tina signaled a passing waiter and ordered us each a pineapple margarita. "I don't care what Felix thinks—we're expensing these," she said when the server was gone. "He can't expect us to spy on the rich and famous on an empty stomach. And of course we need something to wash down the food." She grinned. Felix Dunn was our notoriously cheap editor in chief. I silently wished Tina luck in getting him to pay for our lunch.

"Now, why would you feel bad about snapping a few pics of Joanie Parker? You're just doing your job," Tina reasoned once our order was in.

I shrugged. "I don't know," I said, my face still glued to the viewfinder. "Without all those reality show cameras following her, Joanie seems like a pretty normal girl." I watched the young woman hug the little Pomeranian to her chest. "She's just trying to spend a little quality time with her dog."

"Celebrities: they're just like us," Tina joked. "If we bathed in champagne and ate caviar for breakfast."

I smiled. "I know, I know. The price of fame." It was what Trace had often told me. Did he mind being hounded by paparazzi as he tried to take his girlfriend (God, I loved that word.) out for a romantic dinner? Sometimes. But he said he'd mind even more if the paparazzi suddenly *weren't* interested.

As I watched through the viewfinder, a young woman approached Joanie. She wore a polo shirt with the *Hollywood Hounds Grooming* logo on the breast pocket. The woman took the Pomeranian from Joanie's outstretched hands and carried her over to a large silver basin, where she began to rinse the tiny pup. Joanie took a seat in a chair and flipped through a magazine. I couldn't help but notice her own face was on the cover.

Another woman in the same uniform walked over to Joanie and offered her a clear plastic cup of water. The reality star took a sip and immediately spat it out on the floor at the stunned groomer's feet. Then Joanie shot out of her chair, yelling at the poor woman. Though I'd admittedly acquired decent lip-reading skills over years of spying on celebs from afar, her mouth was moving too fast for my eyes to keep up. But it was clear from the body language that the groomer was getting a heck of a dressing down. I wondered at her crime—serving tap instead of bottled water?

My well-trained trigger finger wasted no time in snapping at least a dozen photos of the whole incident. Photos that were definitely going to land in Felix's inbox before the afternoon was over.

"On second thought, I don't feel so bad about it after all," I told Tina, who had swiveled in her seat to watch the action as well.

"I'll drink to that," she said as our server swooped by to place a margarita in front of each of us.

I smiled and clinked my glass to hers. "Cheers."

*   *   *

Later that evening, I'd traded my jeans and green halter top for a sexy little black number that looked très chic with my blonde hair worn long and loose. Before stepping behind the lens for the *Informer,* I'd made a living (barely) as a model, so dressing up for Trace's shindigs was sort of like saying hello to my former self. And knowing how to pose beside him on the red carpets was like riding a bike: it came back in a way that was almost natural to me. Almost. As much as I enjoyed playing dress-up with Trace now and then, I was keenly aware that I now felt more comfortable being the one taking photos of celebs instead of being photographed.

Tonight, Trace had informed me in the car that he was treating me to dinner at Urasawa, Beverly Hills' most exclusive Japanese eatery. The upscale restaurant was known to be primarily frequented by billionaires and celebrities. Because of this, the parking lot was a feeding frenzy of paparazzi, camping out all evening and jockeying for a position near the entrance, where they could snap the best photos of the evening's patrons. (I knew because I was frequently one of them—the campers not the patrons.) I turned my face away from the parade of cameras as Trace guided me toward the burgundy carpet at the restaurant's entrance.

We had almost reached the open double doors when one photographer called out to us. Well, more specifically, called out to *me*.

"Hey there, Cammy," said a familiar voice. "Give us a smile!"

"Yeah, *pretend* like you belong on that red carpet," came a second, almost identical voice.

I stopped short, letting go of Trace as I turned to glare at the two men pointing their cameras my way.

Mike and Eddie were twin brothers—and twin pains in my rear end. As the photographers for the *Informer's* rival paper, *Entertainment Daily*, it was practically their mission in life to make mine miserable whenever they could. Tonight the bearded brothers were stuffed into matching too-tight black T-shirts, their twin bellies spilling over their wrinkled jeans.

"Turn back around, sweetheart," Eddie said, flashing me a cheesy grin and drawing a circle in the air with his pointer finger. "We wanna get your good side." His gaze drifted down to my butt, and my face burned. More from anger than embarrassment.

"Why don't you guys go back to whatever sewer you crawled out of?" I whirled away from them before they could snap any more photos. Felix would not be happy if my face wound up on the pages of *ED*'s next issue.

"Hey, Trace!" Mike called, not giving up. He used his shirt to wipe Dorito crumbs off his camera lens and then looked up at my boyfriend, a malicious glint in his beady eyes. "Got any big roles coming up?"

Trace, ever the calm one when it came to the press, opened his mouth to respond.

But Eddie ran right over him. "Nah, man. You know no one in town will hire *Piranha Man*."

Trace shut his mouth with a click as the two brothers gleefully filmed the pained look on his face.

I winced at the *ED* brothers' low blow. At his agent's claims that the film would, quote-unquote, "elevate him to Leo DiCaprio status," Trace had signed on as the lead for a superhero project called *Piranha Man*. In it, he played a young scientist living in the Amazon who was transformed into a mutant human-fish hybrid after being bitten by a radioactive piranha. It had been promoted as the box office blowout of the summer. Unfortunately, when the movie finally hit theaters, it was the box office *bomb* of the season. So much so that several publications had called Trace's career "dead in the water." (Not the *Informer*, of course.)

"Let's go," I urged, trying to steer Trace away from the gruesome twosome.

But Trace instead shot the two a bright smile. "I'm not here to talk about my career tonight." He pulled me closer. "Tonight all I care about is spending quality time with my leading lady." Trace pivoted on his feet, sliding a hand around my back, and dipped me in a steamy, sweet kiss that made me absolutely weak in the knees. It was so…Hollywood. *Dreamy sigh.*

Our lip lock was met with a chorus of whistles and cheers from the other photographers and a couple of boos from Mike and Eddie. And, of course, the all-too-familiar *click, click, click* of camera shutters sounded all around us. As Trace released me, I straightened, feeling flushed and breathless. Score one for the Hollywood heartthrob.

"That ought to keep them happy for a while," he whispered to me with a wink as he led me inside.

I'll say!

Once inside the restaurant, Trace and I were seated in plush velour seats on opposite sides of a marble-topped table. A server took our drink orders and then hurried away.

I perused the menu, trying to decide between the California roll and tofu ginger soup. "Everything sounds delicious," I remarked.

"Order whatever you like." Trace reached across the table to take my hand in his. "Tonight is about making you happy." His eyes sparkled as he lightly stroked my fingers, sending shivers all the way to my toes.

"In that case," I said, smirking, "I'll have one of everything on the menu."

Trace didn't flinch. "Sounds great." He pushed his menu aside without even looking at it. "I'll have the same."

I arched a brow at him. "I was kidding."

He shrugged. "Like I said—as long as you're happy, I'm happy."

I narrowed my eyes at him. While the dreamy kiss had been awesome, this line felt out of character. Or maybe I should say it felt more like he was *playing* a character from one of his romantic comedy flicks. In fact, that line felt eerily like the one that he'd delivered to his high school sweetheart in *Only You for Me*.

"What's going on?" I asked. "If I didn't know any better, I'd think you were buttering me up for something."

His expression turned to mock innocence. "I don't know what you mean."

He wasn't *that* good of an actor.

But before I could interrogate him, the server returned and set down our bottle of sake. After we'd ordered not *quite* everything on the menu (though between us, we'd come pretty darn close), Trace met my gaze again. He sucked in a breath and forced it slowly back out. "I've got something I need to talk to you about."

Oh boy. My stomach clenched. I knew when a guy said he wanted to have a "talk," it was never good. Suddenly I wasn't hungry anymore. "What about?" I asked, trying to keep an even tone. Had we *girlfriend-ed* too soon? Had Mike & Eddie hit a nerve? Was I yesterday's news already?

Trace must have seen the apprehension on my face, as he quickly assured me, "It's nothing bad. There's just a career opportunity that's come up, and, well, I think I'm going to take it. But I wanted to talk to you about it first."

Relief washed over me. "That's great," I told him, meaning it. Any opportunity to cleanse the public's palate of *Piranha Man* was a good one. "Is it an action flick? Comedy?" I paused. "Romance?" I silently prayed not the last. Trace had been engaged to his last romantic co-star, an A-list Hollywood starlet. It was when their relationship had suddenly ended that he'd confessed his attraction to me. I'd hardly been able to believe it then. I still sometimes pinched myself, sure I'd wake up any minute to find our whole romance was just a dream produced by falling asleep on my couch after drinking too much Chardonnay while watching his film *You've Got Email.* But the idea of him being with another hot leading lady in intimate scenes didn't fill me with a lot of happy thoughts.

Luckily, Trace shook his head. "No, it's…it's not a feature. It's TV."

"That's new. So, what's the role?" I asked, swirling sake in my tiny glass.

Trace cleared his throat. He looked down at his napkin. He sucked in a deep breath. All of which made a small red flag start to rise in the back of my mind.

"Trace?"

"The role is a man whose relationship is in trouble."

"That sounds like ninety-nine percent of all relationship movies." I thought for a moment. "So I'm guessing more of a drama?"

"Oh, I expect drama alright." I noticed Trace still wasn't making eye contact.

That tiny red flag began waving in the back of my mind. "Who's the lead actress?"

"That's the part I want to talk to you about," he said, eyes still on the napkin, voice low, perfectly white teeth nibbling his perfectly plump bottom lip.

I took a mental deep breath. "Okay. Who?" I asked, bracing myself for the worst. Busty Sophia Vergara? Flirty Emma Stone? Seductive Jennifer Lawrence?

Trace finally lifted his eyes to meet mine. "It's you, Cam."

"Me?" I blinked at him. "I-I don't understand. I'm not an actress," I said, pointing out the obvious.

Trace darted a look around the room. "As you may have noticed, I'm not exactly anyone's first pick for all the top roles lately. Or any roles, for that matter." He gave a self-deprecating chuckle before clearing his throat again. "Anyway, my agent called this morning with an opportunity. You've seen that show *Celebrity Relationship Rehab*, right?"

Celebrity Relationship Rehab was pretty much every woman in America's guilty pleasure—including mine. Tina and I cleared our schedules every Tuesday night at nine to sit on my couch, sharing takeout and a bottle of wine as we watched doomed celebrity couples endure group therapy sessions with the renowned marriage counselors and real-life couple, Doctors William and Georgia Meriwether. Couples talked about their feelings and competed against other famous duos in ridiculous trust-building exercises. Each episode was chock full o' drama, catfights, and those awkward confessionals where each star gossips about the other contestants behind their backs. I absolutely ate it up.

I nodded. "Of course. Who hasn't?" I felt my mental hamster slowing turning on his wheel as it sunk in what Trace was getting at. "Wait a minute…don't tell me…"

"It's just for a week."

"No way!" I shook my head so hard that the restaurant wobbled in my vision.

"My agent says it'll be a piece of cake. We'll only be filming a couple hours a day."

"No."

"The rest of the time it will be like we're on vacation."

I gave him a *get real* look. "Have you seen the show, Trace? Those couples are a train wreck."

He at least had the decency to look guilty. "Just one week," he repeated. "It'll be over before you know it. We do a few silly drills, talk about our relationship, and—bam!—it's over."

Another thought occurred to me. "What will we be saying about our relationship?"

He gave me a blank look.

"It is relationship *rehab*," I emphasized. Okay, so maybe things between Trace and I hadn't been ideal lately, what with the stress of his career teetering on the edge and my odd hours at the *Informer*, but I hadn't thought we needed rehab.

Doubt crept into my belly. Did we? Admittedly we came from different sides of the tracks…or freeways, as the case might be in LA. He was VIP, and I was behind the velvet rope.

Trace studied me for a moment, his expression unreadable. Finally, that boyish grin pulled his lips up at the corners. "Don't be silly," he said, reaching out to cup my chin in the palm of his hand. "We're fine. We're more than fine." He quirked an eyebrow. "You know those shows are completely staged, right? All the arguments between the couples—it's fake. It's just to raise the ratings. People tune in to see who's going to try to rip whose hair out or which couple is going to finally call it quits." He rolled his eyes. "For some reason, people seem to love that kind of crap."

My cheeks colored. Clearly Trace didn't know about my reality TV habit. "Right. So, what does that mean? We just stage a few fights?"

He shrugged. "All the couples do. It's not that hard." He leaned in. "Please. My agent thinks it might be the opportunity I've been waiting for to win back my audience after The Film That Must Not Be Named."

I took a deep breath. I had a bad feeling I was going to live to regret this…

"If you honestly think it will help, I'll do it."

"Really?" Hope lit up his eyes, and my heart melted a little.

"Really," I sighed. Okay, so spending a week with Trace didn't sound all *that* bad. We'd finally have some time to reconnect. Felix was probably going to flip, but if I promised it would be a week-long working vacation full of awkward celebrity photo ops, maybe I could smooth things over. If the show was anything like last season, there was bound to be at least a couple alcoholic starlets, a few Botoxed beauty queens, and maybe even a member or two of a Hollywood royal family—like the Kardashians.

"But you owe me one," I cautioned him.

Trace grinned. "I promise I'll find a way to make it up to you."

"Oh, yeah?" I raised a playful eyebrow at him. "Starting tonight?"

"Anything you want."

"In that case," I said, leaning forward, "have the server box up our food, and let's take this party to your place."

Maybe this wouldn't be so bad after all...

CHAPTER TWO

———

On Monday morning, Trace and I loaded our bags into a chauffeur-driven stretch Hummer and were whisked off to a secluded location tucked away in Malibu. Though it was a short distance, the LA traffic prolonged the trip by nearly an hour. I dozed off, nestling my head in the crook of Trace's neck. I was dreaming of a poolside vacation (complete with warm sun, cool drinks, and my hot, naked boyfriend) when he roused me with a gentle kiss. "We're almost there, Cam."

I blinked at him and yawned, stretching my arms above my head. "Is it too late to stop for Starbucks?" I asked, only half kidding. Caffeine would go a long way toward making the rest of the morning tolerable. When we arrived, we were set to meet the producer, crew, and other cast members for *Celebrity Relationship Rehab*—all of which filled me with anxiety. It didn't help that I'd been up late the night before, hiding out in John Travolta's bushes for a candid photo of him late-night bingeing.

Trace smirked. "You're probably going to want something stronger than coffee. I'm sure there's a bar somewhere on the property."

I knew for a fact that there would be several. I stifled another yawn and turned to gaze out the window as the stretch Hummer pulled up to a large gated property. The driver pressed a button on the call box and gave security our names, and then the double doors swung open to grant us entrance. A long driveway wound through a grove of trees, whose purpose I assumed was to hide the estate from nosy fans—and from the paparazzi.

That irony was not lost on me. Or my editor, for that matter. Felix had reluctantly given me the time off on the condition that I give him all the dirt on everyone as soon as I got back. As he well knew, the encyclopedia-sized set of nondisclosures I'd been forced to sign meant I couldn't leak him anything from the set…but after I got home, it was all fair game. As Felix had reminded me, just because I was away from the office didn't mean I wasn't on the clock. "Week-long *working* vacation," he'd said. "Emphasis on *working*."

As the estate came into view, a low whistle of appreciation escaped me. Though I'd never missed an episode of *CRR*, seeing the property on my tiny television just didn't do it justice. Up close, it made the Playboy Mansion look like a kiddie clubhouse. A cluster of cream-colored buildings stood before us, surrounded by palm trees and exotic flowers of every color imaginable. There was a man-made lake to the left of the complex, with a small island in the middle. Several canoes lined the shore closest to us. I had a sudden vision of a moonlit boat ride with Trace. Maybe the next week wouldn't be so bad.

"Wow, this place is nice," Trace said, craning his neck out the window.

"There are worse places I could spend a vacation," I admitted.

Our driver pulled the car to a stop in front of the largest building. An ornate fountain comprised of mermaid statues stood in front of the marble steps leading to the mansion's mahogany double doors. They swung open just as the driver began unloading our luggage from the back of the Hummer. A man in a sharp gray suit waddled down the steps, waving to us as he spoke into a headset. He was short—I'd put him at around five-foot-two at the most—and from the dirty look he was giving our six-foot-tall driver, I had a sneaky suspicion he had a Napoleon complex.

"Jonathan Reisner," he said in his nasal voice. He took first Trace's hand and then mine, pumping them up and down. "I'm the executive producer of *Celebrity Relationship Rehab*."

"Pleased to meet you," I said, returning his handshake. Anyone who watched reality television knew the man's name. Reisner Productions was the company behind all of the most scandalous shows, from *So You Think You Can Pole Dance?* to *Real Mistresses of Los Angeles. Celebrity Relationship Rehab* was Reisner's most popular project, so I wasn't surprised to see him on the premises. In fact, I'd been hoping he would be there. The rumor around Tinsel Town was that the married father of two was having an affair with his twenty-something assistant, Phillip, though no one had been able to catch them in the act.

Mr. Reisner led Trace and me inside, and my gaze swept the foyer and great hall, taking in the white stone floor, black and gray accent rugs, and sleek, black leather couches and high-backed chairs. I recognized the furniture, which was arranged in a circle pattern, from previous seasons of the show. This was where our group therapy sessions would take place. The room was teeming with life, as nearly a dozen men and women darted about, setting up cameras and other equipment. A slender redhead with a heart-shaped face and bright blue eyes stood behind a tripod, aiming her lens toward the door. She peeked out from behind the camera as we entered. Our eyes met, and she gave me a shy smile before ducking back behind the camera again.

I smiled back and made a mental note to find her later. In my experience, it almost always paid off to befriend the "invisible" staff. Some of my juiciest leads had come from housekeepers, hairstylists, and even a dog sitter. I would need a crew member or two in my back pocket if I was going to score any good behind-the-scenes gossip to send to the *Informer.*

One of Mr. Reisner's assistants clipped a tiny microphone to the collar of my sleeveless blouse, and then the producer led us down a long hallway into a cozy room with a fireplace, shelves of books, three tan leather sofas, and several members of the camera crew already busy at work. Two couples were already seated, sipping champagne as they made sure the cameras caught their good sides while waiting for the rest of the participants to arrive.

My heart fluttered with excitement as I recognized the man settled on the first couch. It was the chart-topping rapper Ice Kreme. I'd trailed Ice a few times over the last couple of years as his music career had taken off. While he was just my height and a hundred pounds soaking wet, his rough-around-the-edges persona could rival any gangsta rapper. His hair was a close-cropped light brown, his jacket two sizes too big, and his designer sneakers a gleaming white that looked fresh off the shelves. He capped off the outfit with a sneer and an unlit cigarette dangling between his lips that looked somewhere between Biggie Smalls and Justin Bieber.

Ice sat with his arm around a gorgeous brunette with tanned skin and brown doe eyes. She looked to be in her midtwenties and sported a rock the size of a nickel on her left ring finger.

The rapper's gaze flitted briefly over my chest as we approached. He made a show of grabbing his crotch to adjust his pants and then sat up straight on the couch. "Dang, shorty," he said, tucking his cigarette behind his ear. "You fly as they come, girl."

"Uh, thanks," I said, moving closer to Trace and squeezing his arm. I glanced at the woman beside Ice, but she didn't seem to mind that he'd been checking me out.

Ice stood up and held out his hand in a fist, bumping it against Trace's. "Yo, dawg! That one movie you did, *Die Tough?* That was awesome!" He grinned. "I tried to get one of my rhymes on the soundtrack, but it didn't work out. I guess my beats are just too fresh."

"Thanks, man," Trace said, flashing him a modest grin.

Ice's fiancée smiled warmly as we took the open seats next to her on the couch and accepted glass flutes of champagne from one of the production assistants.

"I'm Apple," she said, fluttering her long lashes. "Apple Pie."

I nearly choked on my champagne. Ice Kreme and Apple Pie? Really? I wondered which had come first—the stage name or the couplehood with the dairy dessert—as I shook her outstretched hand. "Nice to meet you, Apple." I'm proud to say I didn't bust up laughing as I said the name out loud. I gestured to her fiancé. "How did you two get together?"

She let out an airy giggle. "Ice recruited me for one of his music videos. He's a big fan of my work."

"Your work?" I asked, sipping my champagne.

She batted her fake lashes some more. "I do adult films."

I hid my reaction behind a cough as I looked her over. Apple's profession honestly shouldn't have been that surprising. Her lips and boobs were clearly fake, and her skintight, black leather miniskirt and hot pink tube top ensemble, paired with gold hoop earrings and six-inch stilettos, practically screamed "sex."

"Interesting," I mumbled, wondering what I'd gotten myself into.

I cast a glance at the other couple, seated on a sofa opposite us. A middle-aged man with thick dark eyebrows and jet black (possibly dyed?) hair stared back. I could tell from the expectant look on his face that he was waiting for recognition to strike me. I had to admit, he did look vaguely familiar.

I leaned toward Apple and whispered, "Do you know who he is?"

"Dirk Price," she provided in her own confidentially low voice. "You know, the soap actor?"

"Riiiight." I nodded. While I wasn't a devotee of the daytime drama, anyone who had ever seen *The Charming & the Reckless* would know that name. Dirk had been a fixture on the show for the last twenty-plus years, portraying the handsome Dr. Spencer Carlin.

"Cameron Dakota," I said to the man by way of introducing myself. Clearly the name was lost on him. "Uh, Trace Brody's girlfriend."

Dirk smiled wanly. "Well, I'm sure *I* need no introduction."

"Of course. You're Dirk Price. You play Dr. Spencer Carlin." I sent a quick wink Apple's way. She covered a smile with a sip of champagne.

Dirk didn't seem to notice either, looking pleased. "I've won two Daytime Emmys for the role, you know."

I hadn't, but I nodded anyway.

He squeezed the hand of the woman sitting next to him. "This is my wife, Ellen."

The woman turned to stare down her nose at me. "Ellen *Bents*," she said, as if I should already know her name as well. The fact that I didn't must have shown on my face, as she added, "*Lead* anchorwoman for *US Evening News*." She fluffed her sandy blonde hair and smoothed a tiny wrinkle in her navy blue skirt, which matched her blazer.

"Oh snap!" Ice exclaimed, taking sudden interest in our exchange. "You *are* that news lady. I knew you looked familiar."

That won a half smile from Ellen, though at the expense of her husband's ego. Dirk scowled, seemingly jealous that Ice had recognized her first.

"I always wanted to do the news," Apple chirped.

Ellen arched one eyebrow at Apple, her gaze going to the hemline of the younger woman's skirt which barely covered her panties. At least, I hoped the porn star was wearing panties. "You? Really?" she said.

Apple's cheeks colored. "I auditioned to be a weather girl once, anyway," she added more quietly.

I turned back to study Ellen Bents. Though her outfit, hair, and makeup were perfectly put-together, there were age lines creasing the corners of her eyes and mouth. I put both her and Dirk probably in their late-forties to early-fifties. While Dirk looked excited to be here, his wife fidgeted awkwardly, as if totally out of her element.

The sound of heels echoing loudly down the hallway drew my attention to the room's entrance. "They'd better have champagne in there," a female voice called. "I'm ready to get my drink on." A few moments later, a familiar woman with slick black hair stepped into the room.

I stifled a shout of glee at my good luck. The woman entering the room was none other than my most recent tabloid prey, Joanie Parker! I'd died and gone to paparazzi heaven.

Her hips swayed and her sleek ponytail whipped back and forth as she strutted toward us. Her teacup Pomeranian, Isabelle, peeked its tiny head out of the purse on her arm.

Joanie's husband, NFL linebacker Antoine Parker, trailed in after her. The broad-shouldered hulk took a seat on the couch across the room, his expression stoic. Joanie perched beside him and accepted a glass of champagne when it was offered to her by one of the production assistants. She took a sip and then sighed. "That's so much better," she said, setting her pooch-filled purse on the floor at her feet. "The traffic on the drive here was brutal. If I had to spend another minute in that limo I was going to freaking lose it."

"Well, now that everyone is here…" Jonathan Reisner trailed off from the doorway, making a motion with his hands for the cameras to swivel his way.

Once they did, he stepped aside with a flourish to reveal a man and woman I recognized as the show's hosts entering the room, Doctors William and Georgia Meriwether. The man was tall, his brown hair streaked with gray. He wore a thick mustache that twitched slightly as he looked from Apple to Joanie to me. While I expected a therapist to be assessing in his gaze, something about the way his jaw moved when his eyes lingered on my legs made me cringe. I tugged my hemline before turning my attention to the other host.

She was stick-thin and pale, with dark hair fixed in a tight bun and a pair of maroon glasses perched on the bridge of her crooked nose. Her assessing eyes and arched eyebrows made her look severe and a little judgmental. I wondered if that was natural or created by the makeup team specifically for the show. My cheeks warmed when she caught me sizing her up and returned my appraising look with one of her own. Her lips pulled down in a scowl. Apparently she didn't like what she saw as much as her husband did.

"Everyone, allow me to present your hosts for this season of *Celebrity Relationship Rehab*, Doctors William and Georgia Meriwether," Mr. Reisner said, gesturing to the couple.

Everyone mumbled some greeting or another.

Ice gave a "'Sup."

Trace nodded toward the couple. I did a little wave.

Dirk stiffly shook Dr. Georgia's hand without looking her in the eyes, as if he were already wary of being sent to the principal's office.

Apple jumped up from her seat. "I'm such a huge fan," she gushed, moving to shake their hands. She flashed Dr. Georgia a bright smile. "My name's Apple. Apple Pie. I've read both of your books, Dr. Meriwether. I thought *How to Love and Be Loved in the New Millennium* was especially brilliant. If anyone can help us resolve our issues, it's you."

I felt my eyebrows reach for the ceiling. Apple hadn't struck me as the reading type. A glance around the room told me the rest of the participants seemed equally surprised.

Dr. Georgia studied Apple for a moment. "That's nice." She paused, brow furrowed. "What did you say your name was? Cherry? Pumpkin?"

"Apple." The younger woman's face fell.

"Yes, right." Dr. Georgia nodded. "Apple." She gestured to the sofas. "If you'll take your seat, we can get started."

Dropping her gaze to the floor, Apple uttered a meek apology and returned to the sofa. I couldn't help but feel a little sorry for her.

"Now, then." Dr. Georgia looked around the room, her expression stern. "You're all here because there are aspects of your relationships that need to improve in order to strengthen your bond with your partner. Dr. William and I are here to help you achieve that." She nodded to her husband.

A wan smile appeared beneath his mustache. "Identifying your problems is the first step." He shot a look at Dirk. "Let's start with you."

We watched as, one by one, each couple identified the flaws in their relationships to the doctors and viewing public. I listened to Dirk Price's woeful bravado as he confessed that he and Ellen were looking to rekindle the spark in the marriage. Ellen's expression as her husband spoke about their lack of romance was pure poker face. I wondered how much of what he was saying was truth and how much was for the cameras. Ellen definitely didn't strike me as the overly romantic type.

Joanie and her husband were next, and I struggled not to laugh when Joanie whined that her hulk of a husband didn't appreciate her the way she deserved.

"Do you have anything to add, Antoine?" Dr. Georgia asked after Joanie had voiced her complaints.

The man shrugged his beefy shoulders. "No." He placed a hand the size of a grapefruit on his wife's shoulder, staring at her in adoration. Clearly he was the strong silent type.

"Yo, I always appreciate my woman," Ice interjected, sticking his tongue out in a lewd gesture as he eyed Apple. She giggled and leaned in for a kiss.

"And according to Apple, perhaps you appreciate her a little *too* much," Dr. Georgia said, her eyes flicking to a production assistant who had clearly prepped her beforehand.

Apple frowned. "Well, he does have a violent streak. His anger scares me sometimes."

I bit my lip to keep from laughing. The scrawny Ice Kreme looked about as dangerous as a muppet.

"And you, Trace?" Dr. Georgia asked, turning her attention to us. "What do you hope to improve in your relationship with Cameron?"

I froze. Drat. We hadn't thought to work out a story as to why we were here. I opened my mouth to stall.

But apparently Trace didn't need the help.

"We have almost nothing in common," he said easily. "And our careers are often at odds with each other."

I bit my lip, trying not to take it personally that he could come up with a "flaw" in our relationship so quickly.

Then he added to it. "Plus she's got a jealous streak."

I shot a look at Trace. Don't push it, buddy…

"She gets insecure about me working with beautiful actresses."

I felt my eyes narrow as he struck the teeny tiniest of nerves in me. "Beautiful as opposed to…me?" I asked even as I felt the camera pivot my way, gearing up for action.

Trace's eyes flitted briefly toward me before going back toward the main camera. "Of course not. You know you're beautiful to me, inside and out," he told the viewing audience. Then he sent a look in Dr. William's direction as if to say, *See what I mean?*

I clamped my jaw shut.

"Wait a minute," Joanie Parker piped up from across the room, her eyes narrowing in on me. "You look familiar. Have we met?"

I gulped. Had she spotted me the other day? "Maybe I just have one of those faces," I said, a nervous laugh bubbling out of my throat. I was pretty sure I'd stayed well-hidden during my little photo session. She couldn't have seen me…could she?

"No. Wait a minute." Joanie's brow furrowed, and she appeared thoughtful. A moment later, recognition dawned, and her head jerked back. "Oh, no way!" she said, her eyes blazing. "You're that chick who was snapping pictures of my pimple at the dog groomer. You're freaking paparazzi." She spat the last word as if it'd left a bad taste in her mouth.

Uh-oh. Busted.

All eyes snapped my way, and to my dismay, so did several cameras.

"Ooh, catfight," Ice sang, throwing a few air punches and stomping his glaringly white sneakers on the floor. He nodded at me encouragingly. "Come on, blondie. You can take her."

"I'm not *taking* anyone," I protested.

"Well, I'm not doing this show with paparazzi here!" Joanie yelled to our hosts. "I'm calling my agent!"

"It's alright, Cam," Trace said, directly to Camera One. "I've got your back."

I narrowed my eyes at him. I could have sworn that was a line from *Die Tough*. My boyfriend was in cameras-rolling mode. Then again, wasn't this what we were here for? Create a little on-screen drama and revive his career? Well, I'd checked that box already.

Dirk Price shot a look to the cameras and must have decided he needed a little air time himself. "Ladies, please!" he boomed, coming to stand between us, his hands out as if to block any punches we might throw at one another. "There's no need for such cruel words and violence. For goodness' sake, we've barely known each other five minutes, and already there's so much tension amongst the women."

Ellen Bents rolled her eyes, as if she couldn't believe her husband had talked her into this.

"Chicks," Ice muttered under his breath.

"Well, now that we all know why you're here," Dr. William interjected, taking control of the room again, "my wife and I will do our best to dig deep into your relationships and find the root of your problems. Over the next week, you will participate in activities designed to target your issues and strengthen your relationship. We'll also hold private one-on-one interviews and couples' counseling sessions, and you'll all be expected to visit the confession booth, where you'll reflect on each day's events and your progress toward achieving a rehabilitated bond with your mate."

"It's going to be a lot of hard work," Dr. Georgia chimed in, putting a hand on her husband's arm. "There will be a lot of pain before the real healing can take place, but we're going to do everything in our power to repair each of these broken relationships." She paused for dramatic effect. "Even if it kills us."

CHAPTER THREE

———

When filming wrapped on the introduction segment, we were dismissed to our rooms to get settled and change for the first drill.

Trace moved to grab my hand as we followed Dirk and Ellen up the stairs to the second floor. I pulled it out of his reach.

He shot me a look. "Everything okay?"

"Insecure?" I whispered at him. "Really?"

He grinned, looking almost charming enough to make me forget what he'd told the therapists. "Come on, you know that was for show, right?"

"Why couldn't *you* be the one with insecurity issues and jealousy?"

"Babe." He pulled me in and kissed my cheek. "Look, if it makes you feel better, we'll just focus on our career differences instead, okay?"

I paused, feeling myself soften as I let him grab my hand.

"I mean, I'm sure it won't be hard to convince everyone that a tabloid reporter and an actor aren't suited for each other." He laughed.

I frowned. Why didn't that make me feel any better?

"Hey, by the way, that girl fight?" Trace said. "Very nice."

I did a little mock curtsey. "Thank you."

"Kinda sexy, even." He lifted his eyebrows suggestively.

I gave him a playful punch in the arm as he pushed open the door to the suite. Though any lingering anger I might have had toward Trace melted away when I took in the room. The walls were a pale, silvery blue, and a large window allowed lots of natural light to filter into the room. Furnishings were plush, the closets huge, and the decor interior designer-chic.

"Nice," Trace said, opening the little fridge and grabbing a Corona. He popped the top of the beer and tilted his head back as he took a long swig. "I could get used to this place," he said, looking around the room.

"Me too," I agreed. I slipped off my sandals, relishing the feel of the velvety soft carpet underneath my bare toes. I padded toward a pair of French doors that led outside. Pushing them open, I stepped out onto a private balcony that boasted a breathtaking view of the hills and the ocean in the distance. I inhaled deeply, letting my pulse return to something resembling a normal speed after that introduction-by-fire to the show. While the other participants might be professional actors, this was not my thing. The altercation had been a little too real for my liking, making me all the more nervous for what the next week held.

*   *   *

Almost an hour later, we stood outside in a larger garden behind the main building of the estate, preparing to begin the first Relationship Rehab challenge. Trace and I had arrived first and seated ourselves under the shade of a large palm tree as we watched the crew set up to film the drill. The red-haired camera girl walked past us carrying a boom pole and a shotgun microphone. I caught her attention with a friendly wave. She glanced around to make sure nobody was watching before offering me a shy smile and a little wave of her own. I had a good feeling I'd be able to win her over.

The other show contestants trickled into the garden over the next twenty minutes. Apple and Ice Kreme arrived first, followed by Joanie and Antoine Parker, minus Joanie's canine sidekick this time. Ellen and Dirk were last to enter the garden, with the soap star announcing their arrival loudly and in the direction of the nearest camera. "I'm sorry we've kept you waiting," he said in his booming stage voice. "My wife and I were making sweet, passionate love."

I stifled a snort of laughter at the scowl on Ellen's face, wondering how the drama king and the ice queen had ever gotten together.

I barely heard Ellen mumble to her husband as she joined him on a wrought iron bench. "Save your overacting for your little daytime drama, *dear*."

Dirk's smile froze on his face as he muttered back, "The *little* drama that pays your bills?"

Hmm...interesting. I almost felt ashamed of myself for eavesdropping on such an intimate conversation.

Almost.

"Shut up," she hissed back. "I'm here, aren't I? Doing this stupid little show for you."

Dirk shot a quick glance toward the nearest camera, and it was easy to read his wary expression. We'd yet to be lapel miked, and I could tell he was hoping the boom microphones weren't picking up this particular conversation.

"Drop the attitude and put on a smile," he ordered.

The corners of Ellen's mouth curved up slowly, as if each inch pained her. "What does it matter? This is such a petty, fake reality show. This whole thing is a colossal waste of my time. I don't know how I let you talk me into coming here in the first place."

Dirk raised an eyebrow in her direction. "Don't you?" The two words were loaded with meaning. Exactly what meaning I wasn't sure...but I sincerely hoped I'd have the opportunity to find out. If I played my cards right, maybe I'd even get a killer story out of it.

Dirk and Ellen were still arguing in hushed tones when Mr. Reisner led Drs. William and Georgia Meriwether into the garden a few minutes later. Dr. William immediately took notice of their spat and walked over to them. "Save some of that for the camera, Price," he said.

At the mention of face time on film, I would've expected the soap star to perk up—so I was surprised when Dirk's back stiffened. He narrowed his eyes at the host. "There will be plenty of drama to go around, I'm sure," he said quietly.

Dr. Georgia spoke up as the promised cameras did start rolling. "Now that everyone is here, we can begin our first drill."

I watched all eyes go to her, the same mix of dread and excitement I felt mirrored on my fellow rehabbers' faces.

"This challenge was designed to test your ability to communicate with your partner, both as a listener and when expressing your thoughts and ideas." Dr. Georgia walked over to a table that held four blindfolds. "During this exercise, the women will be blindfolded. We have a small obstacle course set up at the other end of the garden. The men will direct their blindfolded partners through the course by shouting instructions."

The revelation received mixed reactions from the group. Joanie and Ellen groaned simultaneously, and Apple squealed in delight. "Cool! This reminds me of a game I used to play with my friends in grade school," she exclaimed.

"Which was how long ago for you? Last year?" Ellen grumbled. She crossed her slender arms over her chest. "I suppose I shouldn't be surprised we're playing childish games on a show like this."

For a moment, Apple looked wounded, but she quickly recovered. "Well, I think it'll be fun," she said brightly.

"I think so too, sweetheart," Dirk agreed, nodding emphatically. He shot his wife a dirty look.

Ice Kreme's expression darkened. "Don't call my woman 'sweetheart,' old man," he warned. "I can make a phone call to my boys back in the hood and have you curb stomped faster than you can say your own name. You feel me?"

Dirk put his hands up in a surrender motion. "I didn't mean anything by it! I call everyone sweetheart. Don't I, sweetheart?" he asked, turning to his wife.

Ellen shook her head, as if already fed up with the whole thing.

"Alright," Trace said loudly to break the tension. "Let's get this party started."

I couldn't help but notice that he said it right into the camera, accompanied by a high-wattage smile. I barely contained an eye roll.

While the men followed Dr. William toward an open space in the garden, members of the crew assisted the women in securing our blindfolds. My new redheaded, camera-toting friend volunteered to tie the cloth over my eyes. "My name is Bonnie, by the way," she said as she knotted the handkerchief.

"Nice to meet you, Bonnie," I replied, excited that she was opening up.

"Sorry I couldn't talk to you this morning."

"I take it Mr. Reisner doesn't like for you to interact with the guests?"

Though I couldn't see from behind the blindfold, I could hear the sarcasm edging into her voice. "He's worried that we might compromise the integrity of the filming process by giving our favorite contestants more camera time or something like that."

I snorted at *integrity*. Nothing about this process fit that particular word. "Well, I'm definitely not vying for more airtime," I assured her. "I prefer to be behind the camera myself."

"I heard," she admitted. "You're with the *Informer*."

I opened my mouth to respond, but before I had a chance, Bonnie grabbed my hand and carefully led me across the garden. I felt her hand move from my arm to the collar of my shirt as she covered up the microphone. "When you get to the third turn of the obstacle course, make sure you turn right," she whispered.

"Huh?"

"Just trust me," she said. "Your partner will tell you to go left, but you should go to the right."

I nodded my understanding. She was trying to help me. At least, I hoped she was. "Got it." I grinned in what I guessed was her direction. "Thanks, Bonnie."

When the rest of the group was in position, I heard Dr. William's voice. "The couple who completes the races in the shortest time will be treated to a romantic private dinner this evening. For one member of the pair with the worst time, there will be a less desirable fate waiting."

I bit my lip, not liking the ominous tone in his voice.

A shrill whistle pierced the air as our signal to start, followed by a series of shouts from my right.

"Yo, baby, I'm right here," I heard Ice yell to Apple. "Take about three steps forward and then two steps to your left."

"Joanie," Antoine Parker boomed from somewhere on my left.

"Where should I go, baby?" Joanie called in her whiny voice.

"Left" was his only response. Antoine Parker was a man of few words.

I felt my whole body strain to shut out the others and listen for Trace.

"Cam," he yelled. "Walk about four steps forward and then right."

I did as Trace instructed then followed his next set of orders, dropping to my knees and crawling under something that felt slightly damp and sticky. I climbed over hay bales and under wooden obstacles, all at Trace's urging, until I got to the third turn of the course.

"Alright, Cam. You're doing great," Trace called. "You're going to need to take about three steps to the left and then head straight forward. Got it?"

"The left?" I said uncertainly, remembering Bonnie the Camera Girl's warning. *Make sure you turn right.*

"Yes, the left. Come on—Joanie's gaining on you," Trace said.

I took a tentative step to the right, sweeping my foot on the ground in front of me as I felt around for anything that might trip me.

"I said left, Cam. Not right." Trace's tone was impatient. "Hurry up! Joanie's going to pass you."

I sensed movement beside me just moments before Joanie's arm brushed mine. "Out of my way, Tabloid Girl," she grumbled, giving me a shove.

"Hey!" I toppled backward, hitting a hay bale.

"Left," Antoine Parker's voice boomed.

"Thanks, baby," Joanie called. Then there was a shriek, followed by a loud splash. "*Antoine!*" Joanie screeched. "You oversize oaf! You led me into a freaking pit." She groaned. "What is this? Mud?"

My lips twitched at the sound, and I was tempted to adjust my blindfold. But Trace's voice was still urging me on, so I stepped gingerly to the right, around the edge of the mud pit toward him.

Mere seconds before I reached him, I heard Apple squeal with delight.

"I made it!" she cried. "Did I win?"

A hand reached out and pulled me forward. I tugged the blindfold off and looked up into Trace's eyes, noting the faint disappointment there. "It was close," Trace said, squeezing my shoulder. "You almost had it."

I turned to look at the course. Just to the left of my point of indecision was a pit of muddy water, half covered by a camouflaged tarp. The course had been booby trapped by the production team to make some starlet look like she'd just taken a mud bath. I shot a glance at Joanie, silently thanking Bonnie that *she* was that starlet and not me.

Joanie finished the drill, dripping with mud and spouting obscenities at her husband. "This is your fault!" she said, punching Antoine's shoulder. She crossed her slender arms over her chest as she seethed.

I'd have given anything to be able to snap a picture, but with the cameras on us, there was no chance of that.

Ice let out a hearty laugh at Joanie before grabbing Apple and celebrating their victory with a kiss so steamy it probably required an NC-17 rating. I had to look away, feeling my face grow warm.

Ellen was the last to complete the drill, and it was clear from the scowl on her face that she hadn't enjoyed the challenge in the least.

"Alright," Dr. Georgia called the group to attention. "Dr. William will now critique your performances." She gestured to her husband, who stepped forward.

Dr. William's usual smile was gone, replaced by an intense expression of discontent that made Simon Cowell look like Mr. Rogers. "The communication happening during that drill was frankly concerning—from all of you," he said. "I can see my wife and I have our work cut out for us if we hope to salvage any of your relationships."

While I knew this was all fake, I still felt a defensive lift of my chin as he spoke. I thought we'd done pretty well.

"Let's start with the last pair to complete the drill," Dr. William went on, gesturing to Dirk and Ellen. "It's clear Mrs.

Bents doesn't want to be here, yet you, Mr. Price, are so eager to have everyone's attention that you're putting your needs before those of your partner."

Before Dirk could answer, Dr. William turned to address Apple.

"I'm astonished that you felt this was appropriate attire for a relationship drill."

Apple blinked innocently, looking down at her tight shorts and shiny tube top.

"If you thought your scantily clad body would distract the other men long enough for you to steal the victory, it looks as if your plan worked. I caught both Mr. Parker and Mr. Brody ogling you during the race."

I turned toward Trace. Though he raised both hands in one of his signature I'm-innocent looks from his role in *The Defendant*, I detected a hint of color in his cheeks.

"Yo, dawg. You were checking out my woman?" Ice accused. He held up his thumb and forefinger in the shape of a gun and pointed it at Trace.

"That brings me to my next point, Mr. Kreme," Dr. William interrupted. "Her claims that you have crude and overly violent tendencies are certainly not unfounded. Perhaps you should tone down the tough, young punk front. You're trying too hard."

Ice stepped forward, chest puffed out. He got right in Dr. William's face. "Say that again, old man, and see what happens," he threatened, eyes squinting daggers at the host. For the first time, I had the feeling that maybe Ice wasn't all talk.

Dr. William didn't flinch, instead returning Ice's hateful stare. "Before this boot camp is over, you *will* learn to treat others with respect—and not just your fiancée."

Dr. Georgia grabbed her husband's arm and gently steered him away from the angry rapper. "Let's move on to the other couples' critiques, shall we?"

Dr. William turned his attention to Joanie Parker, his eyes lingering on her breasts in a way that made me cringe. "You were so focused on winning by any means necessary—including shoving other contestants and taking off your blindfold mid-race—"

"What?" I said.

Apple gasped. Ellen snorted in disgust.

"—that you not only ruined this drill for your husband," Dr. William continued, "who was working hard to guide you to the finish line, but you've also ruined it for yourself. Due to your cheating behavior, you are the loser of this challenge."

Joanie's eyes brimmed with fire, and she shook her head as Dr. William doled out her punishment.

"And your 'reward' will be to spend the night in the Doghouse."

"The *what*?" The look on Joanie's face was priceless.

Dr. William's face broke into what I could only describe as an evil smile. "The Doghouse is a special room we have set up for contestants who need a little time to reflect on their poor behavior. You like those fancy rooms you all are staying in?"

I watched several of the contestants nod.

"Well, the Doghouse has none of those amenities. It's fit for, well, a dog."

"Oh no! No freakin' way! I'm not staying in some Doghouse. I don't even let Isabelle sleep in a doghouse," she scoffed.

"I'll do it." Antoine Parker stepped forward and slid a protective arm around his wife. Several sets of eyes turned his way—likely as amazed at his selflessness as the fact that he'd spoken a full sentence for once rather than his usual one-word statements.

Dr. William shrugged. "Very well, Mr. Parker. But know that you're enabling your wife to walk all over you, and that is something you're going to have to confront head-on during the next week if you hope to become an equal in your marriage."

He paused, turning his gaze on Trace and me. "Now, that just leaves you two." His jaw clenched. "Miss Dakota, where do I even begin?"

I bit my lip.

"What *is* a member of the paparazzi doing in a relationship with a bonafide Hollywood star, anyway? Is your whole relationship a sham? A clever way for you to infiltrate the most tight-lipped and elite circles in Tinsel Town so you can print their secrets all over the pages of the so-called *news*paper you work for?"

I opened my mouth to defend myself but only managed a little squeak before he rode right over me.

"You failed to listen to Mr. Brody's instructions," Dr. William continued to dress me down, "which allowed Mrs. Parker to catch up to you. On the surface it would seem she got what she deserved for shoving you when she fell in the mud pit, but I can't help but wonder—did you mean for her to pass you? Did you know about the hidden mud pit? I'm sure you would have loved to print a picture or two of Joanie Parker covered in mud."

Dang, he was good. That last part was exactly what I'd been thinking. I suddenly wondered if maybe he wasn't a half-bad therapist at that. I forced myself not to look in Bonnie's direction. "That's absurd," I argued. "I had no idea about the mud pit. I was just disoriented from being blindfolded."

Dr. William tilted his chin, looking unconvinced. He moved on to criticize Trace for his own ineffective communication throughout the race, but I was barely listening.

I was still digesting Dr. William's accusations against me. While he'd been spot-on about my having insider info, the part about me using Trace was just mean. Only now it was also going to air on TV, and half the country would see me that way. I felt my cheeks flame. I hadn't been expecting to care so much what people thought, but as I looked at Trace, I did. His family would see this, his co-workers, his friends. Would they believe what Dr. William said? Sure, it was convenient that our relationship opened doors for a few juicy stories every now and then, but I would never use Trace just to get ahead.

Then again, weren't Trace and I doing just that here on this show? Using each other to further our respective careers?

I shook that disconcerting thought off and tried to tune back in to what the "good" doctors were saying.

Dr. Georgia officially announced Apple and Ice winners of the challenge. "And they will enjoy their prize this evening after our last drill. Which," she went on, "will begin in one hour in the great hall."

We were dismissed to clean up and prepare for the evening session. Trace took off ahead of me, catching up to Ice Kreme, presumably to try to smooth things over after Dr. William's accusation that he'd been making eyes at Apple. "Player" was not the image he'd come here to portray.

Apple fell in step beside me. "Are you okay?" she asked, slipping a slender arm around my shoulder. "That was rough, huh?"

I let out a short laugh. "Am I that easy to read?"

She nodded with a sympathetic smile. "Trace is clearly the only actor in your relationship."

"Well, this wasn't exactly my idea of a good time," I admitted. I met her gaze. "How are you still chipper?"

Apple smiled. "I just don't let it get to me. After all, that's what they do on these shows—at the beginning they have to tear you down so that they can build you back up. Dr. William had to exaggerate all of our issues for the audience so he can make an even bigger deal about our 'improvement' later." She made air quotes with her fingers. "Haven't you watched the show before?"

"Yes," I admitted. "I guess I just didn't realize how harsh the hosts are to the guests until I was in their cross hairs."

"Chin up," Apple said in her girlie voice. "I think I'm going to check out the pool before our next drill. I'll see you later." She gave me a quick smile. "I'm sure you and Trace are going to be just fine."

Yesterday, I wouldn't have had a doubt in my mind either. Today, however, I was feeling on a bit more shaky ground.

Trace wasn't in the suite when I got back. I figured it was taking him a while to soothe Ice's bruised ego. Either that, or there was a bromance brewing and they were sucking down Coronas together somewhere. I wasn't sure which scenario I was rooting for.

I took a shower, dried my hair, and dressed in a pair of skinny jeans, a silk tank, and heels. Then I took that off and put on a wrap dress and flats. Then I took that off and went back to the jeans. Knowing I was being constantly filmed had me second-guessing everything I'd packed. Two more discarded outfits later, I finally settled on gray leggings, a long cashmere sweater, and ballet flats. It was casual yet hip. Chic yet not trying to upstage my boyfriend who needed the camera on him to heal his wounded career.

At least I hoped.

Due to my wardrobe indecision, I was a few minutes late arriving downstairs for the evening challenge. Trace was already in the great hall, laughing at something Dirk had said. Ellen scowled at them, her Ice Queen face firmly in place. Joanie gave me the stink eye, jiggling her three-inch-heel-clad foot up and down impatiently. In contrast, Antoine looked like he was almost asleep in the chair beside her. Apple gave me a little wave from the sofa opposite, and Ice trailed in a few minutes later, a surly expression on his narrow face.

Everyone seemed both physically and emotionally drained after the day's first challenge, which didn't bode well for the rest of the boot camp. We chatted quietly amongst ourselves as we waited for the doctors to appear.

Nearly half an hour later, the hosts still hadn't arrived.

Joanie arched one perfectly shaped eyebrow. "Weren't we supposed to get started around six?" she asked impatiently. "What is the holdup?"

Antoine placed a beefy hand on her leg and squeezed gently. Joanie cast him an irritated glance but shut her mouth.

Apple fiddled with her too-short hem, glancing at the doorway every few seconds. Ice sighed heavily, rolling his eyes. Ellen inspected her nails, casting sidelong glances at the rest of us that I assumed we weren't supposed to see. And Dirk closed his eyes, leaning his head back on the sofa cushions as if he'd consumed one too many glasses of champagne earlier. I had to admit, even I was getting antsy. The longer we sat waiting, the worse tortures I could imagine the doctors inflicting on us.

The crew must have noticed our collective anxiety escalating, as cameras started circling the group like vultures—just waiting for one of us to crack.

Trace glanced at one of the cameras, then me, then the camera again. I couldn't help rolling my eyes at how hyper aware he was of being filmed.

"You know, I wish you had a better attitude about this whole thing, Cam," Trace huffed. Loudly. In the direction of the camera. I barely stifled another eye roll.

Instead, I arched one eyebrow his direction. "Excuse me?"

Trace coughed loudly then whispered to me, "Just play along." He finished his faux coughing fit then in his normal speaking voice addressed the camera again. "You know how much it means to me that we're on the show, trying to fix our relationship."

"Of course I do, *dear*," I said, tentatively "playing along" even though I wasn't sure I liked this particular game.

"If you really cared about me, you'd start taking this seriously."

"I am taking it seriously," I gritted through my teeth.

"I just saw you roll your eyes."

I narrowed said eyes at him. "I was rolling them at you, you—"

Luckily I was cut off by Dr. Georgia appearing in the doorway, putting an end to our fake(ish) argument. Her heels clicked loudly as she hurried into the room. "Sorry I'm late!" she exclaimed breathlessly, tugging at her skirt with one hand and smoothing her disheveled hair with the other. She glanced around the room, and her forehead wrinkled. "Where's William?"

"He wasn't with you?" The question came from one of the crew members setting up more equipment behind the sofa where Trace and I were seated.

Dr. Georgia shot him a look. "No," she said, her cheeks turning the faintest shade of pink. "I haven't seen him. I assumed he was already in here preparing for tonight's exercise."

The stocky cameraman dropped the cable he'd been unraveling and stepped out from behind the couch. He crossed the room and leaned in to whisper something to one of the production assistants, a wiry young man wearing a headset and cradling a tablet in his bony hands.

"Right," he said in response to whatever the older guy had told him. Then he hastily mashed the button on his headset. He spoke in a hushed voice, and I couldn't make out what he was saying. There was a pause as he waited for a response. When it came, he visibly paled. After muttering something to the stocky cameraman, the pair hurried out of the room.

A feeling of dread crept over me. "Something's wrong," I said quietly to Trace. "I can just feel it."

"Relax, Cam," he said, reaching over to tuck a wisp of my blonde hair behind my ear. "I'm sure everything's fine. And I'm sorry about putting you on the spot like that. When we get back to the room, we can put our heads together and plan our next argument."

"Gee, I can hardly wait," I muttered.

Another assistant came around and offered us each a glass of wine while we waited, but the drink did nothing to settle my nerves. I chewed my lip as I watched the minutes tick by on the large grandfather clock in the corner. What could be keeping Dr. William? Perhaps he'd fallen ill, or maybe there was some other production problem that required his immediate attention. But if either were the case, wouldn't Dr. Georgia know about it? The longer we waited, the more dread took up space in my chest.

At a quarter till eight, the doors to the room opened again, and we all turned in our seats, expecting to see the middle-aged host finally making his entrance. Instead, the young production assistant appeared, his complexion slightly greener than before. He scurried over to Dr. Georgia and took her arm, pulling her away from the group. I forced down the lump in my throat as I watched the kid rub the older woman's arm and whisper something in her ear.

Dr. Georgia staggered back a step, the blood draining from her face. She gasped loudly and then slumped to the floor as her knees buckled.

Apple leaned toward me. "What do you think happened?" she asked, her voice laced with fear.

As if on cue, Dr. Georgia Meriwether spoke. "He's dead!" she wailed. "My husband is dead!"

CHAPTER FOUR

———

Within the hour, the entire estate was swarming with police officers and crime scene technicians, making the set of the reality show look more like a crime drama—except for once there were no cameras rolling. The building was on lockdown, with the guests and crew all confined to the great hall—everyone except Mr. Reisner and Dr. Georgia. The producer had escorted her from the room shortly after receiving the news of her husband's death. My heart ached for the poor woman. While Dr. William hadn't been my favorite person, I hadn't wished him dead either.

The rest of us were only permitted to leave the great hall when it was our turn to deliver a statement. One by one, each celebrity or crew member was escorted into the booth where our show confessions were to be taped. When it was my turn to join the detective in the small room, Trace gave my fingers a light squeeze. I could tell the shock was taking a toll on him as well, as the slight crinkles at the corners of the eyes looked more pronounced than usual.

"It's going to be okay," he told me, though I wasn't sure which one of us he was trying to soothe.

I gave him as much of a reassuring smile as I could muster under the circumstances. I knew he only wanted to help calm my nerves, but he was wrong. How could everything be okay? A man was dead. And judging by the tight scrutiny we were suddenly under, I had a feeling it wasn't due to natural causes. People weren't usually interviewed like witnesses if a simple heart attack was in play.

The confession booth was located at the end of long hall near the front doors. Though it was the smallest room in the mansion, it was still plenty big enough to house a long bench facing a camera embedded into the opposite wall. There were no windows, and the stillness of the air around me gave me the feeling that the room was soundproof.

I perched on the bench's plush red cushion. Seated across from me, just below the camera on the wall, was a tall Hispanic man with a crooked nose and short black hair. "I'm Detective John Martinez," he said. "May I have your name please?"

"Cameron Dakota." I silently prayed he wouldn't ask about my profession. Being a member of the paparazzi, I didn't have the best rapport with law enforcement. They generally viewed us as a nuisance at best. Considering the circumstances we were meeting under, I didn't want to know what he might think of me at worst.

Detective Martinez studied me with dark eyes. "This must be upsetting for you, Miss Dakota," he remarked. "Being on the property at the time that a man was killed."

"Does that mean he was murdered?"

He ignored my question. "When was the last time you saw Mr. Meriwether?"

I chewed the inside of my lip. "Several hours ago. At our first drill. After that, I returned to our suite to shower and change for the evening challenge."

"Alone?"

I wasn't sure how he made that one word sound like such an accusation. "Trace was with Ice Kreme. I think."

"Let's just focus on you for the moment."

I swallowed hard, feeling guilty even though I knew all I'd done was take a shower.

The detective jotted something on his smart phone. Then he looked up at me. "Where is your suite located?" he asked.

"Upstairs and to the left," I replied.

"So it faces the back of the property?"

I bobbed my head. "Yes. We've got a nice view of the garden." Despite the cool temperature of the room, I felt a bead of perspiration on my forehead.

Martinez's brows pinched. "Interesting," he said, and I felt even more sweat forming under my arms. If we kept this up, I was going to walk out of here drenched—though, I supposed that was better than walking out in handcuffs. Not that the detective would have any reason to suspect me. I couldn't pinpoint why I suddenly felt so nervous.

"Can you see the gardening storage facility from your balcony as well?" the detective asked.

I blinked. "I'm not sure," I answered honestly. "I mean, not that I noticed. Is it like a toolshed?"

He didn't answer. Instead, he studied me for several long moments and then jotted something else on his notepad. "Alright. I think that's all I need for now. Thank you for your time, Miss Dakota." He rose and held open the door for me. "I'll be in touch if I have further questions. If you think of anything that could help, give me a call." He handed me his card.

"Sure," I said, trying to sound reassuring and not like I was trying to read between the lines of what he wasn't saying. Had William Meriwether been murdered in the gardening shed? If so, what had he been doing out there?

I returned to the great hall and took my seat next to Trace as a uniformed officer escorted Apple toward the door. She cast a nervous glance at me over her shoulder before disappearing from view. Joanie was leaning against Antoine, holding Isabelle in her lap. I found myself wondering how Joanie had obtained permission to bring the little fur ball with her to the set.

Ice was on the sofa next to the Parkers, complaining that he was supposed to be enjoying his romantic dinner prize right now. Dirk and Ellen were deep in conversation, their heads close together. I was pretty sure I overheard Ellen say the words "breaking news story." If I had to guess, I'd say she wasn't excited about being on this side of the news. Mostly because I had the same feeling. I could only imagine that Tina and her competition at the *Informer,* Allie Quick, were both already typing up their takes on the untimely death of Dr. Meriwether. I scanned the room, wondering if there was any way I'd be able to take a few quick shots with my phone to send Felix later. Though, the real story, it seemed, was out at the toolshed.

"I, uh, need to use the little girls' room," I said loudly to the room in general.

Joanie sent me a disgusted look, but no one else seemed to pay much attention. I tried to catch Trace's eye and sent him a *cover me* look. He winked back. I hoped that meant he got the message.

I quickly slipped down the hallway. But instead of going right toward the main floor powder room, I did a quick over-the-shoulder to make sure no one was watching before turning left into the billiard room and out a pair of French doors leading to the side of the house.

I took a minute to get my bearings in the now dark outdoors, but it didn't take long for me to figure out where the toolshed was. Lights and a crowd of people gathered a few yards away, near a small outbuilding almost surrounded by tall bushes.

I quickly made my way over, phone in hand, finger hovering over the shutter to snap any pics I could. No one paid much attention to me. Between the police officers, crime scene techs, and several members of the crew who were milling around on the outskirts of the action, it was a study in chaos. It was also effectively blocking any view I had of the action.

I wrapped my arms around myself to stave off the chill suddenly in the air as I glanced around for my fave female cameraperson. No such luck. I did spot one of the other crew I'd seen filming our obstacle course that day, though. A slightly overweight guy behind a bushy beard that looked like a crumb trapper to me. I quickly came to stand beside him.

"What's going on?" I asked, nodding to the shed.

Beard Guy shrugged. "I guess they're just looking for evidence and stuff. They took the body out a few minutes ago."

So Dr. William had died here. Which begged the next question… "Any idea what he was doing out here alone?" I asked.

Again with the shrug. "He was known to sneak off for a cigarette now and then." He paused, sending me a sheepish look. "His wife didn't like him smoking. This is one of the few places on the grounds where there aren't any cameras to catch him."

I glanced around. He was right—the small cameras mounted throughout the house and outdoor living areas were noticeably absent here. Then again, who wanted to see a toolshed on TV?

"Do they have any idea how he died?" I asked, gesturing to the uniformed officers.

"Dave, that's the sound guy, said he overheard someone say he was stabbed."

I cringed. While I'd covered murder before in my employment with the *Informer*, stabbing sounded messy enough to have my stomach lurching. I involuntarily took a step back from the shed. "That's terrible."

Beard nodded. "Dave said they questioned Carlos— that's the head of the landscaping crew."

"But they don't think Carlos killed him, do they?" I asked.

Beard shook his head. "Nah. They just wanted to know about the equipment. A window was busted in the shed, so they wanted to see if anything was missing or anything like that."

"They think he was stabbed with gardening equipment?" I asked, the lurching in my belly kicking up a notch.

"I dunno." Beard thought about it for a minute. "I guess so. Dave said the police think the doc must have stumbled on someone breaking into the shed and the burglar killed him. Sucks, right?"

I nodded my agreement as I digested that thought. While a theft gone wrong was a great murder theory, I didn't know why someone would try to steal gardening tools when there was a luxury estate just a few yards away. And how had the thief gotten onto the estate grounds to begin with? The set was teeming with cameras and security.

I took a couple quick pics of the crime scene techs then slipped away from the action, figuring I'd learned as much as I could in a believable bathroom break interval, and quickly made my way back to the main house. I arrived back in the great hall just in time to hear Mr. Reisner's assistant, Phillip, speaking to the group.

"…so the producers request that you go to your rooms for the evening. Please do not leave them until further notice."

"They want us to stay *here*?" I whispered to Trace as I slipped into the room beside him.

He nodded. "The detectives don't want anyone to leave the area." He paused. "And Mr. Reisner reminded us that we're still under contract to stay."

I blinked at him, not sure I was hearing right. "Seriously? Our host is dead!"

I must have said that last part a bit louder than intended, as several pairs of eyes turned my way. I lowered my voice before continuing. "They can't possibly be thinking the show must go on?" I asked.

Trace shrugged. "I doubt it. But there's probably going to be a boatload of nondisclosures to sign before they let us leave." A frown settled between his perfect eyebrows. "And none of this will likely air."

"Sorry." I laid a hand on his shoulder as we followed the other couples, trudging upstairs to our rooms. "I know how much you needed this show."

Trace gave me a small smile. "Yeah, well, it could be worse. I could be Dr. William."

"Very true," I admitted.

I watched the other couples disperse to their suites. Antoine did not, I noticed, go toward the Doghouse, instead following his wife into their plush suite two doors down from ours. I guess with our host gone, he was off the hook for that particular punishment.

As we entered our room and got ready for bed, I filled Trace in on what I'd learned outside about the doctor's death. Admittedly, it wasn't a lot. And all of it was hearsay. Felix was going to be sorely disappointed when I left tomorrow without any real info on the Murder at the Mansion (as my soon-to-be-typed-up headline would read). Maybe I could find a way to at least shoot a couple pics of the garden shed in the morning…

"Poor Dr. Georgia," Trace said, cutting into my thoughts. "One of the PAs had to practically carry her out. She was sobbing so hard."

I felt a pang of sympathy for her. I couldn't imagine Trace suddenly not being there. Not that Trace and I had been married for years like the doctors, but I imagined that just compounded her grief. "Did she go home?" I asked.

Trace shook his head. "The detectives specifically said they wanted us all to stay here. Even her."

I chewed my lip. That hardly seemed routine for a cut-and-dried burglary turned homicide. A burglary that just happened to have occurred in the one place on the estate without cameras and where the only loot to be had was gardening tools. If I had to guess, I'd say the detectives bought that theory about as much as I did.

Which meant someone had wanted our host dead...and that someone was likely still here.

* * *

Trace and I awoke early the next morning to a note on our door that we were to meet in the great hall at nine. We hastily showered, dressed, and re-packed both of our suitcases before complying, arriving only a few minutes late.

The air in the room was charged with energy. Dirk and Joanie were chatting animatedly, and even Ellen Bents seemed to be taking an interest in the conversation—at least, compared to her usual dour demeanor.

"What's going on?" Trace asked as we sank onto the couch next to Ice and Apple.

"Yo, check it! They've decided not to cancel the show," Ice said, bumping Trace's fist.

"Wait—what do you mean they're not canceling?" I asked, my mind trying to wrap around the news. I noticed two cameras set up in the far corner of the room. Were they rolling?

"You looked outside lately?" Ice asked.

I shook my head dumbly, admitting I hadn't.

"Dude, there are reporters and paparazzi swarming out there. We're all about to get tons of press." He grinned. "Just in time for me to drop my new album too."

"You're kidding," I said, still absorbing the shock.

"No, girl." Ice looked smug. "It's called *Hott Fudge Sunday*—that's Hott with two *T*s." He arched his brow and licked his lip. "If you're real nice, I might sneak you the track list for your little celebrity paper."

I shook my head. "No, I meant, how can they possibly continue the show?" But I realized I was talking to myself at that point. Ice had turned his attention to Trace, who seemed to have perked up at the news. I swallowed down the conflicted feeling in my gut. While I got that this was what he'd come to the show for in the first place—some press and screen time—the fact that he was getting it because someone had died left me feeling like I'd eaten a bad burrito for breakfast. Then again, it wasn't as if Dr. William had been in the running for Mr. Congeniality either. In fact, I'd have a hard time saying anything positive about the dead man.

I glanced around the room, wondering if anyone else was feeling conflicted.

Dirk seemed nothing but smiles, chatting to Joanie, who looked to be getting bored with whatever the older man was saying. Isabelle was in residence on her lap, squirming as if mirroring her owner's restlessness. Antoine had his arms folded over his chest, eyes at half-mast, looking like he hadn't slept much the night before. Ellen was rolling her eyes at her husband's every other word, as if this entire thing—murder and all—was beneath her. Apple seemed the only member of our party whose attitude had changed. She sat just on the other side of Ice, her brown eyes rimmed with red and the skin around them puffy. If I had to guess, I'd say she'd been crying. I wondered if it was over the dead man or some earlier argument with Ice.

I didn't get a chance to ask her as Jonathan Reisner entered the room, his round face red. "I don't care what newspaper they work for," he said angrily into his headset. "No press are allowed to speak to our hosts, guests, or the crew. If I hear that any of my staff have so much as blinked at a reporter, they'll never work in this industry again. Is that clear?" He didn't wait for a response before removing his headset from his ears and letting it hang around his thick neck. Plastering a smile on his face, he turned to address the celebs. "Good morning, ladies and gentlemen. I hope you all slept well despite the unfortunate events of last night."

"It was no easy task, I assure you," Dirk Price said in his loud, theatrical voice. "What a horrible tragedy."

Apple murmured her agreement.

"Anyway," Mr. Reisner continued. "As you all know by now, Dr. Georgia has decided to move forward with the show."

"This was her decision?" I asked, unable to keep the skepticism out of my voice.

Reisner nodded, not skipping a beat. "Of course. And I fully support her and hope that you will all remain on the estate to join us. After all, it would be a shame if any of you chose to leave and miss out on getting the help that you and your partner need." He gave me a pointed look.

I narrowed my eyes back at him. What he really meant was *you're all under contract and we'll sue you if you leave*.

"We're staying," Trace spoke up, patting my leg. He flashed Mr. Reisner one of his Oscar-worthy smiles. "Cam and I want nothing more than to remain on the show and work toward saving our relationship."

Speak for yourself, I thought. But I forced a neutral expression and nodded my agreement for the cameras.

"Glad to hear it." Mr. Reisner grinned. He addressed the full group. "Mrs. Meriwether will be down momentarily to begin our morning session. And I would appreciate it if none of you mentions the loss of her poor husband. Dr. Georgia only wants to focus on getting the eight of you the help that you need."

Again, I couldn't keep my inner skeptic from reading between the lines. Was the reason he didn't want us to mention Dr. William because it would upset the widow or because Dr. William would be taken out in the show's editing? And what about Dr. Georgia? Did she really want to continue the show even during her grief, or was she too being strong-armed under threat of litigations?

"Ah, here she is now," Reisner said, turning toward the hallway as Dr. Georgia stepped into the room.

I wasn't sure what I expected, but it certainly wasn't the calm, perfectly put together woman who sauntered into the room, staring down her nose at the lot of us. Her dark hair was once again styled in a tight, smooth bun, and her makeup was practically flawless. There wasn't so much as a single wrinkle in her black blouse and beige pantsuit.

"Good morning," she said, her tone somewhere between cheerful and businesslike. "Is everyone ready to begin today's group session?"

I blinked at her. Today's Dr. Georgia Meriwether looked nothing like the sobbing woman who'd apparently had to be all but carried up to her room the night before. Gone was any trace of a woman grieving the loss of her beloved husband. It was possible she was putting on a brave face for the cameras. Or maybe the crying yesterday had all been an act.

"I'm so sorry about your husband." The condolences came from Apple. She blinked her wide doe eyes tearfully at Mrs. Meriwether. Ice nudged his fiancée between the ribs, probably to remind her of Mr. Reisner's warning. Apple realized her mistake and ducked her head, her cheeks coloring.

"Thank you, dear." While Dr. Georgia continued to smile, something less pleasant flashed behind her dark eyes. Though whether it was grief, anger, or guilt I couldn't tell. "Now, let's get to today's first drill, shall we?"

* * *

The morning exercise did not go well. As police continued to filter in and out of the house, bagging and tagging items, we all pretended not to notice them. Some of us more successfully than others, as Dirk made dramatic gestures to the officers each time they came into view, commenting on how his "Emmy-winning complex character" (his words, not mine) on *The Charming & the Reckless* had once dated a detective so he knew all about police procedure. Ice, on the other hand, fidgeted nervously anytime someone in uniform walked through the room. Though whether it was because he had contraband in his suite or had anything to do with our dead host was anyone's guess.

The rest of us did our best to ignore the chaos as Dr. Georgia had us play a game *Newlywed Show* style to determine who knew their partner the best. We were each handed a small dry-erase board and marker. She asked a series of questions, and each time we were instructed to write down what we thought our partner's answer would be. Then we took turns telling the host our personal responses before our partners held up their boards to see if the answers matched.

By the end of the third round, it was apparent that Trace and I didn't know each other as well as we thought. He'd guessed that my favorite color was yellow (it was actually green), my favorite ice cream flavor was mint chocolate chip (it was chocolate hazelnut), and my favorite book was *Gone with the Wind* (it was *The Great Gatsby*). In turn, I'd incorrectly guessed his favorite action film starring someone other than himself (*True Lies*), the model of his first vehicle (Isuzu Rodeo), and his favorite Ninja Turtle (Raphael). Granted, I was pretty sure we were all distracted by the fact that a murder had taken place on the grounds. The silly drills seemed even more silly in light of the heavy situations around us.

And the fact that there was possibly a murderer in our midst.

That thought sent a shiver down my back despite the heated arguments going on around me between the not-so-happy couples over their *Newlywed* game answers.

Apple and Ice Kreme were the winners yet again, though Joanie and Antoine had been a close second—with no credit to Joanie, of course. Antoine had answered each question about his wife correctly, but the diva had only managed to score one point. Dr. Georgia had asked Joanie to name Antoine's favorite pro-football team. I suspected Joanie only knew the right answer because it was the team that currently funded her expensive lifestyle.

It wasn't until the group broke for lunch that I had a moment to myself. The first thing I did was take a totally unsuspicious walk around the grounds, ending at the garden shed. Unfortunately, it was still surrounded by yellow crime scene tape, a uniformed officer, and a handful of crime scene techs. My chances of getting any new info there were slim to waif. So I doubled back toward the house, hoping to find a friendly crewmember who might be willing to give me the latest deets on the police's investigation. But as I made my way past the pairs of lounge chairs beside the swimming pool, a pair of raised voices caught my attention. Joanie and Antoine.

The swimming pool was located behind the opposite end of the mansion from our rooms. Tiki torches lined the brick patio, already burning despite the fact that it was just past noon, and I suspected there were cameras hidden in the bushes.

I skirted the back of the poolside bar, coming up behind the couple from an angle I hoped they couldn't see.

"…keep your fool mouth shut," Joanie hissed at Antoine.

I felt an eyebrow rise. As far as I'd seen, no one could accuse Antoine of being overly chatty. I wondered what, in particular, he was supposed to keep quiet about.

I couldn't quite make out the reply he mumbled, his voice much lower now at Joanie's insistence. I took a step closer to the couple, crouching down behind the bushes.

"If anyone finds out, I swear it will be on you," Joanie warned.

"On me?" Antoine countered, loudly enough for me to hear the sudden anger in his voice. "If it weren't for you, we wouldn't be in this mess."

"Yeah, well, you better just stick to our story." She paused. "Especially now that the cops are crawling all over."

I felt my other eyebrow rise. This was getting good.

"Relax," Antoine told her, back to his usual one-word answer.

"Relax? Easy for you to say. There's no way the police will find out about—"

A soft buzzing emanated from my pocket.

Joanie froze mid-sentence. "What was that?" She sat up straight, her head swiveling around the pool area.

I ducked down, praying the bushes provided enough cover as I fumbled in my pocket to silence my phone.

"What was what?" Antoine asked.

"That buzzing sound? Is someone recording us?"

Antoine shrugged. "It's probably just a bug."

"It wasn't a bug, you idiot. I know what a bug sounds like. And for the record…" The rest of Joanie's dressing down was lost to me as I quickly duck-walked back behind the bar and out of earshot.

I glanced down at my phone. A missed call from Felix.

I looked around the patio. Too many cameras here. I headed toward the stone path to the right before I dialed his number and waited. The call was picked up before the second ring.

"Cam!" Felix barked. "What the hell is going on there?"

"Hello to you too, boss," I said dryly.

"Yes, yes. Hello," he muttered in his lilting British accent. "Do you hate your job?"

My stomach clenched. "No, I—"

"Then if you bloody well want to keep doing it, I suggest you send me something that I can run as soon as possible. Tell me—if I have an employee on site, then why on God's green earth did I have to find out about William Meriwether's death through a Twitter update from *Entertainment Daily*?"

Yikes. "We've been on lockdown," I said, covering my mouth with one hand to obstruct the view of any cameras trying to catch my end of the conversation. "They've instructed everyone not to talk to the press, including the guests."

"Cam, do I have to remind you that you *are* the press?" Felix sounded irritated.

"I know that," I said evenly. The brick path I'd been following ended at the foot of another beautiful garden. I surveyed the area to make sure I was still alone. "But as *you* well know, I can't send you anything, " I said, reminding him about the nondisclosures I'd signed. "If anything shows up in the *Informer*, they'll know it was from me."

"Don't worry," Felix reassured me very nonreassuringly. "We'll just quote an 'anonymous source.'"

I rolled my eyes. "Anonymous? Really? How stupid do you think the producers are?"

Felix paused. "Is that a trick question?"

I couldn't help the snort of laughter that escaped me. Good point.

"Cam, this is a murder," Felix continued. "Every news outlet on the West Coast will be covering it. We can't be the only ones not reporting on it."

He had a point. "I'll see what I can do," I hedged. I was keenly aware that all I had at the moment was a couple photos of crime scene techs. "I'll try to get something good later today."

"I don't need *good*. I need *now*. Do you realize I had to print a stock photo of the coroner's van with Tina's story today?"

"Sorry. But it's not like there's a lot to see here."

"Well, you bloody well send me *something* soon." He paused. "At least tell me you've heard some useful inside info. From the producers?"

I bit my lip. "Not really."

"The wife?"

"Not exactly."

"The police?"

"Not entirely."

I heard Felix sigh on the other end. He may have even muttered a curse word.

"Look," I said, trying to think of anything to calm my boss down. "All I know is that the official theory the police are floating is burglary gone wrong."

"Right. The police report Tina found said some gardening equipment was missing," Felix said. I could hear him typing in the background, no doubt taking notes.

"Well, I'm not sure I agree," I said.

Felix pounced. "Oh? Why not?"

I bit my lip again, hesitant to voice my concerns without more to back them up.

"Dakota? Talk to me," Felix pressed.

I sighed. "Well, the only thing missing is some stuff from a garden shed. And with all of the expensive recording equipment here, not to mention the furnishings and fittings in the house and the designer labels on all the items the guests have brought with them, why would someone steal gardening equipment?"

"Go on," Felix said.

"Okay, and why risk breaking into this place at all? There are cameras practically everywhere—except for the building where William was stabbed."

"Convenient, that," Felix noted.

"Exactly."

"So, you think the killer knew that area was camera-free ahead of time?" Felix asked, following my line of thinking.

I nodded, even though I knew he couldn't see me. "I do. Which means they must be connected to the show."

"Which means this was not about a burglary at all. This was personal," he said, coming to the same conclusion I had.

"Possibly," I replied. "But that still leaves a large number of suspects. It could have been someone on the crew or one of the producers or even one of the other celebrities."

"I like the sound of that," Felix said. "Please tell me Joanie doesn't have an alibi."

I couldn't help a smile. "Wouldn't that be nice?" I thought back to the conversation I'd overheard at the pool. "I don't know about her being a killer, but I do think she's hiding something."

"Oh really?" I could hear the lift in Felix's voice.

"No idea what yet."

"Well then, what are you doing talking to me? Get on it!"

"Gee, brilliant idea." I refrained from saying that I'd been doing just that when he'd interrupted me and blown my cover. Because, well, I *did* like my job. "Listen, the police are being pretty tight-lipped about the details of Dr. William's death. If I had a little more to go on, I might be able to ask more of the right kind of questions," I hinted, knowing Felix had amassed at least a few connections in law enforcement during his career as a reporter.

"I'll see what kind of info I can get from my contacts at the station," he promised. "Check in with me later. I want the inside story on all this!"

"On it!" I agreed before hanging up.

CHAPTER FIVE

———

I slipped back into the house just in time for lunch. A buffet had been set up in the kitchen for the celebs, and I found the rest of our motley crew filling their plates and casting sidelong glances at each other. While it might not have solidified in everyone's heads yet that a killer walked among us, trust was clearly in low supply. Either that or everyone was waiting for the next opportunity to pick a fight and get more airtime.

I grabbed a plate of caprese salad and a bowl of mushroom and green pea risotto and took a seat at the large eat-in kitchen table next to Trace. He was already halfway through his meal and deep in conversation with Ice. It appeared the two were fast becoming BFFs. In addition to the absent Parker couple, I noticed Apple was nowhere to be seen as well.

"No, dawg, you gotta understand the world I come from," Ice was telling Trace. "Ain't nothing ever been handed to me, you feel?"

Except a recording contract, I silently thought.

"It's all about hard work, right?" Trace answered around a bite of pepperoni pizza.

"Totally," Ice agreed, nodding beneath an oversize ball cap.

"That's why we're all here. To put in the hard work on our relationships." Trace shot a look in my direction.

I managed a semifake smile, keeping my lips closed around a particularly large bite. But it didn't matter. I was pretty sure Trace was talking to the camera mounted on the wall behind us and not me anyway.

"Well, that's gonna be harder to do now that the doc's been *iced*."

I paused mid-chew at the way the rapper lingered on that last word, infusing it with meaning. "What do you mean 'iced'?" I asked. After swallowing of course.

The rapper shrugged his shoulders, feigning innocence. "You know, someone took the dude out."

I watched him fiddle with the roll on his plate.

"You think he was murdered?" Ellen Bents piped up, coming to the table with a plate filled with what looked like a Caesar salad minus the croutons, cheese, and dressing.

"Seems kinda obvious, right? Like, what with us bein' interrogated by the police and all."

"Interrogated? Who was interrogated?" Dirk asked, trailing behind his wife with a similar-looking plate of rabbit food.

"The police questioned all of us, right?" I asked.

Everyone at the table nodded.

But Ice said, "There's a difference between questions and accusations, blondie. I mean, I guess with my rep and all and the fact I ain't got no alibi…" He trailed off, letting the statement hang in the air.

"Wait—are you trying to say *you* killed Dr. William?" Trace jumped in. (Presumably he was asking Ice, but he said it to camera.)

Ice held up two hands in an innocent gesture. "Yo, dawg, I never said that. I'm just sayin' I'm the obvious suspect here." He paused then leaned his elbows on the table. "But *if* I did it, you all better believe I'd get away with that shiz."

I raised an eyebrow his way. "'If' you did it?"

He shrugged again. "Girl, I know better than to cop to something like murder on camera." He nodded toward the electronic eye on the wall.

We all glanced toward it, the room growing self-consciously quiet.

Except for Dirk, who presumably didn't want to be left out of any drama, as he jumped in with, "The police asked about my alibi as well."

His wife shot him a look that clearly said *shut up.*

"What? They did." He shoved a bite of salad into his mouth and chewed loudly.

"Did you have one?" I asked in what I hoped was a nonchalant tone.

He shifted in his seat. "Of course. I was with my wife."

Ellen stared at her plate as if undressed lettuce was the most interesting thing in the world.

"Where were you two?" I pressed.

Both of them answered at the same time.

"In the—" Ellen started.

"Upstairs," Dirk said.

Ellen clamped her mouth shut and went back to her staring contest with her lunch.

Ice barked out a sharp laugh. "Dude, you two better get your stories straight."

"There's nothing to get straight," Dirk shot back. "We were *upstairs. In the* bedroom. Napping."

"Sure you were, dude." Ice smirked.

"Well, what about you?" Dirk said, clearly on the defensive now. "You said you have no alibi. Where were *you*?"

"Just chillin'." Ice grinned.

"Chillin' where?" Trace asked.

"Here 'n' there."

If I didn't know better, I'd say Ice was *trying* to look like a likely suspect.

"Was Apple with you?" I asked.

He shook his head. "Nah. She popped a bikini and headed to the pool for some laps."

"You didn't join her?"

Ice shook his head. "Swimmin's not my thing, shorty. Ain't a lot of pools in the hood, you know?"

I thought I saw Ellen roll her eyes. But it might have just been a nervous twitch.

"I don't know how you can all speak so casually about a tragic death," she said, her tone the same one my principal had used in sixth grade when I'd been caught cutting class in the girls' bathroom. "A member of the medical profession is dead."

Ice blew air out through his teeth in a dismissive gesture. "That guy was a chump. You see how he was lookin' at my girl? Ain't nothin' tragic about him getting capped."

"Hey, maybe you should calm down," Trace said, his eyes flitting to the camera again.

"Or maybe I should just get more riled up. See what happens then, huh?" Ice jutted his chin toward Dirk. "I seen *you* lookin' at Apple too, old man."

Dirk paused, a piece of lettuce hanging from the side of his mouth. "Me?" he said, his voice an octave higher.

"You heard me. You keep your eyeballs off my girl. Or, who knows, maybe you'll be *iced* next."

While the last line was delivered straight into the camera, it still sent a small chill up my spine. Clearly Ice was playing the bad boy for the viewing public. But it begged the question: Just how much was an act…and how violent was his jealous temper?

* * *

After lunch, the police and crime scene techs finally all cleared out, and we were corralled into the billiard room to await our one-on-one interviews with Dr. Georgia. The men started up a game of pool, Joanie buried her nose in her phone, Apple told me all about her latest agent and how he was going to get her some "totes big" roles, and Ellen took to the serious business of scowling at everyone over everything. As I halfway listened to Apple, my fingers itched to grab my phone and take some candid shots of the other celebs to send to Felix. While I still didn't really have anything, maybe Tina could come up with some of her creative, alliterative headlines to go with them. Like *Parker Picks off Pompous Prat*. I'll admit, I kinda liked the idea of Joanie as the killer. Sure, I had no evidence, motive, or theories. Just headlines. Oh, how about *Joanie Jumps Jaded Jackas—*

"Cameron?" one of the PAs called my name from the doorway, making me jump as if my guilty thoughts were written across my face.

"Yes?"

"Dr. Georgia is ready for you now."

I let out a mental sigh of relief and got up from the sofa, following him to a small room near the front of the mansion. Two garnet wingback chairs were set up in the center of the room, facing each other. Between them was a small table with a silver tray that held a coffee pot and two mugs. Dr. Georgia was already seated in one of the chairs. On either side of her, members of the film crew were adjusting their cameras. One was facing the host, and the other pointed toward the chair where I would be seated for the interview.

"Please have a seat, Miss Dakota."

I did, studying my host as a sound guy clipped a microphone to my lapel. If she'd been crying, the show's makeup artist had done a bang-up job of hiding it. Dr. Georgia seemed calm, composed, and like it was just another day at the office for her. She skimmed through a sheaf of notes on a clipboard, taking last-minute direction from one of the crew about which way to face under the lights. I thought back to Dr. William's wandering eye and wondered how much of the doctors' relationship had been real and how much had been for the cameras. I felt a sudden pang of sympathy for her.

Once the lights were set, my mike tested, and the crew situated behind the cameras, Dr. Georgia turned to me. "Let's get started." She crossed one leg over the other and leaned forward, studying me from behind her maroon glasses. "In order to get to the root of the problems you're experiencing with your partner, I'll need to know more about your relationship. Tell me, Cameron, how did you and Trace meet?"

"It's sort of a funny story." I paused. "Well maybe not funny, ha-ha," I amended, thinking back to the kidnapping and homicide that had thrown Trace and me together originally. "But more funny, interesting."

Dr. Georgia raised an eyebrow my way.

I cleared my throat self-consciously. "I was working on a story about him for the *L.A. Informer*," I said, keeping it simple.

"I see." A ghost of a smile crossed her lips. "A celebrity photographer and a Hollywood star finding love. I'm sure that made quite the headline."

My mouth twitched. "You could say that."

Dr. Georgia's eyes narrowed. "You've never suspected that perhaps Mr. Brody began a relationship with you in order to control the image portrayed of him in your paper?"

I blinked at her. I hadn't been ready for that one. "Uh, no. I mean, I'm not sure he'd even need to."

"Really?" She arched an eyebrow at me. "And how long have you been dating now?"

I licked my lips. "A few months."

"Not even a year yet?" She raised her eyebrows. "So it's *very* new."

I felt some of my earlier sympathy fading. I forced the smile to remain plastered across my face. "Well, I wouldn't say *very*—"

"Next question," she said, cutting me off. "What do you feel is your biggest challenge in your relationship with Mr. Brody?"

I thought for a moment. "Making time for each other," I replied truthfully. My hours were odd by definition, and Trace had been working hard to repair his image, doing meet and greets, talk shows, and just about anything else his agent could book him to keep his name in the spotlight. Case in point: this farce of a show.

"We're both very focused on our careers, so it's a struggle to balance that with making time for each other."

Dr. Georgia looked off camera toward one of the producers. He waved his hand in the air as if telling her to move on. Apparently my answers weren't interesting enough. She flipped to the second page on her clipboard.

I took the opportunity to jump in. "By the way, I'm so sorry about your husband," I told her.

Her head snapped up, a look of surprise on her face as if she'd forgotten all about him already. "Uh, yes. Thank you."

"I can't imagine how difficult this all must be for you."

She cleared her throat, suddenly looking distinctly uncomfortable. "Yes. It is."

"When did you last see him?" I asked gently. I hoped I wasn't pushing too hard. There was a fine line between sympathetic faux therapy patient and nosy tabloid reporter looking for something to text her editor.

"I…well, yesterday. Afternoon."

"At the obstacle drill?" I asked. "Or…did you see him afterward?"

"I…uh…I don't know. I mean, no. The last time I saw him was at the drill." Clearly Dr. Georgia was not used to being the one in the hot seat.

I nodded. "It's just, well, I heard that Dr. William sometimes snuck a cigarette where the cameras couldn't see."

"Who told you that?" Dr. Georgia's head whipped around the room, silently accusing any crew member in residence.

"Is that what he was doing yesterday?" I asked, avoiding her question.

"How should I know?" she mumbled, her eyes going back to her clipboard.

"Oh, I just thought maybe you'd gone looking for him. I mean, you did show up late to the drill."

"Did I? Oh, well, I guess something came up."

"What sort of something?" I asked.

"Something that is none of your business," Dr. Georgia said pointedly.

Rats. So much for my stealth investigation skills.

"Let's get back to the interview, shall we?" she said.

I nodded. "Sure."

She straightened in her seat, giving an almost imperceptible nod to the camera on her right—I assumed to make sure they got whatever reaction she was about to try to get from me. I steeled myself for the worst.

"Let's talk about the root of your issues with Trace. Trust is the foundation of any healthy relationship. Tell me, has Trace ever done something that violated your trust?"

I paused. "No," I said, though I could sense the hesitation in my own voice.

She raised an eyebrow. "Never? What about the way he was looking at Apple during the obstacle course drill?"

I snorted before I could stop myself. "Seriously? Dr. William made that up. He was the one who was probably ogling Apple."

Dr. Georgia narrowed her eyes at me.

"Uh, I mean not to speak ill of the dead or anything," I backpedaled.

"Hmm." Dr. Georgia made a note on her clipboard. I had a sudden insane worry that this might become part of my permanent mental health record. "Tell me, where do you see your relationship with Trace in five years?"

"Uh…" I drew a blank. I honestly hadn't thought ahead that much. Not that I didn't see Trace and myself continuing to date or maybe even more at some point, but I hadn't mapped our future out in my mind yet. Heck, I was still celebrating the fact we were adding *girl* and *boy* to the word *friend* now.

"You're hesitating. Does that mean you don't see yourself with him long-term?" Dr. Georgia looked practically giddy at the thought.

No, I…just…" I cleared my throat. "Sure. Sure I do."

"So you see yourself with Trace still in five years?"

I nodded. "Sure?"

"Cohabitating?"

"Um, okay."

"Married?"

"Uh…maybe…"

"Children?"

I squirmed in my seat. "Could we start with a dog?"

Dr. Georgia smirked. "I knew you weren't serious about Trace."

"No, it's…it's not that. It's just…" I could practically feel the lens pushing in for an embarrassing close-up as I tried to articulate just what *it* was. I took a deep breath. How had I let this woman rattle me so much? "It's just that marriage and children are a big commitment. I want to make sure we're ready first," I answered lamely.

"I see." She narrowed her eyes at me, clearly probing to see if I'd say more.

For once, I kept my fool mouth shut.

Dr. Georgia's gaze went back to her notes, no doubt scanning for another embarrassing question to ask.

I took the moment of reprieve to scan *her*. I noticed she showed more emotion when it came to possibly catching me in an air-worthy moment than when I'd mentioned her husband. I looked around the room. None of the crew, in fact, seemed to show any signs of grief. No tears, no puffy eyes, no downcast expression of any kind. Sure, Dr. William had seemed like a bit of a tool, but wasn't anyone who knew him sad to see him gone? Friends? Family?

"Did your husband have other family?" I asked.

Dr. Georgia's head shot up. "Excuse me?"

"You know—parents, brothers, sister. Kids?"

The color drained from Dr. Georgia's face. "No," she spat back quickly. "No children."

I blinked. "Sorry. I didn't mean to poke a sore spot."

For a moment I had the feeling Dr. Georgia was going to hit me. The fire in her eyes was nothing short of volcanic. But instead of lashing out, she ground her teeth together then addressed the crew. "I think I have enough from *her.*"

I felt my cheeks warm as if I'd done something wrong. Clearly I'd struck a nerve. But instead of pushing it, I made my way back to the billiard room. Only it appeared deserted. The rest of the rehabbers had already been let go. Apparently Dr. Georgia'd had not only enough of *me* but of everyone else as well.

I made my way back upstairs and found our suite was empty as well. There was a note on the bed scribbled in Trace's handwriting, letting me know he'd gone down to the pool for a swim. I decided to capitalize on the few minutes of alone time.

I walked into the bathroom and turned on the shower. Then I removed the small microphone from my collar and placed it beside the pelting water. If any of the crew were monitoring our conversations for juicy story angles or sound bites, my hope was they'd think I was washing my hair.

I pulled out my phone and dialed Tina's number.

"Well, if it isn't my new favorite reality star," she teased after answering on the third ring. "Sloshed your drink in anyone's face yet?"

"Not yet," I whispered. "But the day is young."

Tina laughed. "What's with the whispering? Big Brother watching?"

"Always. I've got my microphone in the shower," I confessed. "So I'm on borrowed time. And I need your help."

"Yeah, I heard Felix ranting earlier about the murder and radio silence from his 'inside girl.'"

I cringed. "I'm working on something to send him," I told her, sounding more confident that I felt.

"Well, whatever you need on the outside, I'm your girl— as long as you promise to share your info with me instead of Allie."

"Why do you think I called your cell?" I replied. "We both know she's probably got your desk phone bugged."

"Very funny," Tina snarked. Though I could picture her checking it now.

"Anyway, I've got a little research project for you." I quickly brought Tina up to date on all things *Celebrity Relationship Rehab* so far, including Dr. Georgia's icy demeanor, Joanie & Antoine's secret, Dirk & Ellen's shaky alibis, and last but not least, Ice's interesting "if I did it" conversation at lunch.

"Sounds like a fun bunch," Tina said when I finished, heavy on the sarcasm. "How can I help?"

"I was wondering if you could get me some background on my fellow rehabbers."

I could hear her pen moving on the other end. "No prob. I can text you the basic deets on everyone pretty quickly— names, numbers, addresses. More in depth might take me a bit. Anything in particular you're looking for?"

"Maybe prior records? Any history of violence?"

She paused. "You thinking about Ice? Like maybe he actually did *ice* the doc?"

I shrugged. "I don't know. He could just be preening for the cameras, but it's possible he's just clever enough to hide in plain sight."

"On it!" Tina promised. "I'll see if I can get ahold of any arrest records and shoot you a text as soon as I find something."

"You're the best," I said before we ended the call.

Then I turned off the water and re-miked myself. With a quick glance at my phone, I saw I still had an hour before we were due at our evening drill.

And I planned to put it to good use.

CHAPTER SIX

———

Trace had abandoned the pool and was now doing shots at the outside bar with Antoine. Shirtless, I noticed. His female fans were going to love this episode when it aired. I had mixed feelings about that, but I didn't interrupt, instead making my way into the kitchen where Ellen was nursing a glass of white wine while watching Apple attempt to make something. What, I had no clue. But it apparently involved a lot of flour, as her teeny tiny tank and booty shorts were liberally doused with it. Also in residence was a lighting guy, who I recognized as my bearded friend from the gardening shed the day before, and a sound guy (both mesmerized by Apple's floured booty). To their right stood my favorite cameragirl. Just the woman I wanted to see.

While the suspect list I'd just rattled off to Tina had admittedly included just about everyone in the cast, the not-so-grieving widow was near the top of it in my mind. Wasn't it always the wife who done it? And if anyone knew what the dynamic between the victim and his wife had been, my bets were on the ever-present camera crew.

I skirted the mess on the kitchen island, giving Apple a little wave, as I approached Bonnie. I made a big show of covering my mike before telling her, "I never got a chance to thank you for the help at the obstacle course."

Bonnie's eyes darted to her co-workers, but both were much more interested in Apple than our conversation. "No problem," she said, giving me a quick smile. "It was much more satisfying seeing Joanie take the mud bath."

I stifled a laugh. "That wasn't terrible was it?"

Bonnie shook her head, smiling in earnest now.

"So, how long have you worked in reality television?" I asked, trying to feel her out. While she'd seemed happy enough to help me avoid a mess, I wasn't sure how eager she'd be to dish on her bosses.

"Not long, really. I got my start working in children's programming."

"Quite a change going from working with kids to reality stars, huh?"

She smirked. "Not as different as you'd think. Both gigs entail working with spoiled brats. At least the kids were less dramatic."

As if on cue, Joanie walked into the room, Pomeranian in her arms. "God, I need a drink!" she announced to the room at large. Ellen shoved a bottle of Chardonnay her way.

"Terrible about Dr. William, isn't it?" I asked, feeling my window of opportunity with Bonnie quickly closing. As soon as someone starting catfighting in the kitchen (which was only a matter of time with these three), Bonnie's attention would be back to work.

Bonnie's smile faded at the mention of her former employer. She nodded solemnly. "I can hardly believe it."

"What I find hard to believe is that Dr. Georgia is continuing with filming..." I trailed off, hoping Bonnie might pick up the lead.

Instead she just shrugged. "The show must go on."

"Dr. Georgia doesn't seem very upset," I prodded.

Bonnie frowned.

"She and her husband weren't having any problems themselves, were they?" I asked.

"Not that I saw," Bonnie responded, her eyes on Joanie and Apple. She must have had the same thought—any second now the claws would come out. "But it's not like they're close with the crew."

Drat. "Were they close with anyone?" I fished.

"Uh...I heard they used to be friends with Mr. Price."

I blinked at her. "You mean Dirk?" I shot a look toward his wife, Ellen.

Bonnie nodded, her eyes still focusing behind me on the ladies in the kitchen as Apple attempted to roll out dough with another Chardonnay bottle. "Yeah, when they were booking him for the show, I remember Dr. William kept calling him 'our old friend.'"

"Neither of them mentioned that." I could feel a frown settling between my eyebrows.

"Maybe the doctors didn't want you to think they were playing favorites?" Bonnie offered.

I thought back to the interaction I'd witnessed between Dirk and Dr. William. The two had hardly seemed like old friends. In fact I remembered thinking at the time that it seemed tense, but that took on a whole new meaning, knowing they had history together.

I was about to ask more when Apple's "rolling pin" slipped from her doughy grip and crashed to the floor, sending white wine and shards of glass everywhere. Joanie shrieked, and Isabelle the Pomeranian yipped and leapt from her arms onto the counter…right in the middle of Apple's dough. Apple yelled at the dog, Joanie yelled at Apple, and Ellen started cackling at them both as if she'd had one too many glasses already.

In seconds flat, Bonnie was in the middle of the action, capturing every curse word Joanie threw at poor Apple, as the would-be baker scrambled to catch the dog, who was tattooing the kitchen in tiny white paw prints.

"Look what you've done! You ruined my tart!" Apple yelled.

"The tart's making a tart!" Ellen laughed out loud at her own joke.

"It's not her fault," Joanie said, diving for the dog. "You scared Isabelle, you clumsy cow."

"It was supposed to be to cheer Ice up," Apple moaned, ignoring the insult.

A PA stepped into the room, breaking up the scene to remind us all that the next drill was set to film in half an hour. As the women dispersed like flies, off to get their hair and makeup camera worthy, I made a mental note to try to get Ellen alone and ask about her husband's "old friend" status with the deceased. Preferably before she sobered up.

* * *

Exactly half an hour later, we all entered the great hall for another enlightening drill. Dr. Georgia was already standing at the back of the room, cameras focused on her. On the sofas sat four wrapped boxes—each one with a couple's names written on the tag.

"I love presents!" Joanie squealed. She shoved Isabelle (who had clearly had a bath) into Antoine's arms and snatched up the box. "I want to open ours." Without waiting for permission, she tore off the wrapping paper and riffled through the tissue inside. She came up with a pair of earplugs and a surgical mask. "What the…" She trailed off with a glance at the cameras that told me she was thinking decidedly non-network-TV thoughts.

Trace opened our box, coming out with the same. He sent me a questioning look. I shrugged back in response, seeing the other two couples open their boxes with similar results.

"What are we supposed to do with these?" Joanie asked, her nose crinkling.

Dr. Georgia stepped forward. "This evening, you will be completing another challenge designed to strengthen your ability to communicate with your partner." She reached for the open box in Apple's hands and displayed its contents for the camera.

"People don't always say what they mean. It's important for you to learn to read your partner's body language and understand what they are really feeling, even when they can't—or won't—put it into words."

As Dr. Georgia spoke about body language, I couldn't help studying hers. If anything about our earlier interview had shaken the woman up, she was calmly composed again now. Almost too calmly. It made me wonder again if she was stifling her grief or just honestly emotionless over the loss of her husband.

"This drill will take away your ability to hear their words or watch their mouths," she continued. "We'll start with Mr. Kreme and Miss Pie." She gestured for Apple and Ice to join her in the center of the room.

Apple laced her fingers through Ice's and guided the brooding rapper toward Georgia. "We've got this, baby," she said, giving him an encouraging smile.

"Mr. Kreme, I want you to place the plugs in your ears first. Miss Pie, you will wear the surgical mask so that Ice cannot read your lips." She turned to address the rest of the group. "I will give Apple a series of cards with various actions and emotions printed on the back. When the whistle is blown, she will act out what is written on the first card. Without being able to hear her or see what she's saying, Ice will guess what she's trying to tell him. When he correctly guesses an action, Apple will move on to the next card. She will have three minutes to act out as many of the cards as she can. When that time is up, we will move on to the next couple."

"Kinda like Charades?" Apple asked.

"Could we get any more juvenile?" Joanie huffed under her breath.

Ellen shot Joanie a dirty look. I guess I wasn't the only one tired of Joanie's attitude.

"Let's begin," Georgia said, motioning to Ice to put in the earplugs.

The rapper reluctantly placed the plugs in his ears. Apple placed the mask over her mouth and grabbed the first card. When a whistle was blown, she scanned the card with her eyes and began to jump up and down.

Ice blinked at her. "Are you a kangaroo?"

Apple shook her head and continued to hop up and down excitedly. Then she turned around and wiggled her butt. Whatever the clue was, Ice still didn't seem to get it. Then again, his eyes were glued to his fiancée's breasts jiggling as she turned again and continued to bounce up and down.

"Water balloons? Melons?"

My turn to roll my eyes.

"Dude, this is hard, yo!" Ice complained as Apple continued to jump.

"I'll say," Dirk mumbled. I noticed he was studying Apple at least as intently as her fiancé as her Double Ds bounced buoyantly.

Ice flicked a glance toward the soap star. His eyes narrowed, and he yanked the earplugs out of his ears. "You checkin' out my girl again, old man?" Ice slammed the card out of Apple's hand and balled his own hands into fists at his sides. "I warned you about that!"

Dirk's eyes went wide, and he staggered back a step. "Son, I'm afraid you're mistaken," he said, his face reddening. "I was only watching the drill."

Dr. Georgia stepped forward, looking tired. "Mr. Kreme, take a seat. Until you can learn to control that jealous temper, we will be moving on to another couple."

Ice said a few choice words under his breath before slumping onto the sofa.

Apple pouted and reluctantly took a spot next to him. "The word was *excited*," she mumbled. "How can you not know what excited looks like?"

"Mrs. Parker, you and your husband are up next."

As I watched Joanie heave a dramatic sigh and grab her surgical mask, I felt my phone vibrate in my pocket. With a quick glance at the ever-present cameras, I slipped it out, surreptitiously sneaking a peek at my screen. Felix.

"Do you need to take that?" Apple whispered to me.

"Um…" I looked up to find camera number two swiveling our direction. "No, it's fine. It's just…a text alert from my credit card company," I lied.

Apple smiled. "Yeah, I get those all the time."

"Is everyone paying attention?" Dr. Georgia asked in Apple's direction.

The girl's cheeks went pink and she nodded.

"Good. Now, Antoine, take a card please, and let's begin."

As soon as she turned her attention back to the couple, I swiped open the text from Felix.

Time of death 5:41 p.m. Murder weapon=garden shears. Crew alibis out—no one alone. Police have no "official" suspects.

By the quotation marks around the word *official*, I knew exactly what Felix meant: the LAPD were reluctant to point a finger at a celebrity without concrete proof. I glanced around the room. Which celebrity they had their *unofficial* sights on I was dying to know.

* * *

The rest of the challenge went smoothly in comparison to Apple and Ice's fiasco. Antoine and Joanie struggled through their turn, with Joanie unable to interpret her husband's body language as he acted out things like lion taming and even a marriage proposal. Despite her disinterest in previous activities, Ellen fared better—mostly thanks to Dirk's tendency to overact the phrases written on the cards. Ellen Bents actually seemed to be enjoying herself for once. Perhaps her competitive streak had finally kicked in. Either that or the wine.

When it was our turn, Trace was given the earplugs while I put on the surgical mask and acted out the actions on the cards. This put us at a disadvantage since I wasn't the actor in the couple. But to his credit, Trace was better at reading me than I'd expected, and we managed to come in second place in the challenge after he successfully identified three of the four cards I acted out. And Trace only mugged it for the cameras a couple times. And only told me to take our relationship more seriously once. All in all, not the most painful drill we'd done so far.

When the drill ended, I was still itching to talk to Ellen, but Dirk announced to the cameras that he and his wife were going to get their "beauty sleep" now. While he did look tired, I had a sneaking suspicion it was at least partly a cover to get his wife to their room before she did anything else embarrassing in her inebriated state.

Like spill her guts to a tabloid reporter.

"Old people," Joanie scoffed. "It's only, like, ten."

"Wanna hit the bar?" Apple asked, looking like she needed a drink after losing the drill with Ice.

Joanie shrugged. "Why not? I could use a nightcap."

Trace excused himself to make a phone call, saying he was going to check in with his agent about an audition he was waiting to hear back on. Antoine mumbled something about taking a turn in the confessional booth. And as I watched Joanie and Apple walk off arm in arm, I realized something.

I was finally alone.

Well, if you didn't count the cameras.

While the crew was packing up their equipment for the evening, I knew the house was still bugged with dozens of eyes and ears in every room. For their benefit, I gave an exaggerated yawn and stretched my arms up above my head. "Maybe I'll just turn in early too," I said out loud.

I quickly jogged up the grand staircase toward our bedrooms. But when I got to the top, instead of making a right I ducked down below the railing and went to the left, pausing outside the Parkers' bedroom door. Saying a silent prayer to the gods of breaking and entering, I tried the door handle. I almost squealed with glee when it turned easily in my hand. I quickly pushed it open and slipped inside.

I glanced around the room, which looked like a Gucci tornado had hit it. Designer duds littered every surface, and I cringed at the callous way Joanie treated her clothes. My hands itched to reverently hang up the litany of cocktail dresses and silk blouses tossed carelessly around the room, but I knew I had to act fast.

"Uh, Joanie?" I called for the cameras' benefit. "You in here?"

Obviously she wasn't, but maybe the pretense of looking for her would buy me a few minutes before anyone monitoring the cameras questioned my presence.

Honestly, I wasn't sure what I was looking for. A pair of bloody garden shears would be awesome. But one thing I knew for sure was that Joanie and Antoine were harboring a secret, and this might be my one chance to find it.

I quickly began moving clothes around, looking in dresser drawers, the closet, and under the bed. The good news? With the mess that was their room, there was no way they were going to know if someone had rummaged through it. I found an alarming number of false eyelashes in Joanie's bathroom, a bag of designer dog treats in the closet bearing a price tag higher than a lobster dinner at my favorite restaurant in Studio City, and a tub of pimple cream the size of my fist in Joanie's nightstand. All of which might be fun fodder for Tina's gossip column but didn't point to any murderous secrets.

I moved on to Antoine's nightstand and stifled a giggle when I pulled out a prescription bottle of little blue pills.

Though, in his defense, I could see it being difficult for any man to get too excited about Joanie. While it might not be information the football player would want on the front page of the *Informer*, the Viagra was still less than a smoking gun.

I checked my phone, seeing that an alarming amount of time had gone by already. I had no idea how long Apple could keep Joanie at the bar, but considering the diva's short attention span during our drills thus far, I had a bad feeling the clock was ticking.

I moved on to a pile of Joanie's jackets thrown on the chaise lounge next to the French doors to the balcony. I quickly picked up one at a time, feeling around in the pockets for anything that might've been left behind. I came up with breath mints, two balled-up tissues, a dog treat covered in lint, and…a business card.

I quickly turned it over, reading the name on the front.
James A. Johnson, Attorney at Law

Before I could do more than speculate whose attorney Mr. Johnson was, footsteps echoed in the corridor outside the bedroom door.

"…but it's like he doesn't even appreciate me," I heard Joanie complaining just outside the door.

"Ugh. Men, right?" Apple responded.

I paused, my gaze whipping around me for an escape route. Bathroom? Closet? Hide under the bed?

I watched the knob on the bedroom door turn in slow motion, feeling frozen to the spot for a split second before I shoved the card into my back pocket and dove toward the French doors and out onto the balcony. As I flattened myself against the wall, I heard Joanie and Apple enter the suite.

"Well, I can tell you one thing for certain," Joanie said, her voice slurring slightly as if she'd had more than one nightcap. "If it weren't for me, Antoine would be nothing."

Nothing but a well-paid NFL player with a championship ring. But I kept that thought to myself as Apple responded to her.

"Here, here!" Apple cheered, her voice louder than I'd heard it before. "Behind every great man is a great woman, right? Girl power. Woo!"

I felt my eyebrows rise. How many drinks had Apple had?

"Sing it, sister!" Joanie agreed.

I couldn't help myself. I slipped my phone from my pocket and ducked around the corner just long enough to pop off a couple shots of Joanie and Apple in their drunken celebration of womanhood. Joanie's ponytail was crooked, her lipstick smeared, and a dribble of red wine trailed down the front of her pink blouse. Priceless. While the contract I'd signed meant I couldn't print this photo *now*, it didn't mean never.

Flattening myself back against the wall again, I pulled up the contact info Tina had sent me earlier on all my fellow rehabbers. Selecting Apple's number, I sent a quick text off.

Hey, could you and Joanie meet me in the kitchen for a sec?

A second later I heard Apple's phone chime. "Oh, I just got a text."

"Is it Ice apologizing?" Joanie asked.

"No." I peeked around the corner to see Apple frown. "It's from Cam."

"Who?" Joanie wrinkled her nose up.

I rolled my eyes.

"You know, Trace's girlfriend."

"Ugh. That nobody? How she even got on the show I have no idea. I mean, let's face it—after *Piranha Man*, Trace hardly even qualifies as an A-lister anymore."

I narrowed my eyes and thought a really dirty word.

"What does Tabloid Girl want anyway?" Joanie continued.

"She wants us to meet her in the kitchen."

"What on earth for?" Joanie asked, throwing her hands on her hips dramatically.

Apple shrugged. "I dunno."

Joanie did an exaggerated sigh. "Fine. But only because I could go for a snack."

"Ooh! You think they have any more of those chocolates left over from lunch?" I heard Apple ask as the two of them stepped out of the room.

Joanie's reply was lost to me as the door closed behind them. I gave it a three count before I slipped back into the bedroom and quickly crossed to the door. I paused, listening for any sounds of life on the other side. None. I opened it a crack and scanned the empty hallway before quickly leaving the room and shutting the door behind me again. I took the stairs two at a time as I raced down to the kitchen. I hoped I didn't sound too breathless as I caught up to them rummaging through the refrigerator.

"Hey, you got my text," I said as casually as I could muster.

Both women spun around. Apple smiled. Joanie gave me a scowl. Typical.

"Yeah, what's up?" Apple asked, popping a piece of chocolate into her mouth. (Apparently they did have some left.)

"I was…just wondering if…you knew…how we were supposed to dress for the first drill tomorrow?" I lied, making it up on the spot. Even to my own ears it sounded a little lame, but apparently both women bought it, as Apple shook her head vehemently and Joanie scoffed loudly.

"Sorry, I don't think any of the PAs told me," Apple responded.

"Oh. Okay. Well I guess I'll just figure it out in the morning then. Good night!" I said, only slightly too chipper.

As I left the room, I heard Joanie mumbling, "You'd think even trash like her could figure out how to dress herself by now."

I ignored the comment, instead wishing Joanie a very big pimple that night as I made my way up to my room.

As soon as I was safely inside, I quickly pulled up a Google screen on my phone and slipped the stolen business card from my pocket. I searched *James A. Johnson, Attorney* and got a hit for a lawyer in Beverly Hills. A divorce attorney. I felt my eyebrows jump into my hairline. I had assumed that the other couples on the show were all here to boost their own careers or ratings, exaggerating any problems they might be having in their relationships. Were things really so bad that Joanie had contacted a divorce attorney?

Then another thought hit me. If Joanie had already started divorce proceedings, that was a direct violation of the contracts we had signed before coming on the show. Because it took at least three months to film, edit, and air an episode, the producers had explicitly made sure that none of us were in the process of formally separating before coming on the show. The only thing that would ruin the show's ratings would be if a couple publicly split before their last-ditch effort to save their relationship had aired.

Was Joanie in violation of the contract, and had Dr. William found out…and paid the ultimate price for it?

CHAPTER SEVEN

———

    The next morning, I awoke before dawn. I threw on a pair of blue gym shorts and a gray tank and then laced my shoes. It had been days since my last run, and I was determined to put at least a few miles on my Nikes before the rest of the guests and crew were up…and if my run took me past a certain gardening shed, so much the better. I left Trace snoring softly in the bed and quietly made my way downstairs and out of the house. The sky was still a dark blue, and without the lights of the city interfering, I could see the stars. Well, at least a couple of them anyway.

    I did a few warm-up stretches and then took off toward the gardening shed on the far side of the property. While the crime scene tape still fluttered in the early morning breeze, it was the only indication that anything other than pruning and planting had gone on here. I pulled my phone out, using the flashlight app to peek inside. The shed was largely bare, and while I'd had no idea how much was usually stored in it, I had the feeling the police had taken most of its contents with them for evidence or further testing. Knowing a stabbing had taken place here, I'd been afraid of the gory scene I might see, but if there had been any blood in residence previously, it was gone now. In fact, the lingering scent of bleach told me that as soon as the place had been cleared by the police, Reisner had had any hint that a crime had occurred here cleaned out as fast as possible. The entire place looked looted, cleaned, and deserted. If there'd ever been any evidence of who had killed Dr. William here, it was gone now.

    I snapped a couple of shots off for good measure then slipped my phone back into my pocket before resuming my run. While the shed hadn't yielded anything, I knew running was the best way to clear my head so I could process everything that had happened over the past couple of days.

If Joanie and Antoine's secret was that they had already started divorce proceedings, I could see why they would want that kept quiet. Joanie was famous just for being famous—a precarious career position at best. And shows like this one kept the reality star in the public eye and in designer handbags and trips to pampered pooch salons. But did it mean enough to her to kill for it? I'd known starlets to be desperate for screen time before, and let's face it, having the media buzz of a murder surrounding the show wasn't going to hurt its ratings any when it finally did air. I made a mental note to check on Joanie's and Antoine's alibis—I noticed neither had been very forthcoming with them so far.

Speaking of alibis, then there was Ice Kreme and his notable lack of one. That, coupled with his jealous temper, still kept him near the top of my suspect list. As over-the-top as his tough-guy-hood-rat persona was, I'd seen real anger flashing in his eyes—especially where other men's attention toward Apple was concerned. And hadn't he mentioned he had a new album coming out soon? This kind of publicity could only help his "street cred," as he put it.

And of course there were still Dirk and Ellen and their alleged history with the victim. Dirk had seemed decidedly tense around Dr. William. Had their history been a tumultuous one? Had Dirk been harboring a grudge for years and finally had an opportunity to act on it?

And where did Dr. Georgia fit into all of this? As shocked as she'd initially seemed over her husband's death, she'd been all business since then. While I still had a hard time believing it was her decision for the show to go on, she'd been acting more like a woman who'd lost a nail and not a husband. Had their relationship been that cold?

Suddenly I wondered who stood to inherit Dr. William's estate. I had to imagine it was sizeable, considering the type of ratings the show got. If Dr. Georgia was his sole heir and their relationship was on the rocks, a large inheritance beat a messy divorce any day.

I slowed my pace, grabbing my phone from my pocket and pulling up Max Beacon's number. Max wrote the obituaries for the *Informer*, and if anyone would know the details of Dr. William's estate, it was Max—he had informants at every morgue and mortuary from here to San Bernardino.

It rang three times on the other end before Max's sleepy voice picked up. "Beacon," he grunted.

"Hey, Max, it's Cameron. Did I wake you?"

"Nope," he lied, his voice gravelly from sleep and the bottle of Scotch he'd likely consumed the night before. Max's age was somewhere between seventy and a hundred and ten, and he had a liver made of steel that he put to the test on a nightly basis. "What can I do you for, kid?"

"I was wondering what you know about Dr. William Meriwether's estate. Done his obit yet?"

"Finished it last night. You know the boss don't like bodies going cold." He cackled at his own joke. "What do you want to know?"

"Any idea when the will is going to be read?" I asked, hoping I could find a "fly on the wall" to listen in.

But Max answered with, "No will."

"You're kidding?" I asked. Usually people with money on the line like Dr. William were sticklers about assigning it to someone upon their death. Some even enjoyed the thought. Heck, I had it on good authority that Betty White's biggest hobby was rewriting her will.

"I guess the doctor didn't plan on checking out anytime soon," Max said. "He died intestate."

"Meaning by default all of his assets would go to his wife—Dr. Georgia," I surmised.

"Well, not entirely," Max hedged. I heard him shift his phone to the other ear. "Turned out Dr. William came into the marriage with money of his own. Family money. And lots of it."

"Which means…?" Admittedly, I was not up on California estate law.

"Which means it's a little more complicated. The community property is all the wife's, but the family money gets split among heirs."

"But if Dr. William had no children?"

"Then it's all hers," Max confirmed.

Bingo. Hello, motive.

I thanked Max and hung up, still mulling over the ramifications of that as the sun began to peek over the tops of the trees and the sky lightened to a beautiful shade of baby blue.

As I walked absently past the gated front entrance, however, a noise from the other side stopped me in my tracks. It was a sound I'd know anywhere—the distinct clicking of a camera shutter. I whipped my head toward the iron bars, feeling blood rush to my cheeks.

"Well, if it isn't our new favorite reality star," Eddie said, his camera glued to his face as he snapped shot after shot. The *Entertainment Daily* reporter was dressed in a pair of mismatched sweats and flip-flops that showed off his toenail fungus with alarming clarity. "Look who it is, Mike."

"Lookin' good, Cammy," Eddie's brother said through a mouth full of donut. He took another bite, and purple jelly drizzled onto his beard and the front of his dirty white T-shirt.

I tried not to make a face. "A little early for the two of you to be up, isn't it?"

"Not when there's been a celebrity murder," Eddie said, putting down his camera long enough to snag the bag of donuts from his twin brother. "We're working around the clock." He hiked a thumb over his shoulder, where I could just make out the bumper of their car hidden behind the thick brush. "The boss has us on a reality show stakeout. There are at least a dozen other photographers camped out along the road leading up to the property, but we beat them all to the front gate. Now say cheese!" He picked his camera back up and snapped another picture.

I was suddenly acutely aware of the fact that my face was red from exertion and my tank top was probably sporting sweat marks as it stuck to me. I tried to duck my head away from his lens.

"Got any dirt for us?" Mike asked, studying me with his beady eyes. "Heard any drunken late-night confessions about who could've offed the host?"

I gave him a *get real* look and held up a hand to block my face from Eddie's camera. "Why would I tell you?"

Eddie shrugged. "Professional courtesy?"

I stifled a snort. Nothing about Eddie and Mike went with the words *professional* or *courtesy*. "How about this," I proposed. "How about you tell me what *you* know, and I'll share what's going on inside the house."

Mike narrowed his eyes at me. "How do we know you've got anything good?"

My turn to shrug. "Maybe I do. Maybe I don't." I tried to give them my sweetest smile. Which, granted, while trying not to look at Eddie's toes and Mike's jelly-stained shirt was more of a grimace.

The two brothers shared a look, doing the sort of silent conversation thing I'd seen twins do in the past, with a lot of nodding, shrugging, and eyebrow raising. Finally they turned to me, and Eddie nodded. "Okay we'll show you ours if you show us yours, doll face."

I rolled my eyes at how dirty Eddie had made it sound. "You first."

"Why us?" Mike whined.

I crossed my arms over my chest. "Because you're the ones who need a story." Which was a total bluff on my end. I was acutely aware of the fact that I'd yet to send Felix anything more incriminating than a few shots of crime scene techs.

"Fine!" Eddie relented. "Alright. How about this: Reisner Productions is refusing to turn over the video footage from the day Dr. William died."

I frowned, unable to keep the surprise from lacing my voice. "Why would he do that?"

"Why indeed." Mike nodded and winked at me.

"Wait, you don't think that Reisner had anything to do with Dr. William's death, do you?" I'll admit that was an angle I had not yet thought of. Had there been some sort of falling out between the host and his producer? While I was sure Reisner would be getting some great publicity out of this when the show aired, I didn't see it doing him much good if the star of the show was dead.

Eddie just shrugged. "Beats me. All I know is that the police produced a warrant yesterday for Reisner to turn over all recordings from the day of the murder. Only, what they got was short the two hours before Dr. William was killed. The official statement from Reisner Productions is that the footage is 'missing,'" he said, making exaggerated air quotes with his pudgy fingers, "and they are 'looking for it.'" More air quotes.

I bit the inside of my cheek as I digested that bit of information. While it felt like a long shot that Reisner was involved in Dr. William's death, it was quite possible he was covering it up for someone else. Or even for the sake of his own ratings—imagine the media frenzy he could create by airing footage of a murder about to happen on his show. I wondered just how "missing" the footage really was and just how difficult it might be to slip into the control room and poke around for it myself.

"Your turn," Mike said, shoving half a donut into his face.

"What?" I responded, lost in my own thoughts.

"We showed you ours. Now you show us yours, Cammy. What's the dirt on the inside, girl?"

"Oh. Right." Truth was, I didn't really have any. At least none fit for sending to my own editor. I quickly racked my brain for anything that might feel even slightly newsworthy to the two trolls of the tabloid world. "Well…" I drew out. "You know Joanie Parker?"

A pair of heads nodded in my direction.

"I know for a fact that she…" I dramatically looked over both shoulders before leaning in, as if sharing national secrets.

Mike and Eddie leaned in as well. Close enough for me to smell the stale coffee and faint hint of Cheetos on Mike's breath. Ick.

"…Joanie sleeps with a tub of pimple cream in her nightstand."

Mike and Eddie blinked at me as if still waiting for the punch line.

"That's it?" Eddie asked.

I shrugged. "What? I think that's pretty embarrassing."

Mike scoffed. "What does that have to do with Dr. William's murder?"

"Nothing," I admitted. "But that's the best you're getting from me." I sent them a saccharine sweet smile before turning on my sneaker heels and heading back toward the house. I could have sworn I heard Mike mumbling something derogatory about me, my mother, and a goat as I jogged away, but I ignored him. Instead my mind was focused on just one thing: how to get hold of that missing footage.

*   *   *

As soon as I returned from my run, I was met in the foyer by a grim-faced PA who scolded me for not putting my obligatory lapel microphone on that morning. As much as I tried to protest that I'd like to get a shower first, my sweaty tank top was miked for sound before I was allowed back upstairs to our suite. Trace was already in the shower when I entered, so I went to the bedside table and checked my phone while I waited for him. I'd had a missed call from Tina and a text from Felix while jogging. I read the text first.

Send something usable. Now. If I don't have something incriminating or embarrassing by the end of the day you're fired.

I groaned. While I was 90% sure he was kidding about the "you're fired" part, I was 100% sure he was serious about needing a story now. And I hated to admit that Felix was right. Even I had expected to be able to send more juicy tidbits to my editor by now. What I had were more questions than answers when it came to Dr. William's death. Not that I'd had a whole lot of opportunity to run down said answers, what with the incredibly therapeutic drills, the violent outbursts, and my camera-hungry boyfriend. But I made a mental note to catch someone—anyone!—doing something incriminating or tabloid-worthy embarrassing today as I checked my voicemail for Tina's message.

"Hey, chick," Tina's recorded voice said. "I've got the deets on your favorite flavor of ice cream. Call me."

I smiled at her thinly veiled code. With a quick glance up at the camera mounted in the corner of the room, I grabbed my phone, along with Trace's cell and a pair of ear buds, and went out onto the balcony. While I had no doubt there were cameras out there as well, I hoped I could at least muffle the sound of my call enough so that it wasn't air-able. I connected the earbuds to Trace's phone and pulled up his workout playlist before draping the buds around my neck…so that the energetic, upbeat music played directly into my lapel mike. Then I quickly dialed Tina's number on my own phone.

Two rings in she answered. "Cam, are you gonna love me, girl," Tina said, excitement accenting her words.

I grinned. "I hope so. What did you find?" I asked in hushed tones.

"Well, it turns out that Ice Kreme does not have a police record."

"So he is all bark and no bite?" So much for my Suspect Number One.

"Not necessarily," Tina said. I could hear the sly smile in her voice, giving me a lift of hope.

"Spill it," I directed.

"Well, 'Ice Kreme' may not have a record, but Morton Steinberger does."

"Who?" I asked, pacing the balcony.

"Morton Steinberger. Child of the burbs, went to private school, sang in his junior high choir, and was the captain of the chess team. Oh, and then went on to take a dessert-themed stage name as a rapper."

"Oh em gee." I felt my face break into a smile to match Tina's giddy voice. "Are you telling me that Ice's real name is Morty and he was a chess geek?"

"Bingo, girlfriend. And that's not all. Turns out our Morty *does* have a bit of a violent side."

This just kept getting better. "Do tell!"

"Well, we've got three arrests in Orange County for battery. Two that look like bar fights, and one—get this!—an altercation after the Southern California Chess Masters Open."

I snorted. "He beat up another chess player?"

"Looks like it. He also has a drunk and disorderly in Hollywood and a restraining order taken out by an ex-girlfriend in Burbank."

"Wow. Girl, when you deliver, you deliver." I heard Trace getting out of the shower in the room behind me. "Hey, I gotta go. But thanks, and I'll let you know if anything else comes up."

"No prob," Tina said before hanging up.

I leaned on the railing and stared out at the picturesque view, churning this new information over in my head. While the idea of Ice Kreme being a private school-raised chess player was enough to make me giggle, a history of violence certainly didn't seem out of character for someone who might snap...say at a therapist he believed was ogling his girl?

"Hey, beautiful."

I spun around to find Trace, freshly showered, wearing a towel wrapped around his waist. And nothing else. My mind suddenly emptied of all thoughts. Talk about distracting.

"Hey, yourself," I responded, taking a step toward him. But remembering how sticky and sweaty I was, I limited myself to a quick peck on his cheek. Though the scent of clean soap and warm man melted my insides.

"How was your run?" he asked.

"Huh?" I'll admit I was having a hard time focusing on anything other than the half-naked movie star standing in front of me.

Trace grinned, one dimple forming in his left cheek. "Your run?" he said, glancing at my workout attire. "You did go out this morning, right?"

"Right. Yeah. Sure. Good run."

Trace took a step closer, sliding his arm around my middle. "You know if you've still got a little energy to burn off, I can think of some other forms of exercise we could indulge in."

Be still my beating heart. While I was suddenly full of energy and totally in an *indulgent* mood, I couldn't help my gaze flitting up to the camera in the corner of the room.

Traces eyes followed mine, understanding lighting them. Mixed with a healthy dose of disappointment.

I gave him an apologetic look. "Rain check?" You know, for sometime when we wouldn't be making a celebrity sex tape.

He nodded. "Sure." He cleared his throat, taking a step back and turning toward the closet, where he pulled out a pair of jeans and a T-shirt.

I swallowed down a large lump of my own disappointment, suddenly needing a very cold shower as I watched him get dressed.

"By the way, one of the production assistants stopped by while you were out," Trace told me. "We're supposed to dress for a physical challenge and meet out by the lake at ten."

I glanced at my phone readout. That gave us just over an hour. While Trace left to find breakfast, I jumped into the shower and did my best to tame my hair into something camera worthy. I slipped on a little teal bikini underneath a pair of spandex shorts and a cute off-the-shoulder top that I hoped looked girlfriend-of-a-movie-star but not trying-too-hard-to-look-like-the-girlfriend-of-a-movie-star. Then I grabbed a pair of lace-less Converse and made my way downstairs.

Joanie and Ellen were in the kitchen, arguing over whether Isabel would be eating the leftover filet mignon from last night's dinner (Ellen's choice) or the chicken sausage intended for today's breakfast (Joanie's insistence). Ellen had a cup of coffee in one hand and her other hand pressed to her temple. Hangover, perhaps? Bonnie was busy filming the action, and I could only imagine she was wishing she was still working with clowns and puppets versus divas and…well, divas. I spied Apple slipping into the confessional booth down the hall, her eyes looking puffy and red, as if she'd been crying. I wondered if she and Ice had fought again. Now knowing that her boyfriend had a real violent streak, not just a fake one, I suddenly felt a little protective toward the girl. As sexy as her career and wardrobe were, there seemed to be a certain naiveté about Apple that was endearing. I made a mental note to find her later, suddenly wondering if she knew about Ice's past.

Speaking of Ice, I noticed he was nowhere to be found. As much as I was itching to track down the rapper, we only had a few minutes left before our next drill was supposed to start, so I made my way outside by the pool area, where a small breakfast buffet had been set up. Trace and Antoine already had their plates filled and were sitting together at a table under a large umbrella, chatting about Antoine's team and their playoff chances this year. Dirk was lingering near a tray of fruit, a half-empty Bloody Mary in one hand. I grabbed a plate and made my way toward him.

"Good morning," I said, loading my plate with sliced pineapple and melon.

Dirk nodded and smiled in my direction.

I tried again to engage him. "This all looks yummy."

He shrugged, downing the last of his drink.

"The, uh, bar open already?" I asked, gesturing to his glass.

Dirk sent me another watery smile. "It's always open here at Relationship Wreckage Manor," he slurred.

And if I had to guess, he'd been hitting it pretty hard. Perfect.

"In that case, how about we start the day off right," I suggested, setting down my plate. "Do a couple shots with me?"

Dirk raised an eyebrow my way. "A bit early for that?"

"Come on," I pushed. "It's five o'clock somewhere." I winked at him. And might have even bent a little forward so that my off-the-shoulder showed just a *hint* of cleavage.

Dirk's face broke into a full-on grin. "Alright. If you insist, little lady."

I led the way to the poolside bar, where it appeared Dirk was right—the crew had made sure we were well stocked with all manner of liquor, along with fresh lemon and lime wedges, mixers, and glasses ranging from champagne flute to stubby shot glass. I quickly grabbed a bottle of top-shelf tequila, the lime wedges, and a small bowl of coarse salt. I poured two shots then put on my best dumb-blonde face and turned to Dirk.

"I always forget the order you're supposed to do these," I lied.

Dirk grinned. "It's easy." He lifted his hand to his mouth and licked the fold of skin between his thumb and index finger. Then he grabbed a pinch of salt and dusted it over his moist skin. "First you lick the salt off your hand. Then you take the shot, and you chase it with the lime wedge. Like this." Dirk brought his hand to his mouth again and flicked his tongue over the salt. Grabbing the shot glass, he tilted his head back and poured the tequila down his throat. Then he plucked a piece of lime from the bowl and pressed the juicy citrus wedge to his mouth. "That," he said, his whole face puckered from the sour taste, "is how you take a proper tequila shot."

"Well done." I gave him a small clap.

"Your turn," he said, nodding to my shot.

I made a big show of licking my hand, adding salt, getting my lime wedge ready. And just as I was about to take the shot, I let my eyes focus on a point just behind the pool area. "Is that Apple in a bikini?"

"Where?" Dirk spun his head away.

I tossed the tequila onto the ground.

Just as his head swiveled back. "I don't see anything."

I shook my head. "Sorry. Must have been a shadow or something.

Dirk's eyebrows furrowed together, and his mouth opened as if about to question that lame excuse.

But I cut him off by leaning forward and showing more than a hint of cleavage this time as I seductively licked a lime wedge.

His eyes glazed over as he blinked at me.

"Am I doing it right?" I asked.

Dirk just grinned and nodded.

I giggled. "Do another shot with me please, Dr. Spencer Carlin?" I asked, using his soap opera character's name. Yes, I was laying it on thick.

"Anything for a fan," he told my boobs.

I watched him go through the whole complicated process again, this time a little less steady with the salt (which mostly ended up in his lap), and throw back another round of tequila.

"Isn't this place fun?" I said as he sucked a lime wedge chaser.

He nodded, lips puckering.

"I know Trace's agent had to push hard to get him on the show," I said, not entirely making it up.

Dirk shrugged, filling our shot glasses up again. "Well, he did make that stinker. I'd imagine most of Hollywood would pause over booking him."

I cringed at the truth of that but managed to keep a flirty smile on my face. "How did you and your wife get the gig?" I asked.

Dirk snorted, tossing more salt around. "It's all about who you know, my dear. Hollywood thrives on connections." He gave me an exaggerated wink.

"I imagine you've amassed a few of those in your time."

Another wink, and then he threw back a third shot. I was getting queasy just watching him. Luckily, he didn't seem to notice that my glass was remaining untouched.

"Like the Meriwethers?" I pressed.

Dirk slammed the empty shot glass back on the bar loudly enough that Trace and Antoine both glanced our way. Trace shot me a questioning look. I gave him an innocent little wave before turning back to Dirk.

"Um, so, the Meriwethers?"

"What about them?" Dirk asked me.

"Just wondering if the Meriwethers were your connection to get on the show. You know, Drs. William and Georgia?"

"What do you know about that?" he asked. Though, it came out more like, "Waddayaknow 'bout dat" as he swayed on his barstool. Forget making the morning drill—this guy wasn't going to make it past breakfast without passing out.

"You are old friends, right?" I asked slowly, trying to gauge his reaction through the booze.

Finally he nodded. "Yeah. Yeah, we were friends. Once."

"Once? Not anymore?"

Dirk's eyes went to the bar top, and he fiddled with a discarded lime wedge. "It was a long time ago."

I cleared my throat. I feared I was quickly losing my audience. "How did you meet?"

"Who?"

"You and the Meriwethers?" I reminded him. Yeesh, this guy was far gone.

He smirked. "Bill—that's what *Dr.* William went by then. Bill and I met on the set of *Late Night USA*. We were guests on the same episode, if you can believe that."

"Really? I love that show," I lied. While I'd heard of the late-night talk show, I was usually asleep before the monologue ended. "When was this?"

Dirk waved his hand in the air. "Oh, years ago now. Let's see, I was promoting the second season of *The Charming & the Reckless*, and he'd been asked to host a special relationship-advice segment to promote his first book." Dirk stared off into the distance, his eyes unfocused, a small smile playing across his lips. "God, we were young then."

"So, you met on the show and became friends?" I pressed.

He nodded. "We had a lot in common back then. Both just starting out in our fields, making a name for ourselves, the underdogs of TV, if you will, not quite invited to the prime-time events yet. Heck, Bill actually introduced me to my wife at the first Daytime Emmys we attended together." He paused. "I have two, you know. Emmys, that is."

"Yes, I've heard." Several times since I'd arrived in fact. It seemed to be his favorite subject. "So, the four of you were friends?" I clarified, trying to get him back to *my* favorite subject.

Dirk gave me a lopsided grin. "Oh, yes. We spent a lot of time together back then. We used to vacation at their house in the Hamptons every summer. Their annual anniversary dinner party every June was one of my favorite occasions." Something shifted behind his eyes, and his smile vanished. "Those were simpler times," he said, his words tinged with sadness.

I suddenly found myself feeling just a tad guilty for prodding him about Dr. William's murder when it was clear he'd cared deeply for his friend. At least at some point. "I'm so sorry for your loss," I said sincerely.

Dirk shook his head and dropped his gaze to the patio tiles, his bushy brows turning down. "No. It's not *my* loss. We weren't close anymore," he said, suddenly sounding more sober. "We hadn't talked in…well, it's been at least twenty years. A lifetime ago. Trust me, I didn't even know the man anymore."

"It sounds like you had a falling out," I said, not having to feign the sympathy in my voice.

Dirk shrugged. "It was a complicated situation." He ducked his head. I wasn't sure if his cheeks were flushed from the booze or embarrassment at whatever conflict he was reliving in his mind.

I almost felt bad pushing him…

Almost.

"How complicated?" I asked. "Dirk, what happened between you and William?"

"There you are," a woman's voice cut across the pool area, startling me so badly that I nearly fell out of my chair. I turned to find Ellen Bents walking briskly across the patio toward us. Any sign of a hangover was gone as her sharp eyes were laser focused on us. "They're about to start the drill. We should get a little coffee in you first," she said, accurately assessing Dirk's state. Her gaze settled on me, and her eyes narrowed. "I hope Miss Dakota hasn't been grilling you for gossip."

Dirk shook his head, his lower lip sticking out. "No. No, Cam and I were just enjoying a little morning pick-me-up." He grinned my way. Or at least in the direction of my chest.

"Hmm." If Ellen's eyes narrowed any farther, she wouldn't be able to see out of those suckers.

She laced her arm through Dirk's and gently coaxed him out of his seat. "Come, darling. I've got coffee in the kitchen," she said with a disapproving glance at the remnants of our tequila party.

I watched Ellen help a stumbling Dirk back inside the house, wondering if her timing had been fortunate or calculated. She'd interrupted just as I was about to learn what had happened to end Dirk's friendship with William Meriwether. I might say it was coincidence, but I didn't usually believe in the phenomenon. Maybe she really did suspect I was fishing for tidbits to run in the *Informer*—or maybe there was something in Dirk's past that Ellen wanted to keep hidden.

CHAPTER EIGHT

———

I quickly grabbed a yogurt and a bagel before heading inside to see if Apple was done with her confessional yet. The booth was empty, and there was no sign of Apple. I did, however, see Joanie Parker waving to me from down the hall.

"There you are, Cam. I've been looking for you."

I raised an eyebrow. I wasn't sure which was more surprising: that she remembered my name this morning or that she was actually seeking me out.

She power walked toward me, her heels clacking on the tile floor as she waved a cell phone in one hand and a mimosa in the other. (Was everyone drinking already this morning?)

"Good morning, Joanie," I said, attempting to be civil.

She smirked, coming to a stop in front of me. "Oh, it is for *me*!"

I narrowed my eyes at her. Something in her tone raised a red warning flag in the back of my mind. "Hmm. So, where's your better half this morning?" I asked.

Joanie scowled. "Better?" she scoffed. "I'm the best thing that ever happened to that man, and he knows it."

I was pretty sure the best thing that had ever happened to Antoine Parker was actually his multi-million-dollar contract with the NFL, but what did I know?

"Speaking of better halves," Joanie said, her taunting grin returning. "Has Trace seen it yet?"

There went that red flag again. "Seen what?"

Joanie blinked in mock innocence. "Oh, you mean you don't know?"

"Know. What?" I ground out, my patience starting to wear.

"Oh, honey, for a reporter you are sorely out of the loop."

"Joanie, I've got things to do this morning," I said, seeing Apple slip in through the French doors at the end of the hall. "So if you have something to say to me, just say it."

But her smirk just grew. "Let's just say you should check out *Entertainment Daily,*" she said, sneering. "And, uh, maybe invest in a good antiperspirant," she said, mock-whispering the last part as she walked away, swigging her mimosa.

Oh. No.

I slipped my phone from my pocket and pulled up *ED*'s page. It looked like Eddie and Mike had wasted no time in uploading their shots from my morning run. There were several images of me standing at the gate, my hair matted to the sides of my face and dark sweat rings under my arms. The text underneath read *"Cameron Dakota was spotted sporting stinky sweats this morning at the location of the murderous hit reality show,* Celebrity Relationship Rehab, *where she and hunky Hollywood star, Trace Brody, are struggling to fix their failing relationship. Considering Dakota's current look, we can see why. Trace, you could do so much better! Or is this how low Piranha Man has sunk?"*

I groaned. Felix wasn't going to like the competition scooping me… Especially with pictures of me! And this was pretty much the opposite of the good press Trace was looking for.

I thought a really bad word. No doubt Joanie was on her way out to the pool to shove the pics in Trace's face even as I stood there. I was tempted to head her off, but as I spotted Apple head up the stairs to her room alone, I set my ego aside and decided to save my job first. Felix needed a story, and it was just possible Apple needed a warning about her boyfriend's violent past.

I took the stairs two at a time, knowing our next drill was starting soon. But as I approached Apple and Ice's suite, I heard raised voices on the other side. They were too muffled to make out what they were saying, but it was definitely Ice and Apple. And Ice was mad. I paused, doing an eeny-meeny-miney-moe about whether to knock or let them duke it out in private. I was just about to walk away when I heard a loud noise and Apple cry out.

I instinctively banged my fist on the door. If Ice had done anything to her...

"Apple!" I yelled.

Immediately the two on the other side went silent.

I was about to knock again when the door abruptly opened and Ice Kreme peered out at me, his nostrils flared, his eyes flashing. I had sudden second thoughts about confronting the guy, realizing just how menacing he was in close quarters. What he lacked in height and girth, he made up for in pure anger.

"What do you want?" he asked, irritation evident in his tone.

I licked my lips. "I, uh, wanted to ask Apple if I could borrow her curling iron," I said, thinking quickly.

Ice narrowed his eyes in suspicion. I stared back at him, fighting to keep my expression neutral.

"Babe," he called over his shoulder. "You got a curling iron?"

"Yeah," she replied from somewhere inside. I heard the sound of bathroom drawers opening and closing, rustling of clothes. More drawers closing. More rustling.

As the seconds stretched on, Ice rolled his eyes. "Dang, that girl couldn't find her own head if it wasn't on her skinny shoulders." He shook his head, glancing once back toward the room. "I'm outta here, shorty. You do your own thing."

Ice gave me one last long look before brushing past me and heading down the stairs. A beat later Apple appeared in the doorway. Her eyes were still wet with tears, and she was sniffling.

"You okay?"

She dropped her gaze to the floor. "Thanks. Yeah, I'm fine." Apple stepped aside and allowed me to enter the suite. It looked identical to the one where I was staying with Trace, with the same pale walls, velvety carpet, and gorgeous balcony. The only difference was theirs looked like two teenagers lived there—clothes, makeup, and empty soda cans littering every surface. My inner snoop itched to look under the piles of junk for a pair of bloody garden shears.

Apple followed me into the bedroom and resumed her curling iron search. I didn't have the heart to tell her it was just a ruse.

"You sure you're okay?" I asked again.

She shrugged. "Ice and I got into kind of a fight." She sighed, blowing out a puff of air that ruffled her bangs. "Over Dirk checking me out. Can you believe it? I told him Dirk's harmless. I told Ice he was just talking to me, and besides, that guy's old enough to be my dad."

I couldn't help a grin. "Sorry. Ice certainly has jealous streak, doesn't he?"

Apple plopped down on the bed. "At this point, I should be used to it. I mean, last month he thought the busboy at a restaurant was hitting on me. Then the caddy at the golf club. And before that it was the checker at the grocery store. It's like, any guy I see, Ice wants to pounce on, you know?"

"Apple, does he ever get violent with any of them?" I asked slowly, hoping I was treading lightly enough to maintain her trust.

"Well…he did hit that rollerblader at the Venice Boardwalk a few weeks ago when he catcalled me. But it almost wasn't his fault. I mean the guy did sorta roll right into Ice's fist."

Yeah, I'll bet. "Apple, he doesn't get violent with *you*, does he?"

Her head shot up. "Oh no! I mean, not the way you're thinking. He'd never hurt me. He just…well, he gets loud. Yells a lot. Breaks stuff. And cusses."

My thoughts must have been plain on my face about that, as she quickly continued. "But it's just because he's so passionate. He's an artist, you know?"

I was proud to say I stifled my eye roll. Ice's biggest contribution to the *arts* was the song "All My Hos Better Pay Out." He was a regular Beethoven.

"Have you guys fought a lot since you've been here?" I asked.

Apple nodded. "Constantly! At first I thought it was mostly for the cameras, but I can tell he's getting really upset now. Especially when I…" She paused, suddenly looking guilty.

"When you what?" I prompted.

She shook her head. "It's nothing."

When someone said it was *nothing*, it was always something. I put a hand on her arm, doing my best to project a friendly, non-threatening vibe. "You can tell me, Apple."

She sighed loudly, her eyes flitting to the camera mounted in the corner. Then she held a hand over her mouth so the eye in the sky couldn't see her lips move and whispered, "Ice won't tell me where he was when the doctor was murdered."

I raised an eyebrow at her. It was one thing to admit you didn't have an alibi. But it was another thing altogether to refuse to say where you were. Especially to your girlfriend in private.

I put my hand over my own mouth and whispered back. "Where do *you* think he was?"

"I don't know." But the worried look in her eyes told me she was thinking the same thing I was. Just how *passionate* had Ice been that first evening? Enough to kill?

* * *

After Apple finally found her curling iron and offered it to me (Hey, I couldn't very well refuse it at that point.), a PA tracked me down in the hallway outside our rooms and informed me the next drill was starting. I quickly stashed the curling iron in my room and headed outside where the rest of the celebs were assembling on the lawn in front of the man-made lake at the edge of the property. The men were all dressed in athletic shorts and T-shirts, with the exception of Dirk, who'd paired board shorts with a hot pink polo shirt straight out of 1989 and a pair of loafers without socks. Ellen stood next to him, her bare arms crossed in annoyance over her tasteful Lululemon top and cropped yoga pants. Her hair and makeup looked like she was about to report the evening news rather than expend any physical exertion. Joanie had on a pair of short-shorts and a crop top that showed off her belly ring, and Apple wore a bikini so tiny I had a feeling parts of her body would have to be blurred out in editing in order to even air on cable.

As I approached, Dirk gave me a small wave, still swaying slightly on his feet from the tequila aftereffects.

Trace gave me a scowl.

"What?" I whispered, coming up beside him.

"Forget it," he muttered under his breath.

I was about to ask more when Dr. Georgia took that moment to grace our group with her presence. "Alright, rehabbers, today we'll be doing a drill that tests your ability to communicate, even when confronted with uncomfortable or unpredictable situations." She paused for dramatic effect.

I had to admit, the drama worked. The "uncomfortable or unpredictable" part had me wincing a little.

"Today you and your partner will be tasked with paddling a canoe through a series of obstacles."

"Wait—on the water?" Joanie asked, her eyes big and round.

Dr. Georgia nodded. "Yes, on the lake." She gestured behind her.

"Oh no. No, no, no, no, no," Joanie said, shaking her head so hard that her long black ponytail swished behind her. "There is no way I'm getting these extensions wet. Do you have any idea how much these cost?"

I did. I'd followed her to the salon and bribed her stylist that day. But I figured the question was rhetorical and kept my mouth shut.

"If you and your partner can effectively communicate, you won't be getting them wet." Dr. Georgia grinned, and I could tell she was really hoping no one communicated effectively.

"Dawg, I don't swim!" Ice piped up.

"You will all be wearing safety vests," Dr. Georgia assured us. On cue, a crew member appeared then, handing out bright orange life vests to each of the celebs.

"You have to be joking!" Ellen said, looking at the thing as if it were a snake, not a piece of safety equipment. "You want me to wear this? On camera?"

"Darling, it's just a precaution," Dirk assured her, struggling to fit his over his paunchy belly.

"It's orange!"

"Orange is the new black!" Apple said, giggling as she slipped hers on.

Ellen rolled her eyes and swore under her breath.

I put my own vest on, noticing that Trace had been unusually quiet. While all the other rehabbers were making a show for the cameras of getting their vests on, he'd slipped his on under the radar and was standing at the edge of the group.

I looked over both shoulders, assessing just how much the closest microphone could pick up. (Thankfully they'd gone with boom mikes today instead of trying to attach lapel mikes to the strings of our bikinis.) "You sure everything is okay?" I asked again.

Trace glanced out the corner of his eyes at the nearest camera before turning his mouth away from it. "That sure was a scene you put on today."

I blinked at him, not sure what he meant. "With Joanie?" I asked, thinking I'd handled the diva pretty well considering she was gloating about *my* face on a tabloid.

Trace frowned. "No. You and *Dirk*?"

I frowned back at him. "What do you mean?" I whispered.

"I saw you flirting with him at the bar."

I glanced at Mr. Miami Vice and couldn't help the snort of laugher that escaped me.

Dr. Georgia spun her head my way.

I quickly covered my mouth.

She frowned but continued her instructions to the group on how to navigate the drill.

"You think I was flirting? With *Dirk*?" I asked Trace.

He was less amused, eyes narrowing at me as his forehead creased. "I know what I saw."

I couldn't help it. I laughed again. "Trace, I was just pumping him for information."

"You weren't pumping. You were licking a lime!" he whisper-yelled at me. "With lots of tongue. Suggestive tongue."

"Trace, you can't seriously think I'm interested in Dirk."

"It doesn't matter what I think," he whispered back, eyes darting to the cameras again. "It matters what they think."

"The crew?"

"The viewers!"

My turn to narrow my eyes. Okay, it was kinda flattering thinking that he was jealous of Dirk. Kinda cute, even. But as I realized it was less jealousy and more worry over how this would play out in the public, it became way less cute. Slightly annoying, even.

"So, you're worried that your fans might see me flirting with Dirk and it will reflect badly on *you*?"

"I'm sorry, was there something you want to share with all of us?"

Both Trace and I looked up to find Dr. Georgia watching us. In fact, as I looked around, everyone was watching us. I bit my lip. Making a scene had not been on my to-do list this morning.

"Sorry," Trace said, stepping forward. "Just a little disagreement."

I swear Dr. Georgia's eyes looked practically giddy. "Do share with us all. That's what we're here for."

Camera One pushed in on Trace.

"Well, I saw Cam here this morning—" Trace started.

But before he could finish, I jumped in with "—on the *Entertainment Daily* website looking a mess."

Joanie smirked. Apple shot me a look of sympathy. Trace frowned and shut his mouth with a click. Clearly that wasn't what he was about to say, but the last thing I wanted was to try to explain to the entire group how I was pumping Dirk for information and not hitting on him.

"It was super embarrassing," I continued. "I mean, not just for me but for his image."

"Trace, how do you feel about that?" Dr. Georgia said, turning to him.

Camera Two pushed in now too.

Oh brother.

I shot Trace a *play along!* look and mentally crossed my fingers.

He stared at me for a long moment. Then uttered just one word. "Betrayed."

Ouch. While he hadn't outted me, I could tell the word was aimed at me like a weapon. It was all I could do to keep my mouth shut for the cameras and not fall all over myself trying to apologize.

"Well," Dr. Georgia said, seeing she'd gotten all the drama she could from us, "maybe we'll have a chance to redeem that feeling in the drill. As I was saying…" she said, shooting a pointed look our way.

I made a big show of doing a zip-the-mouth-shut thing.

"…we all know that each of our couples have fallen into destructive patterns of communication. But what happens when they're faced with a whole new way of communicating in a whole new situation?"

I chewed my lip, trying to decipher what she meant.

"We're about to find out as we…switch partners!"

This was met with an equal number of groans and sighs of relief from the crowd. I was on the fence until I found out who I was trading in my *betrayed* partner for.

"Dirk, you'll be with Apple, and Ellen will paddle with Ice."

Ellen snorted in disgust and rolled her eyes again. If I had to guess, she was wishing she'd been hitting the shots that morning instead of her husband—who was currently beaming at Apple with what I could only describe as pure joy.

"Mr. Parker, you'll be paddling with Cameron," Dr. Georgia informed us.

Antoine gave me a nod. I nodded back. This would be a quiet ride at least.

"And that leaves Joanie riding with Trace."

Joanie sent me a triumphant grin before flouncing toward Trace. "My favorite movie star. I'll try not to be too gushy of a fan-girl on you," she purred. I had a feeling she was only half-kidding.

I glanced at Antoine. But if Joanie's display was aimed at getting a rise out of him, the starlet had failed. He was as stoic as ever, eyes on Dr. Georgia as she gave us last-minute instructions on how to paddle the canoe. Let's face it… The poor guy was probably used to Joanie's childish behavior. After all, her ridiculous antics had been displayed all over national television (not to mention the *Informer*) on a regular basis. I had to wonder what the guy saw in her. But it was clearly something. From the way he acted, it seemed as if he worshiped the ground she walked on and would do anything for her. In fact…

Squinting, I studied the large, muscled man. At well over six feet tall, his wide frame loomed over the rest of the guests. I'd seen some of the hits he'd delivered on the football field, and they'd been brutal. Off the gridiron, though, he seemed to be a gentle giant. A man like Antoine Parker was physically capable of killing a man, but he'd have to be given the proper motivation.

I watched as Joanie giggled at something Trace said, wondering if his wife was capable of giving him that motivation. If Joanie had wanted Dr. William dead, would Antoine have done it for her?

I tried to shake that disconcerting thought off as I stepped into a canoe with him, the rest of the rehabbers following suit. With the help of about a dozen crew members, all four boats were soon on the water as we tried to paddle through a set of buoys, rocks, flags, and other obstacles set in our path.

I could hear Joanie already starting to shout at Trace over veering too near to the banks. So much for their love affair. To our left, Apple was struggling to paddle the boat basically on her own as Dirk swayed in the seat behind her, his oar dragging in the water and his eyes glazed over. Ice was swearing up a storm over anything and everything, and Ellen was threatening to push him overboard as their canoe swayed unstably.

All things considered, I thought Antoine and I had a pretty decent chance of winning. I felt a little competitive streak kick in as I rowed. Not only did I have the strongest physical partner, but Antoine and I had zero drama, and having grown up a bit of an outdoorsy girl myself, I wasn't a total stranger to paddling a boat. Okay, not something I did every day in Hollywood, but I found it was starting to come back to me as we developed a quiet rhythm.

So quiet and rhythmic, in fact, that it took me a moment to realize our boat was taking on water.

Uh-oh.

I looked down to see several small holes in the bottom of our canoe. They must have been covered with something that had slowly disintegrated as we'd paddled farther from the shore, now leaving us leaking like a faucet. We'd been sabotaged.

The "unpredictable" part of the drill. I should have known.

"I think we're sinking," Antoine said, realizing at the same time.

"You paddle. I'll bail," I suggested, trying to scoop handfuls of water out of the canoe.

I glanced up, seeing the other boats starting to take on water at the same time. Joanie screamed, lifting her feet. Ellen shouted obscenities. Apple and Dirk both started giggling as if it was the funniest thing ever.

I bailed quickly, realizing that I was wrong about our chance in this drill—Antoine's size was going to work against us. His weight was pushing our boat lower and lower into the water as we furiously tried to bail and row and finish the drill without sinking at the same time.

"I get it," he said suddenly, still paddling as we neared the farthest obstacle.

"Get what?" I asked, pushing hair out of my eyes with the back of my wet hand.

"It's symbolic. Our sinking relationships."

I paused. "Wow. You're right." I wasn't sure if I was more surprised at his philosophizing or the fact he'd strung together more than two words to make a sentence. Even as the water was starting to seep into my shorts, I decided to take advantage of his unusually chatty moment.

"Have things been sinking for a while with you and Joanie?" I asked, trying for sympathy and not nosiness.

Antoine shrugged. "Maybe." Back to the one-word answers. Dang.

I tried again. "I can tell she means the world to you."

Antoine's expression softened. "I do love her."

He was so sincere I suddenly felt sorry for him. "And does she love you?" I pushed, remembering the divorce attorney's card in her pocket.

He blinked back emotion. What emotion was hard to tell, as he ducked his head. "She married me, right?"

I bit my lip, treading lightly here. "Getting married is one thing. It's harder to *stay* married…" I watched his reaction carefully.

He paused so long I thought maybe he wasn't going to answer. Then finally he said, "That's why we're here, right?"

I hated to tell him that he was probably the *only* person here actually looking to repair a relationship. Everyone else was all in on camera time.

Speaking of which…

As we rounded the end of the obstacle course, the sunlight reflected off several camera lenses in the bushes. Not that I should be surprised, but I could have sworn one of them was smaller than the others. Not mounted but moving slightly. I squinted toward the patch of oleander on the shore, a few feet away.

"Dude, what did I tell you about hands on my girl?!" Ice yelled.

I snapped my head around as Ice and Ellen's canoe came up behind Dirk and Apple. Dirk had both arms around Apple's middle, the two still giggling like middle schoolers.

"He was just catching me, Ice," Apple protested though her laughter. "We're sinking!"

"Yo, we all sinking. You don't see me grabbin' on Grandma here."

"Hey!" Ellen shouted in response.

"We're just having fun, Ice," Dirk said, splashing Apple like they were two kids in a bathtub. Apple squealed and splashed him back.

"That's it, Dawg. That's the last straw. I'm comin' for you!" Ice stood in the canoe, pointing a finger at Dirk.

Ellen screamed, "Sit down, you buffoon!" She grabbed the sides of the canoe as it tipped precariously to the side.

Antoine tried to paddle left, out of the way, as they headed straight toward us. Not that they had much choice. Joanie and Trace were coming through the narrow course from the opposite direction.

"Trace, go left! No, right! Slower! Turn!" Joanie shouted directions, tossing her paddles everywhere.

"Watch out," I warned as one hit our canoe.

"You dead, old man," Ice yelled, still gunning for Dirk. He reached out a paddle and shoved the side of their boat.

Dirk and Apple tipped to the right.

Antoine struggled to veer left.

I watched in horror as Joanie's oars went wild, shoving at the front of our boat. Antoine's giant weight shifted, the boat teetered into Ellen and Ice's, Ellen screamed, Ice lost his balance, and over we all went.

The next thing I felt was cold, wet, muddy water washing over me. I heard Joanie laughing, Trace diving in to help Ice who was screaming about how he couldn't swim, and Ellen sputtering about lawsuits and slimy algae…and a camera shutter clicking.

My head spun around to the oleander bush. Just as a pair of unkempt heads ducked down…one suspiciously dusted with Cheeto crumbs.

Mike and Eddie.

Just. Great.

CHAPTER NINE

———

Needless to say nobody won the canoe drill. Except maybe Reisner Productions. I had a feeling that eight soaking wet celebrities were going to make for great ratings when this episode finally aired. *If* it aired. This season felt like the biggest fiasco ever, and I was starting to have doubts that any of this would be worthy of actually showing on TV.

Once we dragged ourselves out of the lake, everyone trudged through the pristine house, creating a trail of muddy water behind them that caused at least one crew member to groan out loud. Then we hightailed it up to our rooms to clean up, change, primp, and become camera worthy again. I quickly showered and threw on a pair of skinny jeans and a flowy white top before pulling my hair back into a no-fuss ponytail. A swipe of mascara and a little dab of red lipstick later, and I figured I looked about as camera ready as I was going to. While Trace showered, I took the opportunity to head downstairs to see if I could catch any of our rehabbers alone before our next drill.

Luck was on my side finally, as I found Ice and Dirk in the billiard room. It looked as if they might have been playing a game of pool, but it had turned into a bit of a standoff—Ice wielding one billiard cue in his hand almost like a sword as he again read Dirk the riot act over keeping his eyes off his woman. Though I noticed the tirade was directed more toward the cameraman standing in the corner of the room.

With a quick glance over my shoulder, I ducked behind one of the bookcases and pulled out my phone, pointing it at the two. It was hardly a smoking gun, but at least the snippet of video footage was something I could send Felix later. I got about thirty good seconds of Ice threatening Dirk with a pool cue before Dirk's gaze turned my way and I had to duck back behind the bookcase again. I shoved my phone into my pocket and quickly backtracked down the corridor toward the great hall. Which was currently empty. It appeared that the female half of our rehab group was taking a bit longer to recover from the mud bath than the males. Go figure.

It also meant the house was largely empty.

To the left of the great hall sat the kitchen, dining area, and the lounge, as well as a couple of common areas where a large bar had been set up near foosball and ping-pong tables that, so far, no one had touched. Behind me was the billiard room and beside that the staircase that led up to our suites on the second floor. To my right was a small hallway I'd yet to explore. But I had seen the staff and crew filtering in and out of it. Presumably storage rooms for the multitude of cameras and lighting and sound equipment…and possibly the video control room?

I looked around, making sure no crew members were in the vicinity, before quickly slipping down the hallway to the right. While it was almost inevitable that some of the mounted cameras around the house might see me heading that direction, I crossed my fingers that no one was watching the live feed.

There were four doors down this wing of the mansion, all closed. None of them labeled. Rats. As I scanned the length of the hallway, though, I didn't see any mounted cameras here. Which made sense. Celebrities weren't supposed to be in this area, so there would be no need to film it. Feeling like I was on borrowed time before someone saw the footage of me ducking into forbidden territory, I put my ear to the first door. Silence. I tried the knob, but it was locked. I filed that info away for later and moved on to the next door, pausing outside to listen for any sounds within. Unfortunately I heard them. Two voices. What they were saying was too muffled for me to hear, but I could tell they were both deep and male. I quickly moved on to the next door.

No sounds on the other side of this one. I tried the handle and said a silent *thank you* when it turned in my hand. Darkness met me as I opened the door, so I quickly slipped inside, praying no one else was there.

I closed the door behind me and felt up the side of the wall until I hit a light switch. When I flipped it on, I swear I almost heard a chorus of angels singing above me. It was a small room, but one entire side of it was filled with a bank of a dozen or more monitors, all showing black and white footage of various parts of the house and grounds. An electronic control panel sat on a large desk in front of the monitors, and two office chairs made up the entirety of the rest of the furniture in the room. The evidence of several take-out meals sat crumpled to one side of the desk, spilling onto the floor. Someone had spent a good deal of time sitting here.

Watching us.

I blinked at the wall of images, suddenly realizing just how monitored we all were. I clearly saw Ice and Dirk still in the billiard room, Apple putting on her lipstick in her bedroom, Joanie on her cell phone in the kitchen screaming a silent tirade at someone, Trace getting dressed in the bedroom (I'll admit, I paused a few moments to watch that monitor more closely. Be still my beating heart!), and even Ellen in a steamy shower in her bathroom.

Wait, they had cameras in the bathroom? I suddenly felt violated. And vowed to shower in a bikini from now on.

There were also several monitors, currently void of rehabbers, showing the other rooms in the house, as well as the pool, bar, and outdoor seating areas. Anything anyone did on the grounds was being recorded. And, by the take-out evidence, watched live as well. I felt a shudder run down my spine at the thought. While I had known what I was signing up for when I'd agreed to do the show, the sheer magnitude of it hit me now, making me feel like I'd been living in a goldfish bowl.

However, it was also very convenient when investigating a murder.

I quickly sat down at the control panel, knowing whoever usually manned this area would probably be back soon. If I wanted to search for the "missing" footage from the day of the murder, it was now or never.

While I was no stranger to working a camera, the control panel in front of me was a bit more complicated than I was used to. Definitely out of my league. I randomly tried a few different buttons and saw things flit across the screens as the view switched from one camera to another. I tried some more and was able to move a couple of the outside cameras around. So they could follow us as well. Creepy.

After about five minutes of guess-and-check, I finally figured out how to pull up past footage. I scanned through our first drill, trying not to laugh too hard as Joanie fell in the mud again.

I watched the drill end and witnessed Dr. William's last moments with the group as he told us all how terribly we had each done. I tried to zoom in on each contestant's face, reading their expressions. If I had to guess, at that moment no one had been a fan of the good doctor. When he'd finished we all dispersed up to our bedrooms, and I watched the various monitors from different camera angles as Apple went to the pool house to put on her bikini, Dirk and Ellen wandered toward the bar in the great hall, Trace pulled out his phone and made a call in the lounge, and I went upstairs to shower and change. Antoine surprisingly went toward the confession booth. I spotted both Joanie and Ice coming into the house, but the cameras lost them then. I tried to pull up footage from various parts of the house, but I never caught ether one of them again.

Then suddenly the screen showed us all gathered in the great hall, waiting for our hosts to arrive for the evening drill. I frantically pushed different buttons trying to get the footage for the critical time between when we'd dispersed and when Dr. William's body had been found. Unfortunately, every camera seemed to have cut out at exactly the same time.

I sat back in the seat, staring at the monitors. Had someone tampered with the recording functions in the control room that night? Or had the footage really been lost? Or, perhaps, had it been deleted after the fact? The truth was it hadn't been *that* difficult to get into this control room. And while it had taken me a few minutes to figure out the system, I was far from a computer expert. Almost any one of our rehabbers could have had the same opportunity. So who had erased proof of their guilt?

I was still pondering that when I heard the two voices from the room next door grow louder.

And closer.

Uh-oh.

My eyes darted around the sparsely furnished room. Truth was, there was nothing to hide under or behind. I watched in horror as the doorknob turned, a crack of light showing as the two men pushed the door open.

I jumped up from the chair and instinctively flattened myself against the wall behind the door as it fully opened.

"…the heck does she expect us to do? Magically make up a new drill?" I heard one voice saying.

"Yeah. And fast," said a second voice.

"Reisner seriously didn't have anything planned?" Voice Number One asked.

"Sure. Tomorrow was supposed to be Secrets Day."

"What's that?"

I watched the back of Voice Number Two's head shake back and forth as the two crew members came into the room, standing just inside the open doorway. "Dude, didn't you at least watch the show before you applied for this job?"

Voice Number One must not have responded as Voice Two continued, "Dr. William always has a file of secrets on all of the rehabbers. Stuff they *didn't* divulge in their initial interviews. Secrets Day is when he springs it on them."

I thought a really dirty word. Of course. Secrets Day! I had forgotten all about it. Honestly, I had always thought that the rehabbers' reactions to the "secrets" the doctors revealed were choreographed ahead of time. There was no way the rehabbers didn't know these things were going to be brought up in the house. Or at least that was what I had previously thought. My mind was already rewinding all of my most embarrassing moments, trying to pinpoint anything that Dr. William would have considered scandalous enough to expose on the show. Aside from a mountain of unpaid parking tickets, I didn't have any skeletons in my closet that I could think of. Did I?

"Sounds mean," Voice Number One responded. "And awesome."

"I'm sure it would have been."

"So, why are we scrapping it now?"

"Dr. William was the guy who had the secrets. So now we're stuck coming up with something last minute."

There was a pause. Then: "Wait—Reisner doesn't know the secrets? What about the lady doc?"

I saw Voice Number Two's head shake again. "No, he always played them pretty close to the vest. Afraid something would leak before he had a chance to spring it on the unsuspecting celeb-u-idiots."

The two men moved toward the control panel, and I said a silent prayer hoping they didn't notice someone had been playing with the footage. At least not until I could make my escape.

"Dude, you been messing with the cameras again?"

So much for the power of prayer. I bit my lip, calculating the odds of being able to slip away unnoticed.

"So, how did Dr. William find out these secrets if the rehabbers didn't tell him?" Voice Number One asked, thankfully changing the subject as his buddy fiddled with the controls and repositioned cameras around the house for optimum spying on the guests.

"I dunno. Dave told me he hired some private eye in the Valley."

"Well, he must have a record of them somewhere," Voice One pressed. "Something we can use?"

Voice Two sighed. "If he did, it's probably on his laptop. The police have that. So, no two ways around it, we've got to come up with something. And tonight."

This was met by a loud groan from Voice One. "And I had Lakers tickets tonight."

"Welcome to glamorous Hollywood, kid."

The rest of their conversation was lost on me as both men focused on the monitors, and I grabbed my moment to sneak out unnoticed, all but sprinting back down the hallway toward the main area of the house. When I hit the great hall I finally slowed down, nonchalantly walking toward the kitchen where Apple and Joanie were pouring themselves glasses of wine.

I grabbed one myself and did my best at looking calm, cool, and collected…when inside all I could think about was those now-lost secrets. And if one of them might have been worth killing over.

*   *   *

Two glasses of wine and an hour of listening to Apple and Joanie both complain about their men later, we were all gathered into the great hall, where it was announced that there would be no further drills that afternoon after all. Instead, Dr. Georgia would begin filming our couples' interviews. Where I knew from my viewer experience she would ask pointed and uncomfortable questions designed to instigate fights between them.

Ellen and Dirk were called in as the first victims, leaving the rest of us to heave a collective sigh of relief.

I took the opportunity to step into the billiard room alone and update Tina on what I'd heard about the possible private investigator Dr. William had hired. I pressed speed dial and waited for her to answer.

"Cam!" an airy voice exclaimed into the phone. "How are you?"

I frowned. It wasn't Tina. "Allie? Why are you answering Tina's cell phone?"

There was a pause. "Oh. She's in Felix's office," Allie said easily. Almost too easily.

I narrowed my eyes at the phone. "And *why* are you answering her phone again?" I asked.

"I was walking by her desk and saw your name on the caller ID. I figured it must be important if you were calling from the set. So, tell me—how are things going on the show?" she asked, and I detected a hopeful tone in her voice.

"Everything's fine," I hedged. While I actually genuinely liked Allie, she had been known to angle for…well, an angle. And I had promised Tina an exclusive on anything that happened.

"You call a murder among celebrities *fine*?" She snorted. "Gee, your idea of *exciting* must be pretty intense."

I couldn't help a grin. "Okay, 'fine' was a poor word choice. *Grating, emotional, ridiculous*. Those all might fit better."

"Oh yeah?" she asked, and I thought I heard bubblegum snap between her teeth. "Do tell…"

"Sorry," I said, meaning it. "I promised the story to Tina this time."

Allie sighed. "Of course you did," she said, sounding deflated.

I honestly did feel a little bad. Before Allie had started working at the *Informer*, Tina and I had been a two-man crew. She got the deets, and I got the pics. And while Felix often reminded us that Allie was now a member of the team and should be treated as such, sometimes Tina and I fell into old rhythms. I could understand how Allie sometimes felt like the odd man out.

"Well, if you need a hand with anything—anything at all!—I'm here. You know, just hanging around. Waiting on a tip. Even an itty-bitty tippy," she tried.

"I will," I told her, mostly meaning it. "But when Tina gets out of Felix's office, could you tell her to call me, please?"

"Yeah. Sure," Allie said. But it didn't hold much conviction. If I was a betting girl, I'd lay odds that Tina wouldn't be getting my message.

* * *

I returned to the great hall just in time to see Dirk enter and cross the room to the bar. His face was red, and his hands were shaking as he poured himself a generous four fingers of Scotch. A moment later, Ellen's heels sounded as she clacked purposefully toward the stairs, mascara staining her cheeks in tell-tale tear tracks. Yeesh. Dr. Georgia must have done a number on the couple.

"Cam and Trace?"

My head snapped up as a PA with a clipboard walked into the room.

"Yeah?" Trace rose from the sofa, a look of trepidation on his face that exactly matched the way my insides were churning.

"You're up next."

Oh boy.

I gave Trace a wan smile as he grabbed my hand, and we followed the PA down the hall and into another room.

It was the same one I'd had my one-on-one interview with Dr. Georgia in the other day, only now it had been outfitted with a cheesy red love seat in the shape of a heart. Trace and I sat down on it, the two of us barely able to fit. Clearly it was designed to maximize discomfort. Dr. Georgia sat across from us, an electronic earpiece just barely visible beneath her hair, which was worn loose this afternoon. If I had to guess, I'd say Reisner was somewhere on the other end of that contraption, ready to feed her embarrassing questions. Behind her stood a couple of camera operators, a guy holding a boom mike, several lighting and sound techs, and a handful of PAs. All in all, it felt like we were about to face a firing squad.

Trace gave my hand a reassuring squeeze. I squeezed back.

Okay, we got this. I mean, what could she really say that would be so awful?

"Trace, I'd like to begin with you. What exactly do you think of the fact that your girlfriend sells your secrets for a living?"

I blinked at her, not sure I'd heard her right. "I *what*?"

"Well, you are a tabloid reporter, are you not? A member of the dreaded paparazzi?"

"Uh…" Trace trailed off, looking from me to Dr. Georgia.

"Yes," I answered. "I mean, no, we're not *dreaded*."

"You are by celebrities."

"Well, maybe some."

"And Trace here is a celebrity, aren't you, Trace?"

Trace shifted uncomfortably beside me. "Um…"

"That's beside the point," I jumped in. "Our relationship is completely separate from my professional life. I would never print anything Trace told me in confidence."

"Really?" Dr. Georgia said, her eyebrows rising.

"Really." I sat back in my seat, giving Trace a reassuring smile.

He smiled back, but it held less confidence than when we'd entered the room.

"Then why exactly are you here? Exploiting your relationship for your career gains?"

"Ha!" I said, though there was zero humor in it. "Listen, lady, this was not *my* idea to be here."

"Oh no?" she asked, those eyebrows going up again.

"No. It was Trace's idea to come on this show. All his."

I felt him shift uncomfortably again as Dr. Georgia turned her attention on him.

"And why did you feel your relationship needed help, Trace?" she asked.

"No, it wasn't that he—" I started.

But Dr. Georgia cut me off. "Is Trace ever allowed to speak for himself?"

I froze, mouth hanging open in way that I'm sure was incredibly unattractive. And being recorded. I shut it with a click and did my best not to roll my eyes. I may or may not have succeeded.

"Now," Dr. Georgia continued, "Trace, what is it that made you think your relationship was in trouble?"

Trace sat up straighter, and I felt him shift from Real Trace to Celebrity Trace, no doubt channeling the loveably heartsick billionaire he'd played in *My Heart Belongs in Manhattan*.

"You're right. About everything, Dr. Georgia," he said.

I felt my stomach drop. "She's *what*?"

But no one was paying attention to me now. Dr. Georgia's eyes shone with anticipation, and Trace was in full-on camera mode.

"Go on," she prompted, practically salivating.

"I just don't feel like I can trust Cam. I mean, you're right. She has exploited our relationship for her own career gains."

I felt my cheeks heating, not believing what I was hearing. "You have *got* to be kidding me. What do you call this?" I asked, waving my arms wide. Which was no small feat while squished on the tiny loveseat. I almost hit Trace in the nose. And it was almost not on purpose.

But, again, I was ignored.

"So she has violated your trust in the past?" Dr. Georgia asked.

Trace nodded. "She has."

"I have not!"

"Yes, you have, Cam."

"Have not!" I realized I had sunk to playground-level arguing, but my blood was boiling. It was one thing to fabricate some minor issue to get ratings. It was another to tell the viewing public that I was untrustworthy. The news business survived on trust. No way was I going to let him take down my professional character just to boost his career in front of the cameras.

"Tell me, Trace," Dr. Georgia cut in. "When did she violate your trust?"

"When she published nude photos of me in her paper."

"*What*?!" I jumped up from the sofa. "I never—"

"Taken of me in my swimming pool from the bushes outside my property."

I froze mid-sentence. And sat back down. Oh God, he was right. "But...but that was so long ago. I mean, it was before I even met you!"

"Are you saying you didn't know who Trace Brody was at the time?"

"Well, no," I hedged. "I knew. I just didn't *know* him. I mean, we weren't even dating yet."

"It violated my privacy," Trace pressed, his face doing that cute frown-slash-pout thing that had won over audiences' hearts in the scene where the billionaire bared his soul to his secretary in Times Square.

"But...but..." I sputtered. "I mean, you were a celebrity, and I was..."

"The paparazzi," Dr. Georgia finished for me. "Which begs the questions—can the two of you ever really trust each other? Or will your career always get in the way, Cam?"

"Yes!" I paused. "I mean, no. We... This was forever ago. We're fine *now*. I mean I would never do that now." I was floundering again, and I could feel Camera One pushing in to capture every embarrassing moment of it.

"Sure," Dr. Georgia said, nodding sympathetically with an emotion that was anything *but* sympathy dancing in her eyes.

"You're fine now. But Trace...he's not fine. And unless you start acknowledging his feelings, I don't think you ever will be fine together as a couple."

I opened my mouth with a rebuttal, but Dr. Georgia stopped me once again. "That's all for these two," she told the crew. "Please bring in Ice and Apple now."

"But...I..."

Dr. Georgia stood, gesturing to hair and makeup for a touch-up. Trace got up from the sofa, not looking me in the eye, I noticed, as he quickly stepped out of the room.

And I sat there on the cheesy red velvet loveseat, wondering what the heck had just happened. This *had* all been for the cameras, right? Because it had felt a little too real. And personal. Did Trace really still harbor some resentment about my job? About photos I'd taken before we'd even said a word to each other? Could it be we really weren't totally fine? This reality show was totally messing with my own sense of reality.

A PA finally took me by the hand and guided me off the loveseat and back out to the great hall. Ice and Apple were being escorted away by another PA, and Dirk and the Parkers were the only occupants of the room.

"Where's Trace?" I asked lamely.

I was met with three shrugs.

Which left me two choices: search the house myself for Trace and face whatever grains of truth were behind his reality show confession or pour another glass of wine.

I crossed the room to the bar.

CHAPTER TEN

———

The rest of the afternoon went by in a blur, possibly due to the Chardonnay. After Ice and Apple's turn in the hot seat, Apple ran crying to her room, and Ice came out swearing a blue streak that used all of George Carlin's seven forbidden words. Several times. In ways I never thought they could be used. Honestly, it was the most creative thing I'd ever heard him do.

Joanie and Antoine's stint with the doctor ended much the same, only it was Antoine huffing away outside to cool off and Joanie charging for the bar.

By the time we gathered for dinner, the group had shrunk considerably and those of us who were left were either sulking, drunk, or both. I picked at my food, the uncertainty in my gut growing with each passing moment that Trace was absent from the group. While part of me desperately wanted to go after him and be reassured that this had all been for the cameras, my pride held me back. He'd humiliated me on national television. And, worse yet, he'd been right. I had violated his privacy. But my motto had always been that the celebrities we photographed needed us just as much as we needed them. It was an unspoken agreement we had. We took scandalous, embarrassing, and yes, sometimes nude photos of them, and they tolerated us doing it because it kept them in the news and in the public eye.

How many times had celebrities used us in publicity stunts to promote their latest movies or in "impromptu" photo ops to reveal their latest beau or baby bump? Plenty! So had I crossed a line in publishing those photos of Trace? Possibly. Would I do it now? Never. Which of us was *currently* exploiting the other for career gains? Trace!

And how many glasses of wine had I had? I was afraid that in my current state I couldn't count that high.

By the time dinner was over and Mr. Reisner came in announcing there would be no evening drills, we heaved a collective sigh of relief. The emotional day had taken a toll on us all, and everyone mumbled excuses to go up to their suites and retire early.

As soon as I opened the door to ours, I spotted Trace pacing the floor while talking on the phone.

I swallowed down a lump of trepidation as he turned and spotted me. I did a little wave in his direction and attempted a smile.

He didn't smile back.

"I gotta go. I'll call you later," he told the person on the other end of his call before hanging up.

"Hey," I said. "Who was that?"

"My agent."

"Oh. Cool. Got a new offer?"

"No. He's doing damage control."

"Over what?" I asked, sitting down on the bed. Admittedly, the room had started a spinning a little.

"Over my *girlfriend* showing up on the *ED* website looking like death warmed over."

I cringed. "Oh yeah. I forgot about that." I paused. "'Death warmed over'? Isn't that a little harsh?"

Trace ran a hand through his hair. "Sorry," he said, "but this whole thing has headed south on me. This was supposed to make me look *good* to the viewing public. Now I've got tabloids saying we're breaking up and the producers making me look like a sap."

I snorted. "I think you did that all on your own."

Trace paused, eyes narrowing my way. "And what was that in there with Dr. Georgia?" he asked.

I felt my eyebrows head north. "My thoughts exactly! You killed me in there."

He angled his body away from the camera. "That's what we're here for, remember?" he hissed. "No drama, no air time. No air time, no career for me."

"Yeah, well, what about my career?" I asked, not even caring if the cameras heard me. "You just called me out as a liar and a sneak in there. How does that bode for my journalistic career?"

"*Journalistic*?" Trace asked. "Come on, Cam, you're a tabloid photographer!"

The Chardonnay and I narrowed our eyes at him. "Okay, pal. You want drama?" I stood, angling myself toward the camera mounted in the corner of the room. "I'll give you drama!"

"What's that supposed to mean?" Trace took a step backward.

"It means all you've done since we've entered this house is preen for the cameras." I waved my hands toward the lenses I was sure were picking up every juicy bit of what had somehow escalated into a fight. "I've seen Heartbroken Romantic Hero Trace, Encouraging Coach Trace, Action-Star-Slash-Buddy-Flick Trace. Your whole range of characters. But you couldn't be real if your life depended on it!"

"That's not fair, Cam," Trace protested, eyes darting to the cameras.

"You want to know what's not fair? This whole thing has been *you* exploiting our relationship for *your* career gains. And then you have the cojones to accuse me of it? My career is tanking, if you didn't notice! My editor is threatening to fire me, my face is all over the *other* tabloids, and I'm stuck in a nut house with a bunch of spoiled has-beens and a killer on the loose!"

"'Has-beens'? Me included in that?" Trace's eyebrows were hunkered down over his eyes, his Adam's apple bobbing up and down. Maybe he was a better actor than I'd given him credit for. He was nailing Wounded Boyfriend Trace right now. "How much have you had to drink tonight, Cam?"

"Not enough to deal with your ridiculous, fame-seeking bullsh—"

"Okay, that's enough!" Trace shouted, hands going in the air. "Out!" He pointed toward the door.

"Huh?" I'll admit, the wine was making my thoughts a little cloudy.

"Look, you need some time to cool off before you say something you'll regret."

I narrowed my eyes at him, thinking a whole lot of *regretful* words already.

But before I could voice any, he continued. "I think you should…" He paused, looking toward the cameras again. "I think you should take the night in the Doghouse to cool down."

I blinked at him. "Wait—what? Are you serious?" I asked, lowering my voice and angling away from the camera. "This is just for show, right?"

But if he was acting, Trace didn't break character. "Just go, Cam. We both clearly need some space," he said, his voice deep and dark. Then before I could respond further, he stalked out onto the balcony.

I stared after him for a beat, for the second time that day wondering what had just happened. Had this been a staged fight or real? I'd thought I was supposed to be the one mad at him…but *I* was in the Doghouse?

Fine. If it was space he wanted, he'd get it. I stood back up, only wobbling slightly, and made my way to the door. Which I slammed extra hard on my way out as some sort of last word. Take that, Wounded Boyfriend Trace!

News of our fight must have traveled among the crew members quickly, as a camera was waiting for me at the bottom of the stairs along with Dr. Georgia. I groaned out loud. As if this evening couldn't get any better.

"I've been informed that Mr. Brody has banished you to the Doghouse for the evening." It was said in her usual clinical tone, but her eyes shone with excitement as if she couldn't believe her luck. Two fights from golden boy Trace in one night!

"Banished is a harsh word," I defended.

"I'll walk you," Georgia said.

I saw Bonnie peek out from around the camera and give me an apologetic look.

I shrugged, too tired to care about further humiliation at this point. "Lead the way then, Doc."

I followed Georgia past the great hall and to the end of the hallway on our left to a room I'd not been in before. Dr. Georgia unlocked the door with flourish, sweeping it open with a faux welcoming gesture.

Though I'd seen the Doghouse on previous seasons of *Celebrity Relationship Rehab*, it was ten times cheesier in person. The floor of the large room was covered in Astroturf, in the center of which sat a larger-than-life-size doghouse. It was painted fire engine red and had a *Beware of Dog* sign hanging on the door. Georgia stopped just outside the entrance and turned to stare down her nose at me. "I hope you'll spend your time here thinking about how you can be a better partner to Mr. Brody," she said stiffly.

"I sure will." My tone sounded more insincere than I'd intended, and the hostess eyed me skeptically before turning to leave.

Bonnie stayed, following me silently inside with her camera.

The interior of the Doghouse was just as silly as the outside. Every inch of the floor was covered with newspapers, and the bed was actually a large beanbag mattress that resembled a dog bed. The small bathroom off the back housed a toilet that looked like a fire hydrant, and the walls were decorated with framed paintings of dogs not only playing poker but also Go Fish, Old Maid, and…was that Uno? I shook my head at the ridiculousness of it and flopped back onto the dog bed with a sigh.

At least the beanbag was comfortable.

After it became clear I wasn't moving, Bonnie turned off her camera and set it down on the oversize pillow beside me. "I'm so sorry Trace kicked you out," she said, giving me a sympathetic pat on the shoulder.

I sighed. "I suppose I might have deserved it a little." Had I just called my boyfriend a has-been fame-seeker? Ugh.

Bonnie's forehead wrinkled. "Blame it on the booze. It flows like water around here for a reason."

I shot her as much of a smile as I could muster. "Thanks. But I think I can only partially blame it on the wine."

She shrugged. "Cheer up. At least you don't have to spend the night filming Dirk and Ellen in their bathrobes." She did a mock shudder.

Thank God for small favors.

* * *

"Seriously, Cam. Are you *trying* to run my paper into the ground?"

I groaned, blinking into the barrage of morning light coming through the window as I held my phone to my ear. I'd been tempted to not answer it, but the incessant ringing had not only woken me up from a deep, dreamless sleep but had also caused a headache to brew instantly behind my eyes.

"Good morning to you too, Felix," I croaked out in response.

But my boss was not about pleasantries today. "You're practically delivering scoops to *Entertainment Daily* on a silver platter. Why don't you just give them my bank account info while you're at it so they can take *all* of my money?"

"What did Mike and Eddie do now?" I asked, sitting up and rubbing my eyes.

"Are you telling me you haven't even seen *ED* yet today?"

I shook my head even though he couldn't see me. Bad mistake. The headache spread to my temples. I was never drinking again.

"No. Why? What did they do?"

"Only post information that the first rehabber of the season had been sent to the Doghouse in a knock-down-drag-out fight with her boyfriend that just might end their relationship." He paused. "Any idea who that rehabber might be?" he asked, sarcasm dripping from his English accent.

I glanced at the dogs playing poker in a frame on the opposite wall. "I have a guess."

"Why, in all that is holy, did you not tell me first!?"

I took a deep, cleansing breath. Ouch. Was it possible to have a headache in your lungs too?

"It's not a big deal. We're not breaking up." I hoped.

"I don't care what you are or aren't doing. I care that *ED* is printing it first!"

While he had a point, the last thing I wanted to do was discuss the status of my relationship with my boss. On the other hand, I did like having a job. "Sorry," I croaked out.

"Sorry? Sorry!" Felix muttered a few cursed words.

In the background I could hear Tina yelling, "Swear pig!" at him from across the newsroom. I grinned, wishing I was there instead of in this oversize doghouse of horrors.

"Look, I promise I'll get you something soon. Something big," I said.

Felix paused in his tirade. "Big?"

I bit my lip. "Yeah."

"How big?"

"Big as in…I'm getting close to figuring out who killed Dr. William." I cringed. I hated lying.

"If you're stringing me along, Cam, I swear I'll—"

"Oh, sorry, someone's at the door." Well, if I was already lying, might as well go for broke. "Gotta go. Sorry. Talk to you soon, Felix."

"Cam, I—"

I quickly stabbed the *Off* button on my phone.

Then flopped back onto the bed again.

The truth was, all I had about who'd killed Dr. William was speculation—I was woefully short on proof. And without evidence, if Felix printed any of my theories, the *Informer* could potentially be sued for libel. Not an option.

"Okay, Cam. Think. What do I know so far?" I asked the card-playing dogs.

Suspect number one: Dr. Georgia Meriwether. No solid alibi but nothing solid to pin her to the crime either. The only things I'd learned so far were that she likely inherited a boatload of money and she wasn't exactly grieving her husband's death. And she was a sadist when it came to instigating conflict in relationships. Which didn't make her my favorite person ever, but it didn't mean she was a killer either.

Then there was Ice Kreme. Ice had no alibi and a violent temper—two things that added up nicely on my suspect list. Ice certainly hadn't hidden his disdain for Dr. William or the fact that he thought the sleazy host had gotten what he deserved. But was a wandering eye where Apple was concerned really enough to kill over? Not sure.

I wasn't about to count Dirk and Ellen out of the mix either. Dirk had admitted to knowing Dr. William, and I'd gotten the impression that the friendship had ended on bad terms. How bad was a question mark, but it wasn't out of the realm of possibility that it had been enough to hold a grudge for all these years. For that matter, if the grudge was real, why had Dirk agreed to do the show? Had the soap star seen it as an opportunity to right some past wrong?

And then there were Joanie and Antoine. Joanie was hiding something, and I had a feeling it had to do with the divorce attorney, though I had no idea how to find out for sure. It wasn't like the starlet would confide in me. How much Antoine knew and was hiding for her was still up for debate. And it hadn't escaped my notice that, like Ice, Joanie had slipped off alone and unaccounted for during the time of the murder. I wondered if the police had asked for her alibi.

I had no idea. All I knew was that I needed coffee—stat!

I made my way out of the Doghouse, still dressed in my clothes from the day before, and padded into the kitchen.

Joanie was already there, feeding her dog tiny bites of croissant. She gave me a big, fake smile as I approached.

"Well, look who it is, Izzy," Joanie cooed to the little pup. "Our very own little doggie out of her house."

I shot her a look. "Coffee. If you want to live, point me in the direction of coffee."

"Well, someone got up on the wrong side of the dog bed," she mumbled, smirking to herself.

"Here," Apple said, appearing beside me with a fresh cup of strong, black deliciousness.

"Bless you," I told her, electing to ignore Joanie. At least until I had some caffeine running through my brain.

"Rough night?" Apple asked, her eyes sympathetic.

I shrugged. "I'll survive," I said, watching Dirk and Ellen filter into the room. Dirk eyed the bacon but, under the watchful gaze of his wife, only added fruit to his breakfast plate. Ellen followed suit as Apple grabbed her own cup of coffee while telling me all about her latest fight with Ice the night before.

"…and then I told him for the millionth time that I'm not interested in Dirk Price. I mean, come on. The guy is a gazillion years old." She paused, looking over her shoulder at Dirk, whose frown said he'd heard her. "No offense or anything."

"None taken," he mumbled, cheeks going red.

"Anyway, it's like Ice just doesn't hear me. He's got a one-track mind."

"Where is Ice this morning?" I asked, noticing that most of the rehabbers were at the breakfast table munching away. I spotted Trace pushing eggs around on a plate, carefully avoiding looking my direction. Smart man. I couldn't be responsible for what might come out of my mouth this morning without at least another gallon of coffee.

"He said he needed some alone time. He went out for a walk around the grounds."

I raised an eyebrow her way. "How long ago was that?" I asked, half an idea brewing in the back of my mind.

Apple shrugged. "I dunno. He was leaving just as I was coming downstairs. Maybe ten minutes ago?" she said, filling a plate with pancakes and breakfast potatoes.

"Huh." I paused, glancing back at the assemblage of rehabbers. "Excuse me. I'm just gonna go freshen up…" I said, trailing off as I backed out of the kitchen.

I set my now-empty coffee cup down on the nearest ledge and made a beeline for the stairs, taking them two at a time. If Apple was busy with breakfast and Ice was out for a walk, I sensed a perfect opportunity to slip into their room unnoticed. I paused at the top of the stairs, coming face to face with two mounted cameras. Well, almost unnoticed.

Thinking fast, I went left, ducking into Trace's and my suite first. I quickly grabbed the borrowed curling iron from our bathroom counter then stepped back out into the hallway, making my way to Apple's suite. I made a show of knocking on the door, even though I was 99% sure she was downstairs enjoying breakfast potatoes.

"Apple?" I called in the direction of the cameras. "Apple, I just wanted to return your curling iron."

I turned the doorknob and peeked my head into the room.

No Ice. No Apple.

No time to waste.

I quickly stepped into the room and shut the door behind me. I tossed the curling iron onto the king-size bed then dropped to my knees, checking under it. Nothing but a couple pairs of Apple's heels and a discarded soda can. No bloody gardening shears. No smoking gun.

I stood, acutely aware of the cameras in the room cataloging my every move. I cleared my throat, loudly announcing to the empty room, "I was hoping to borrow a…" I paused, racking my brain. "Tampon?" I cringed. "Yeah, maybe not borrow, but you know, if you had some extra…" While it sounded kinda lame even to my own ears, at least it felt like a subject Voice Number One and Voice Number Two in the control room wouldn't want to investigate further. I dug through a pile of clothes on the chaise near the French doors. "Just wondering if you have some somewhere…" I trailed off for the camera's benefit again.

I opened a few drawers, glanced around the bathroom, shifted more clothing and dirty dishes. I knew I was on borrowed time to find something—anything!—incriminating and/or tabloid-worthy before one of the room's occupants came back. So far the worst thing I'd determined was that the couple lived like pigs. I wiped my hand on my pants after coming into contact with a partially sticky side table.

Running out of places to look, I crossed over to the closet and poked my head inside. On the left was a row of hangers holding tight leather skirts, skimpy dresses, halter tops, and a few pieces of racy lingerie. I swore Apple didn't own any clothing larger than a handkerchief. I felt my cheeks heat just looking at her wardrobe. Apple's luggage and a pile of sexy boots and stiletto heels were on the floor underneath. Ice's oversize T-shirts and baggy pants hung on the right. I blew out a frustrated breath. Nothing to see here.

As I was turning away from the closet, a dark spot on the carpet caught my eye. I glanced at the camera, hoping I didn't look too suspicious digging for tampons in Ice's closet, before kneeling to get a closer look. One small, rust-colored stain marred the creamy carpet just inside the closet doors. Two more trailed farther into the closet, toward the right. I pushed Ice's suitcase aside to reveal a pair of gleaming white sneakers. I recognized them as the same shoes that Ice had been wearing the day of the murder. With excitement growing in my belly, I also realized I'd not seen them on the rapper since. I gingerly picked up one of the shoes, turning it over to look more closely. Rust-colored stains tainted the insole of the kicks. I felt a chill zip down my spine. Stains that looked a lot like dried blood.

CHAPTER ELEVEN

———

After I carefully put the tainted shoe back where I'd found it, slid Ice's luggage back in front of it, and told the cameras I'd go ask Joanie if she had tampons instead, I slipped out of the suite, my hands shaking as my mind raced over what I'd just found. Had Ice stabbed Dr. William and gotten blood on his shoes? It looked a lot like he'd been trying to hide them. From Apple? Had the police seen them? I knew they'd gone through all of our rooms that first day, but if Ice had been wearing the shoes, maybe they hadn't noticed? The detective certainly hadn't searched my clothing that closely during our interview.

I slipped into my own suite and pulled my phone from my pocket.

You busy? I texted to Tina's number.

I took deep breaths as I stared out the window at the deceptively serene gardens, trying to get my heart rate back to normal as I waited for a response.

A minute later my phone buzzed in my hand.

I'm here. Got news?

Boy did I.

I stepped into the bathroom, grabbed my hairdryer, and turned it on, filling the room with white noise as I dialed Tina's number.

"*Please* tell me you've got something good," Tina answered in lieu of a hello. "Allie just scooped me on the royal baby bump story. I'm going to shoot myself if she finds out the gender before me." She paused. "Or maybe just shoot her."

I grinned. "Cheer up," I said over the noise. "I just found something."

"Oh, do tell… Hey, where are you? What's with the racket?"

"Hair dryer." I put one finger to my other ear, trying to block some of the noise.

"Clever."

"Thanks. Anyway, listen to what I just found." I quickly filled her in on my search of the other couple's suite and the bloody shoe in Ice's closet. Tina made the appropriate gasping sounds on the other end.

"So you think it's Dr. William's blood?"

"I don't know. Maybe." I bit my lip, wondering if we should call the police. On the other hand, what did I really have? A shoe with a spot of something that might possibly be blood on it. Was that even enough to run a headline with?

"Didn't the police already search his room?" Tina asked, voicing my thoughts.

"They searched all of our suites, but I don't know if the shoes were in the closet then or not."

"Well, if Ice did it, he had to have hidden the murder weapon somewhere on the grounds too, right?"

I nodded in the empty room. "I didn't see it in his room." I paused. "But he did go out for a walk today."

"You think he tossed it?"

"It's possible."

"Okay, good. We're getting somewhere." I heard Tina scribbling down notes. "So what's Ice's motive? Just mad the doc was checking out Apple?"

When she put it that way, it did seem rather petty. Sure, Apple said he had a jealous streak, but it wasn't as if Dr. William had even touched her. "Maybe there was something in his Secrets Day file…something about Ice?"

"Ohmigosh, you guys haven't done Secrets Day yet?" Tina gasped.

I shook my head and told her what I'd overheard in the control room.

"So Dr. William was the only one who knew what the secrets were?" Tina asked when I was done.

"It appears that way. He didn't want anything leaking and getting back to the rehabbers before he could play his cards for shock value."

"Well, when you put it that way, it sounds like any one of our rehabbers' motives could be in the doc's hidden files, right? I mean, who there isn't hiding something?"

"Good point." I paused. "Speaking of hiding something, I was wondering if you could help me with something. Something a little…devious."

"That's my favorite kind of something." I could practically feel Tina perk up on the other end of the line.

"I need you to track down a divorce attorney for me." I quickly filled her in on the card I'd found in Joanie's pocket and how our contract expressly forbid exactly what I suspected the reality starlet of doing.

"You think if Dr. William found out, maybe she killed him to stay on the show?"

I shrugged. "Shows like this keep her in Prada and Birkins."

"You know I love the idea of Joanie being the killer."

I had to admit—I kinda did too.

"Okay, so how can I help?" she asked.

"I'd love to know exactly what Joanie was seeing the attorney for." While it was a great theory, it only worked if a) Joanie had indeed even contacted the attorney yet and b) had started proceedings. Otherwise it was just a business card and hardly a motive.

I heard Tina tapping her pen cap against her teeth. "That's not gonna be easy. Attorney-client privilege is kind of hard to get around."

"I know," I admitted. "Which is why I'm asking you. If anyone can get the deets, it's you. Surely someone in your network of informants knows a clerk there or a janitor or a receptionist at the firm?" While it was something of a long shot, Tina's network of informants was pretty legendary.

"No promises, but I'll see what I can do," she said.

"That's all I can ask."

* * *

I took a quick shower as I mulled over my conversation with Tina. She was right—the Secrets Day file could very well be the key to our killer's motive. And, well, I'll admit there was still a teeny part of me that wondered what he had on *me* as well.

I threw on some jeans, a bright red V-neck shirt that was a lot cheerier than I felt, and a pair of strappy sandals before ducking back into the bathroom to do my hair and makeup. I vaguely heard Trace come into the suite and rummage around the bedroom for something while I was drying my hair (for reals this time), but I ignored it. I wasn't ready to face that challenge yet today. Once dried, I strategically pulled my hair up into a messy bun, adding several bobby pins to hold it in place.

By the time I came downstairs I was informed by a PA that Dr. Georgia was conducting more one-on-one interviews that morning. The other couples had dispersed around the ground floor, anxiously awaiting their turns. Apple and Joanie were in the great hall, trying to tie ribbons in Isabella the Pomeranian's long hair. Without much luck. Ellen sat in a chair in the corner with a book, though she seemed more interested in shooting daggers at the younger women than reading. I spotted Dirk through the French doors, already hitting the bar by the pool. Trace was swimming laps. Which I'll admit had me pausing to watch for just a moment. What was it about a hot guy flexing his muscles that made me just a little bit hazy about why we were fighting? I found Antoine napping in the lounge as I walked by, which meant our missing member, Ice, was probably being grilled by Dr. Georgia as her first victim. Everyone else was accounted for.

Everyone, that is, except one little tabloid reporter on a mission.

I did my best nonchalance thing as I stepped down the corridor on the right, out of the cameras' eyes and into the crew's hallway. Luckily, it was empty—everyone off filming angry confessionals. I knew from my last visit into this territory that the third door held the control room. The second one was where Voices Number One and Two had come from the other night— possibly an equipment room or break room of some sort. Door Number One had been locked.

I did a quick over the shoulder before trying the knob now. Still locked.

Luckily, I'd come prepared.

I slipped one of the bobby pins out of my bun and straightened it with my teeth before sliding it into the lock.

In my line of work, you picked up a few tricks every now and then to help you get into places you weren't necessarily supposed to be. I'd once used a paper clip to get into a certain star's pool house so I could snap a few photographs of her latest tattoos before she went public with them. Not naming names, but let's just say it rhymed with "smiley papyrus."

I gently pushed the pin, bending the end into a small hook. Then I pulled a second pin out of my hair and bent it to a 90-degree angle, creating a sort of tension wrench. I stuck the bent pin into the hole, turning it just a smidge in order to hold the set of pins inside the lock. Then I stuck the hooked end of the first bobby pin into the lock and began gently rocking it back and forth, up and down, until I felt the locking pins begin to set. I tried not to let my nerves take over as seconds ticked by. I did a couple of deep breaths in and out, channeling my inner yogi, trying to keep my hands steady. Finally I felt the last pin set and the knob turned in my hands.

I let out a long breath, shoved both bobby pins back into my pocket, and slipped inside the empty room.

It looked like I'd entered an office. While the curtains were shut, enough natural light still filtered in for me to make out a desk and several large file cabinets in the opposite corner of the room. No computer equipment. No laptops or tablets. The police had no doubt already been here.

But maybe they weren't looking for the same thing I was.

Voice Number Two had mentioned Dave saying Dr. William got his Secrets Day info from a private investigator in the Valley. While there were no doubt dozens of those, somewhere there had to be records of who that particular PI was. A number in an address book, an invoice, a business card—something.

I opened the top drawer of the first file cabinet and riffled through the loose papers inside. They were mostly food service invoices for the production crew. Nothing seemed particularly interesting, other than the fact the crew was apparently single-handedly keeping the donut industry alive. The next few drawers also contained a lot of paperwork—mostly contracts and several printed emails from the producers to the staff. I scanned a few, but they all seemed to have to do with production dates, schedules, and props needed for various drills. Nothing that mentioned Secrets Day or any private investigator.

I moved on to the next file cabinet. Nearly two dozen full folders took up most of the drawers. I lifted the first folder and flipped through it. Various forms and questionnaires that the contestants had filled out upon being accepted on the show—all identical to the ones Trace and I had filled out. I read a couple of them, but they didn't seem to contain anything that wasn't already common knowledge among the household. Joanie thought Antoine didn't pay her enough attention. Apple thought Ice was jealous. Dirk wanted to put the spark back in his and Ellen's marriage. I couldn't help sneaking a peek at Trace's forms. He'd listed "career differences" as his concern about our relations. Huh. So even before we'd arrived, he'd had in his mind what our problem was. I suddenly felt very left out of the loop that he hadn't shared it with me. All I'd put down was that maybe I'd girlfriend-ed too soon—something I really *was* questioning at this point.

I shoved that uncomfortable thought aside and dove into the next file cabinet.

Ten minutes later, I'd scoured every drawer and come up empty. I was starting to feel the anxiety of the ticking clock. Any minute now some PA would come looking for me to take Dr. Georgia's hot seat. And it would be very hot indeed if they found me here.

I let my gaze travel around the room. The only place I hadn't scoured was the desk itself. I opened the top drawer, coming up with the usual pens, paper clips, rubber bands, and loose stamps. The next two drawers were similar, yielding only a variety of office supplies.

That anxiety was building to full-on panic as I pulled open the last drawer. A stack of Post-its, some loose-leaf writing paper, an owners' manual for a fax machine… and an old-fashioned check register. I pulled the register out. It had been at least a decade since I'd seen anyone but my grandma use one of these. Surely I wouldn't get that lucky… I flipped it open and almost squealed with glee. Someone had actually written check numbers, recipients, and amounts by hand. I checked the date of the last entry. It had been dated just a couple of weeks ago.

I quickly flipped through, noting checks written to some of the crew, a couple of department stores, a notable restaurant downtown, some various people whose names meant nothing to me. And then the heavens broke, angels sang, and I spotted it. Check number 2735 made out to a Thomas Charles Investigations. I did a mental fist pump, taking a picture of the register with my phone before quickly shoving it back into the drawer where I'd found it. Two beats later, I was stepping back out into the hallway and closing the door behind me.

Not a moment too soon. Bonnie rounded the corner and stopped short at the sight of me standing in the crew's forbidden corridor.

"Cam." She blinked. "What are you doing here?"

"I was just looking for Mr. Reisner," I lied.

Her eyebrows drew down in a frown. "Mr. Reisner? Why?"

"I wanted to…make sure that…he knew I wasn't very happy with the temperature in the Doghouse last night. It was too cold. I almost froze." Okay, the temperature had been the last thing I'd noticed about that place, but it was the best I could come up with on short notice.

"Oh." Bonnie eyed me as if she didn't buy that line much more than I did. "Okay. Well, I'll be sure to let the crew know. Uh, in the meantime, I think you should stay in the great hall until Dr. Georgia is ready for you."

"Right. Will do!" I agreed in my most chipper voice. Maybe too chipper. Bonnie eyed me suspiciously again. But I didn't wait around to be questioned, instead practically speed walking back out into the great hall where the rest of our group had assembled, before plopping my butt into one of the chairs facing the pool. Which was vacant now, I noticed. Trace paced near the French doors in a pair of jeans and a black T-shirt, though his hair was still damp. He looked almost good enough to eat…if I wasn't still miffed at him. Especially when he found a piece of lint on his pants so interesting he still couldn't make eye contact with me.

Joanie, however, looked up from the pooch in her lap and narrowed her beady little eyes at me. "Where have *you* been?" she asked, her voice pure accusation.

All eyes turned my way. Including Trace's.

"Uh, who me?" Somehow my voice had gone up an octave.

"Yes, *you*," she said, shifting on the sofa beside Antoine to face me. "One of the crew was looking for you."

"They were?" I squeaked out. I cleared my throat, willing my voice to go back into a less-guilty register. "Uh, why?"

Joanie rolled her eyes. "For your interview, duh! No one could find you, so they took Apple instead."

"Oh." I felt my shoulders relax. "Sorry. I was…in the bathroom."

Ellen snorted from her chair in the corner. Joanie wrinkled her nose in disgust. Antoine's mouth curled up in a half smile like he enjoyed potty jokes.

But Dirk frowned from his spot in the club chair opposite his wife's. "You know that was actually the first place they checked. You weren't there."

"Did they?" I asked. "Well, I was in a different bathroom."

"Which one?" Joanie pressed, clearly liking the idea of catching me in a lie.

I shrugged. "Upstairs. Does it matter?"

Trace frowned now. "Not the one in our suite. I was changing up there alone."

I threw my hands up. "Seriously, no one has anything better to do than discuss my bathroom habits?"

Ice cackled from his perch on the arm of the sofa by the window. "Yo, shorty, you look like you been busted."

I shot him a death look. "I'm not busted. I have nothing to hide." I paused, remembering the shoes in his closet. "Can *you* say the same thing, Morty?"

Ice's face paled at the use of his real name. Or maybe the guilty knowledge that he'd *iced* our host. He jumped up from the sofa. "What do you mean by that, girl?" While it was phrased as a question, the tone came out pure threat.

I shrugged. "Dr. William was murdered. Doesn't that mean someone here has *something* to hide?" I looked pointedly around the room, assessing reactions. Ellen had found her book suddenly interesting. Dirk was still frowning, but he seemed more lost in thought than directing it my way now. Antoine had his poker face on, totally unreadable. Ice was still scowling, and Joanie was still staring daggers at me. Only Apple looked unaffected by the statement, confusion etched on her brow as she mouthed the word *Morty* in a questioning manner.

"Maybe we all have something to hide," Trace added, infusing the words with about as much accusation as I had.

The room grew silent, no one wanting to touch that statement.

"Cameron?"

I practically jumped when a PA walked into the room, calling my name.

"Yeah?" I asked, putting a hand to my hammering heart.

"Dr. Georgia is ready for you now."

I let out a sigh. "Right. Okay. Let's get this over with."

"Where were you earlier?" the PA asked, leading me away from the Suspicious Six.

"Bathroom," I said loudly to the entire room, daring anyone to argue it.

Luckily they were all lost in their own thoughts this time—some more guilty than others.

CHAPTER TWELVE

———

After thoroughly interrogating me about my stay in the Doghouse, Dr. Georgia finally let me go just before lunch. The dour mood of the group seemed to carry over, as everyone chewed their sandwiches quietly…those who didn't opt for a liquid lunch, that was. I was dying to run down PI Thomas Charles's contact info, but it seemed every time I tried to slip away for a quiet moment with my phone and my helpful friend Google, someone was at my elbow. It was almost like they were all suddenly keeping tabs on me.

After an awkward meal, we were instructed to assemble outside in the back garden for the afternoon drill.

As soon as we arrived on the lawn, we were met with the sight of four canoes filled with life vests.

"Oh no. Oh *hizzle* no!" Ice shouted, echoing all of our thoughts. "There is no way you're getting me in one of those things again."

"This is outrageous!" Joanie threw her hand up in the air. "I'm calling my agent."

"I'm done," Ellen simply said, crossing her arms over her chest. "This ridiculous farce has gone on long enough."

"Everyone, please, settle down," Jonathan Reisner said, emerging from behind one of the cameras. "We're just using the canoes as a means to get you over to the island in the center of the lake. That is where your next drill will take place."

"What kind of drill?" Apple asked, the skepticism in her voice overriding her normally cheerful countenance.

Reisner's eyes gleamed. "A treasure hunt."

Ellen opened her mouth to question our producer further, but he waved his arms in the air, staving off any more replies. "Please, we need to get started or we will lose the light. Each couple get into your canoes, and the crew will follow you across the lake to the island."

I watched each of the couples eye each other skeptically but eventually comply. Apple grabbed Ice's hand and murmured something in his ear that calmed the reluctant rapper down enough to step into the canoe. Ellen threw her hands into the air in surrender and followed an unsteady Dirk (clearly one of the ones who'd had a liquid lunch) into their canoe. Joanie protested something about not getting her shoes wet, and Antoine picked his wife up and carried her into their canoe.

I glanced at Trace.

He nodded back. Well, I guess nodding was a step up from not making eye contact.

We all got into our boats and somehow managed to row the short distance to the small island in the middle of the lake. Even if it did take us all three times as long as it should have. Apple and Ice rowed in circles, unable to coordinate left and right. Dirk dropped his oar in the water twice and had to have a crew member rescue it. Joanie yelled at Antoine to paddle slower so he didn't splash water on her outfit. And Trace and I rowed in awkward silence, though I wasn't sure which of us was officially giving the other the silent treatment.

By the time we finally hit the shore, Dr. Georgia and the rest of the crew were already waiting for us.

"Every relationship needs adventure," Dr. Georgia announced, commanding our attention as we all gathered on the shore. "That's why this afternoon our couples will be searching for buried treasure." She gestured to eight shovels lined up in the sand behind her. "Each couple will receive a pair of shovels and a treasure map. You will then be escorted to different parts of the island to begin your hunt. The couple who finds the treasure chest first will be rewarded with the mystery surprise inside. Though, I will warn you," Georgia added, holding up her index finger, "there will be obstacles along the way. Watch out for booby traps, and be sure to have your partner's back."

"This sounds like fun!" Apple said, sounding more like her upbeat self now that we'd all made it safely onto dry land.

"I always wanted to be a pirate," Ice said beside her. He grinned at his fiancée. "Yo, girl, let me get that booty." He reached over and tapped her behind.

"Baby, stop," Apple protested, her cheeks turning pink. "Not in front of the camera."

Ice grinned. If Apple thought for one minute Ice wasn't aware of the cameras, she was more naïve than I thought.

Ice just smiled wider…that is until he turned his attention to Dirk. "Yo, *you* can keep your old eyes off my girl's behind."

Dirk blinked innocently. "I…I wasn't looking at her behind. I was just…"

"Yeah, well you can just *not*, dawg. Or ain't all of us makin' it off this island alive, you feel me?"

"Ice," Apple protested. "Please."

Dirk ducked his head away, still mumbling his innocence as the rest of us grabbed our shovels.

A crew member led each couple to a different starting point for the treasure hunt. Trace and I were taken to the opposite side of the island and given a rolled-up sheet of parchment paper. When our crew escort got word through his walkie-talkie that the other couples were in place, he gave us the signal to start and headed back toward the shore.

Leaving Trace and me alone.

Awwww-k-wwwward.

I crossed my arms over my chest as I glanced his way, not sure I was yet ready to be the bigger person.

Clearly neither was Trace, as he avoided eye contact and instead turned his attention to the map. "The treasure is somewhere in the center of the island," he said, going into Indiana Trace mode. He took off through a cluster of trees without even glancing behind him to see if I was following. I rolled my eyes, fully prepared for an afternoon as his silent sidekick.

We marched through the man-made island, coming up against all manner of trees and vegetation that I was pretty sure were not native to California. The crew had done their best to mimic some sort of African rain forest, only the occasional seagull flying overhead giving away our true location. About ten minutes into our trek, Trace's shin rubbed against a thin wire that stretched between two trees. There was a whooshing sound from the bushes to our left.

"Look out!" I exclaimed, grabbing Trace's arm and jerking him backward as an object sailed past the spot where his face had just been. It smacked into a tree across the path and slid down the length of its trunk, leaving a trail of white goo. It was a pie plate full of whipped cream.

Trace laughed. I felt my cheeks go red. Okay, I don't know what I'd been expecting to come hurtling toward my boyfriend (yes, I was still using that word, even if it was a big assumption at this point), but I realized my reaction was a little high strung for pie.

"Don't worry. Their insurance wouldn't let them put anything really dangerous out here," Trace assured me.

"Thanks," I mumbled, following him again as he continued his trek. On the upside, he'd actually said it to my face this time and not the lint on his pants. Progress?

"I'd have thought our camera guy would be following us," he said over his shoulder. "Think we lost him?"

"They've probably got cameras set up around the island," I replied, my eyes scanning the tree line.

"Big Brother's always watching, huh?"

I stifled a shudder, thinking about the wall of monitors I'd seen in the control room the day before. He had no idea.

We resumed our silent trek through the vegetation, with Trace navigating with the map while I kept an eye out for any more booby traps. It took us at least an hour, trying to read the map that seemed as if it had been designed to purposely throw us all off track, before we reached what looked to be the center of the island. Trace squinted at the parchment in his hand and then pointed to a flat patch of earth. "If I'm reading this right, we should start digging there." He handed off the map to me and then rolled up his sleeves.

"We're the first ones here," I noted, surveying the trees around us. Though I could hear voices somewhere to our left.

I shoved the map into my back pocket and gripped my shovel. Trace broke through the dirt, and I joined in, scooping up shovels full of earth and dumping them off to the side.

We'd been digging for a few minutes when Apple appeared from behind a tree. "Oh, thank goodness I found you guys." Her shorts were ripped, and she had mud on her cheek. Clearly she wasn't the outdoorsy type.

"You okay?" I asked her.

She nodded. "Have you guys seen Ice?" she asked. "We got separated."

I shook my head. "Nope, sorry. How did you lose him?"

She grimaced. "We got into a fight about that booty comment he made earlier and him accusing Dirk of checking me out again. I told him he shouldn't be so crude on television. I mean, my mom might watch this."

I wasn't sure if it was charming that she was so concerned about modesty, given her profession, or if she herself was putting on her own act for the cameras.

"Anyway, he took off through some bushes," she continued, "but when I tried to follow him, he'd disappeared."

"It's a small island," Trace said, wiping sweat from his forehead with the back of his hand. "He couldn't have gone far."

Apple nodded, but she didn't look convinced. "Would you help me look for him?" she asked me, her doe eyes pleading. "We could split up. Whoever finds him can send him back here. Two heads are always better than one, right?"

I stopped digging and looked at Trace. But he'd already gone back to checking the map. If he was concerned about Indiana Trace having a sidekick, he didn't register it.

"Please, Cam?" Apple pleaded again. "He could be stuck in a booby trap."

The thought of Ice getting a whipped cream pie in the face was too much to pass up. "Okay, let's go look."

I put down my shovel and followed Apple back the way she had come.

"Here's where I lost him," she said, turning around in a circle. Her forehead wrinkled. "At least, I think so."

I pointed at the trees to our left. "Why don't you go that way, and I'll head to the right. Maybe we'll run into Dirk and Ellen or Antoine and Joanie. Somebody has to have seen him."

Apple nodded, and we each took off in our designated directions. I could hear Apple calling Ice's name as she stomped through the brush. I swiveled my head from side to side as I scanned the small island forest. Reisner had been right about us losing the light. Getting all of us to the island had taken a while, and I could see the setting sun reflected off the lake water a couple hundred yards away.

Being the first moment alone I'd had all afternoon, I pulled my phone from my pocket as I hiked toward the shore, eyes scanning for Ice. I was getting one whole bar out here. Well, one was better than none. I pulled up Google (agonizingly slowly due to the one bar) and typed in *Thomas Charles Investigations LA area.* After watching a loading symbol that seemed to take an eternity, I got a hit, and a *Yelp* listing for the PI popped up. He had 3.5 stars. Not bad. Not great either, but considering he probably followed cheating husbands around half the day, I was surprised he didn't have more complaints. I noted an address in Burbank and a phone number, saving both to my contacts. I was just about to try the number when a rustling of leaves brought my attention to the bushes on the right. "Apple?" I called. "Ice?"

There was no response. I shoved my phone back into my pocket, walked over to the cluster of vegetation, and pulled back the branches. No one was there. As I peered through the thick brush, I heard heavy footfalls behind me. Someone was hurrying in my direction. I started to turn around.

But before I could see who that someone was, pain exploded at my temple. I cried out, dropping to my knees as the intense sensation ripping through my skull blurred my vision. I struggled to stand up, but my legs wouldn't work.

"Cam?" I heard Apple call from somewhere in the distance.

All I could respond with was a low moan. Blackness formed in the corner of my vision and spread inward until I was enveloped in darkness.

CHAPTER THIRTEEN

———

"Cam? Cameron, please wake up."

Something cold and damp pressed against my forehead. I cracked open an eyelid and immediately shut it again as a wave of nausea crashed through me. I winced, and a groan escaped my throat.

"Oh, Cam." I recognized Trace's voice, which was thick with emotion. "Thank God you're okay." His fingers gently stroked my hair, and I flinched and let out a hiss of pain as they brushed the sore spot on the side of my head. He immediately drew his hand back. "I'm sorry, babe," he murmured.

I forced my eyes open and stared groggily up at the cluster of faces looming over me, illuminated by a flashlight. Trace, Dr. Georgia, and Apple were staring down at me with concerned expressions. Mr. Reisner stood behind them, his cell phone glued to his ear as he muttered something about lawsuits.

"This is all my fault," Apple said tearfully. She met my gaze with wide eyes.

"Did you find Ice?" I asked. My mouth felt like it was full of cotton balls.

Her expression darkened. "Yeah, he stomped off to the other side of the island to cool off. The crew found him smoking a cigarette at the canoes." She dropped her gaze, looking guilty. "If I hadn't asked you to help me look for him, you wouldn't have fallen and hit your head."

"What?" I blinked, trying to pull the last few moments into focus.

"You fell," Dr. Georgia explained as if talking to someone with amnesia. "And you must have hit your head on this rock right here." She pointed to a small boulder on the ground beside me.

I tried to sit up, but another wave of pain pushed me back into the dirt. "I didn't trip," I said, wincing again as memories came flooding back. "Someone hit me over the head with that rock."

Reisner dropped his cell to his side and frowned. "You must be mistaken," he said slowly, giving me a skeptical look. "There's no one out here except the other guests and the crew."

I gave him a pointed look. "Well, one of *them* hit me."

Reisner started to shake his head in the negative, but I cut him off.

"Check your cameras," I said, irritation edging into my voice. "I didn't fall down."

Reisner offered me a tight smile. "I'm sure that bump on the head just has you confused."

"If she said she didn't trip, then she didn't," Trace snapped. He rose stiffly and took a step toward the producer. "And if someone attacked her, you need to do something about it."

Reisner's face paled. "Of course we'll look into it," he said, holding up his hands in a placating manner.

"You'd better." Trace glared at him. Then he looked back down at me. "And I'm calling her an ambulance."

"No." I managed to sit up slowly. I reached up and gingerly touched the bump forming on my head. "No, I'm okay. I've just got a nasty goose egg."

"Maybe you shouldn't move." Apple chewed her lip.

Trace hooked his arms under mine and carefully lifted me to my feet. I swayed for a moment but managed to regain my balance.

By the time Trace and Apple had helped me to the shore, the other guests had already returned to the main house. Dr. Georgia, Reisner, Apple, and one of the cameramen were the only other people still on the island. The hostess and producer climbed into a canoe together while Apple shared a boat with the young crew member, who filmed her as she tearfully rowed across the water, presumably upset that Ice had left without her.

Trace helped me into our canoe, gently settling me on the front bench. "You sure you're okay?" he asked, eyes roving my face.

I nodded, instantly regretting it as the throbbing in my head kicked up a notch.

Trace must have seen it reflected in my expression as he gently reached out a hand and brushed a strand of hair from my cheek. "Oh, Cam. I'm so sorry." He paused. "About everything."

I raised an eyebrow his way. "Go on."

Trace let out a sigh and ran a hand through his hair. "Look, this whole show was a bad idea. I realize that now. And last night, I just… I got carried away, okay? You were right. Totally right."

I raised the other eyebrow, really liking where this was going.

"I do fall into playing characters. Honestly, I don't mean to, but it's just so hard to turn them off sometimes, you know? I spend months inside their heads getting ready for a role, and then it's not so easy to just forget all that. For crying out loud, every time I go swimming now, I swear I almost feel piranha fins on me."

I bit my lip, trying to stifle a laugh at that image.

"Anyway," Trace said, running his hand through his hair again until it stood up in adorable tufts. "what I'm trying to say is I got carried away playing the role of the actor in relationship trouble. So much so that I created relationship trouble. And I never meant to hurt your career just to boost mine."

I felt my anger thawing. "I know you didn't," I reassured him.

"I'm so sorry. I've felt like a jerk over it all day. Heck, I've felt so guilty I couldn't even look you in the eye."

Forget thawing, I was close to melting at that point. "It's okay. I mean, I might have gotten a teeny tiny bit carried away last night too."

The corner of Trace's mouth lifted in a half smile. "Just a smidge?"

I returned his grin with a sheepish one of my own. "I'm sorry I called you a has-been."

He cringed a little as I said the words out loud again. "I've been called worse."

"Still." I grabbed an oar.

But Trace took it from me. "No, *I'm* the bad guy. *I'm* the one who owes you an apology for the whole Doghouse thing. *I'll* row us back to shore."

I grinned in earnest now. "I won't fight you on that one."

Honestly, I was grateful, considering my head still ached and the already gentle rocking of the boat was making me feel ill. I gripped the sides of the canoe and closed my eyes.

"Who found the treasure?" I asked, trying to take my mind off the latest wave of nausea to roll over me as we headed toward the house.

"I did," Trace replied. "Joanie and Ellen caught up to me pretty soon after you took off. Apple had bumped into the Parkers and recruited Antoine to help look for Ice, and according to Ellen, Dirk discovered one of the hidden cameras and decided to show off by staging an action sequence. Apparently he's auditioning next month for a movie about Tarzan's later years, and he thought he could impress the casting directors with footage of him swinging from branch to branch." He shook his head. "When we realized you were missing, Dr. Georgia took the treasure chest and told me the crew would film us opening it later."

"So, every couple split up," I said slowly. Which meant any one of the pretend pirates could have attacked me. I was suddenly dying to sneak into the control room again and look at the footage from the island. Surely some camera somewhere had caught my attacker.

"You know, Cam, I honestly think we should just leave the show," Trace said, breaking into my thoughts.

I spun in my seat to face him. He looked serious. "I don't know," I hedged. "You think Reisner would even let us?"

"I don't care. Let him sue us. Cam, it's too dangerous here. Someone hurt you tonight."

The genuine emotion in his voice warmed my insides, but I felt myself shaking my head. "No, we can't leave now."

He frowned. "Why not?"

I leaned forward, tightening my grip on the boat to steady myself when it rocked slightly. "I'm close to finding out who killed Dr. William. And, until I do, I can't just leave."

"You mean until you get your story." Some of the emotion seemed to seep out of Trace's gaze.

"Well, sure, yeah. I mean that too."

Trace dropped his gaze to the water. "Cam, if something were to happen to you..." He broke off and cleared his throat loudly. "Look, we're leaving tonight. I'll tell Reisner as soon as we get to shore."

"You're not hearing me," I said, my head starting to pound again. "I can't leave, Trace."

"My mind is made up, Cam."

While the concern was touching, the alpha thing was starting to grate on my nerves. "So, when it was *your* career on the line, we were staying. But now that it's my career in jeopardy, none of that matters?"

Trace shook his head, his features hard in the fading light. "So not the same, Cam. Look, I told you that was a mistake. And I'm sorry. But my career isn't getting anyone hurt. Besides you're just—"

"A tabloid reporter?" I finished for him, anger starting to replace the warm fuzzies I'd felt just moments ago. "The paparazzi? The insignificant little nobodies who keep big stars like you in the public eye?"

He clenched his jaw. "I was going to say a magnet for trouble."

Oh. Well, he had me there. I did seem to be attracting it lately. Including sticking my foot directly in my mouth just now.

I closed my eyes, that headache going full force on me. "Look, I'm staying here. You can leave if you want, but I'm seeing this through."

"You're being unreasonable, Cam," he ground out.

"Oh, am I?" I snapped back. "Well, how's this for reasonable? I'd rather stay in the Doghouse again tonight, thank you very much," I added for good measure.

Trace shook his head. "Cam, you don't need to do that."

"Well, maybe I want to!"

He shook his head at me again like he was looking at a stubborn child.

I was about to open my big mouth and tell him just how stubborn I could be, but we hit the shore with a jerk that threw me off balance and made my stomach lurch again.

A crew member helped me out, and I did my best to stomp away in a huff on unsteady legs. Which probably looked a lot more like a giraffe calf taking his first steps than the indignant exit I was going for. But I didn't care. A hailstorm of emotions pounded through me as I trudged inside: anger over Trace's unfairness, heartache at how concerned he'd been about me, embarrassment that I'd reacted exactly like a reality show couple on the brink of disaster, and mixed in with all of that was a small but growing fear that whoever had attacked me was sleeping in the very house I was insisting on staying in. Maybe Trace was right. Was I risking too much to stay?

On the other hand, the fact that someone had attacked me meant I must be getting a little too close for their comfort. The problem was, I had no idea which someone it was. Ice had been the first to split off from Apple during the treasure hunt challenge. Was it possible he had snuck away with the sole purpose of attacking me? Or maybe it had been Dirk, who had also separated from his wife during the drill. Joanie had been on her own for part of the treasure hunt as well, so it could have easily been her. Even her scrawny arms could have swung that rock hard enough to cause the pain still hammering behind my eyes.

Of course, there was always Dr. Georgia herself. Who knew where she'd been when I'd been hit on the head.

As soon as I arrived back in the house, Reisner insisted I be taken to the lounge, where an on-site medic checked me out. I'd like to think Reisner was sincerely concerned, but I had a feeling his worry was over his insurance and not my well-being. The medic looked barely out of high school and informed me that he'd taken the job to tide him over while his agent tried to get him on a sitcom. While I might have questioned his credibility, it was pretty clear what my diagnosis was: bump on the head equals big headache. He gave me some Tylenol for the pain and told me to ice the bump. Thank God the kid had gone to med school. (Clearly the sarcasm center of my brain was unaffected by the blow.)

As soon as I was cleared by the medic, I made my way back through the house. The majority of the rehabbers seemed to have congregated in the billiard room, where another bar had been set up in our absence. Joanie and Dirk were playing pool, Apple was pouring drinks, Ice was telling Antoine how unfair it was that football players got paid more than "artists" like himself, and Ellen was again pretending to read while actively engaging in scowling at everyone and everything. Trace was noticeably absent. I had mixed emotions about that.

"Cam!" Apple called from the bar. She held up a margarita in one hand. "Have a drink with me?"

As much as I usually might have enjoyed the frosty refreshment, all my pounding head wanted tonight was my soft bed and a good night's sleep. "No thanks," I said, waving her off. "I think I'm just gonna turn in early."

"Are you sure? They're yummy!" Apple pouted.

I nodded. "I'm fine. See you in the morning," I told her, leaving before she could protest.

"Hope you feel better!" she called to my retreating back.

I held a hand up to wave again as I made my way toward the staircase. Only, I froze on the bottom step. Crap. I wasn't going to my soft bed tonight. I'd said I was sleeping on a dog bed.

I bit my lip, visions of the plush suite at the top of the stairs warring with my pride. I could just apologize to Trace. Tell him I'd overreacted a little to his suggestions we leave. After all, he'd just been being protective, right?

And stubborn, and controlling, and just the teeny tiniest bit condescending.

I sighed. Nope, my pride just would not let me climb those stairs tonight. Instead, I slunk with my tail between my legs to the Doghouse again and flopped on the lumpy beanbag, the pooches playing pokers seeming to mock me.

"I know I'm being pigheaded," I told them. "But so is he!"

Their little beady eyes just stared back at me.

I ignored them and pulled my phone out of my pocket. I swiped open the contact I'd saved just before being assaulted— Thomas Charles Investigations. I hit the *Call* button and waited as it rang on the other end. Four rings in, it went to an automated voicemail system where a pleasant computer-generated voice told me that the recipient's mailbox was full and then hung up on me. I glanced at the dog bone-shaped digital clock on the wall. It was almost eleven. Maybe a little late for business hours. I put my phone away and resolved to try again in the morning, before I closed my eyes and sank into blissful sleep.

*   *   *

I awoke with a start, my heart pounding. My eyes shot open in the dark, blinking to try to make out shapes. A fire hydrant in the corner. My sandals by the door. Dog bone clock on the wall, the digital numbers showing 2:32 a.m.

Then I heard it again. A sound outside my window that must have originally jarred me out of sleep. I jumped up from the dog bed and padded barefoot to peek out. Unfortunately the moon was on the other side of the house, and all I could see were shadows. I was about to go back to bed and chalk it all up to my overactive imagination when one of the shadows moved. Then it lit up a cigarette, the red glow bright against the darkness. I ducked back down below the window, my heart pounding. I knew Apple said Ice had snuck off for a cigarette earlier. Could it be him out there now? The Doghouse was on the far side of the mansion. An inconvenient place to step outside just for a smoke…but a great place to be if you didn't want anyone else to see you. Like, possibly hiding evidence of a crime? A pair of bloody garden shears perhaps?

I pulled myself up again and squinted out the window. But the shadow had his back to me, and I couldn't tell if he was carrying anything or not.

I quickly slipped my sandals on and tiptoed out into the deserted hallway, out the French doors at the end, and into the darkness. I kept close to the house, not wanting to give away my position to anyone whose eyes might have adjusted to the night faster than mine.

I spotted the figure easily, thanks to the glowing red beacon. That is until the figure dropped the butt to the ground and crushed it under a foot. Then it moved away from the building and crossed the lawn toward the pool house. As it did, he passed by one of the decorative up-lights, and I caught a glimpse of his face. Disappointment hit me harder than the blow I'd taken to the head. It wasn't Ice but one of the crew—Phillip, Reisner's assistant. He pulled his phone out of his pocket as he neared the pool house, the screen casting a bluish glow on his young face as he tapped away.

From what I could tell, he hadn't noticed me. I turned to go back inside, but before I could, a second figure suddenly appeared on the scene. Emerging from the shadows near the outdoor bar, Jonathan Reisner briskly crossed the tiled pool area, navigating the loungers as he made his way toward the pool house. Phillip looked up as he approached, and a smile played at his lips. The older, shorter man stopped as he reached the young assistant. He said something, though I was too far away to hear exactly what. But judging by the way Phillip ducked his head shyly, I could make a few guesses. Phillip leaned forward, and Reisner stood on tiptoe to plant a kiss on the young man's lips.

I knew it! I fought back the urge to cheer triumphantly. The rumor about Reisner's affair was true. And, I thought as I pulled my phone from my pocket and discreetly snapped a few pics, now I had proof. Felix was going to kiss me for this.

I watched as Reisner looked over his shoulder to make sure the coast was clear before grabbing Phillip's hand and leading him inside the pool house.

I took one last pic of them ducking inside together before I re-traced my steps to the main house. I slipped back inside, scrolling through the photos for the perfect one to gift my editor.

I was just rounding the corner toward the Doghouse when I saw a large figure emerging from my room.

I froze.

Seriously? Was anyone *not* slinking around in the dark tonight?

I flattened myself against the wall as I watched the figure leave *my* room, wondering what on earth they'd been doing in there. Looking to steal a priceless work of dog art? Or… A scary thought hit me. Had my attacker from earlier that night come back to finish off the job?

That thought sent a chill up my spine as I watched the figure slink toward the great hall. On instinct, I followed.

As I watched him cross the great hall to the east wing of the house, I realized it was indeed a *him*. A 6'4", 250-pound-plus him to be precise. The slim moonlight filtering in through the windows on this side of the house illuminated his profile as he crossed the room to the hallway on the right. I tried to hold in my shock at seeing him. What had Antoine Parker been doing in the Doghouse? Of all the rehabbers to be sneaking around after dark, my money had not been on Antoine. And *sneaking* he definitely was, looking over his shoulder in a paranoid fashion before slipping down the crew's forbidden hallway.

It appeared I wasn't the only one who was breaking the rules in this house.

I waited until he had rounded the corner then sprinted across the great hall as quietly as I could, seeking the cover of the thick velvet drapes by the French doors. I peeked my head around the corner just in time to see Antoine trying the knob on the door to the control room.

Wow. Caught red-handed, big guy.

My mind was racing as fast as my heartbeat as I watched Antoine jiggle the locked doorknob. Why was he trying to get into the control room? Had Antoine been the one who'd attacked me on the island and was now looking to delete the incriminating footage? Had Joanie put him up to it? According to Apple, she'd found Joanie alone on the island, which meant Antoine had been unaccounted for during at least part of the drill too. He'd had the opportunity. But why? Was Antoine covering up for Joanie? Or had he been the muscle to her mastermind all along? He certainly seemed devoted enough to the pampered starlet to do whatever she asked. Did that include murder?

"What are you doing here?"

I jumped hearing the voice of a crew member booming behind me, but as I whipped my head around, I realized he wasn't talking to me. It was Voice Number One, and he was directing the question at Antoine. The crew member crossed his arms over his chest, clearly trying to project an authoritative air even though the football player had a good six inches on him.

Antoine shrugged nonchalantly. "Nothin'."

"This area is for the crew only." Voice Number One frowned, his eyes going to the locked door. "Why were you trying to get in there?"

A very good question. I held my breath in my hiding place, waiting for the answer.

But Antoine just shrugged again. "This isn't the confession booth?"

Some of the fight relaxed out of Voice Number One's shoulders. "No, man, you got the wrong hallway. The confession booth is down the hall near the front doors."

"Sorry. My bad."

I squinted through the dim light to make out Antoine's features. But years of facing down violent opponents on the gridiron had perfected his poker face. If Antoine was lying, he didn't show any signs of it. However, I knew for a fact from the footage I'd spied on my own trip to the control room that Antoine had visited the confessional booth before. On the day of the murder no less. How he could get so turned around now to accidentally wind up at the control room was hard to figure.

"Yeah, no worries. In a place this big, it's easy to get lost. Come on. I'll walk you over there," Voice Number One offered.

I held my breath as both men shuffled past my hiding spot, hoping neither of them looked too closely at the lumpy curtains. Luck was with me, and they didn't as they crossed the great hall and made a sharp turn toward the entrance to the house. I waited till they rounded the corner to leave my hiding place and quickly sprint across the room again. I watched as Voice Number One opened the door at the end of the hall for Antoine and then shut it behind him. But instead of leaving, the crew member opened the door to the room right next door and stepped inside.

I felt my left eyebrow rise. Could it possibly be that the monitor connected to the camera in the confessional booth was housed right next door?

I bit my lip. I could have gone back to my lumpy dog bed, but being the sort of tabloid girl I was, curiosity got the better of me. I quickly tiptoed down the hallway, stopping outside the second door. Voice Number One hadn't been expecting visitors, and he'd left the door ajar just the tiniest sliver. Just enough for me to peek inside the room.

It was small, almost the same size as the tiny confessional booth. And, to my glee, it did indeed house a bank of monitors, similar to the ones in the larger control room. There were only four here, and three of them were dark. The only monitor showing a live image had a large black and white picture of Antoine's face sitting in the confessional booth next door.

The helpful crew member sat in an office chair in front of the monitor, his back to the door, eyes on the screen as Antoine started to speak.

"That woman is driving me crazy," Antoine said, licking his lips as if he really did feel guilty talking about Joanie behind her back. "First she insists on bringing that rat dog with us, and then she wanted me to draw a bubble bath for it in the bathroom sink?" His nose wrinkled. "I brush my teeth in that sink, woman!"

I stifled a laugh. This was the first time I'd ever seen Antoine say a bad word about his so-not-better half.

"It's always something with her. Rub my feet, bathe my dog, get me a drink. And tonight, she took it too far. She even threatened to kick me out of our suite if I didn't obey her every command." He gave the camera a disbelieving look. "I know, right? Joanie told me to go spend the night in the Doghouse. I reminded her that Cameron is already sleeping there tonight, and she told me she didn't care. That I could find somewhere else to sleep." Antoine shook his head at the camera. "That woman is nuts. And you know what? I'm getting off the crazy train tonight. Maybe I'll actually get some rest without her snoring in my ear all night. I'm gonna go find a nice lounger by the pool and catch some Z's. Peace out." He rose, saluting the camera.

I took that as my cue to make myself scarce and quickly ran back toward the Doghouse. I heard footfalls behind me just as I ducked down the second corridor, and I caught Antoine's shape crossing the great hall, as promised, toward the French doors.

I didn't wait to see whether he found his poolside lounger or not, figuring my luck was due to run out anytime, and instead hightailed it back to my nice cozy Doghouse. Once inside I flopped back down on the bed, staring up in the semidarkness at the card-playing pooches.

While I'd found Antoine's confession highly entertaining—especially the information that Joanie Parker snored like a lumberjack—it had also been highly convenient. Had Antoine made that up on the spot, knowing Voice Number One was watching? Or had he really forgotten where the confession booth was? I closed my eyes, trying to calm some of my suspicions. Was it possible Joanie had kicked him out and Antoine had innocently gone to the Doghouse, forgetting it was already occupied? And was it just a coincidence that he'd gone to the control room next instead of the confession booth? I didn't know. But one thing I did know was that in my line of work, where there was a suspicious coincidence, there was usually a nefarious reason behind it.

CHAPTER FOURTEEN

———

"Your call has been received by an automated voicemail system. The user you are trying to reach has a mailbox that is full. Please try again. Goodbye."

The starting-to-be-less-pleasant computer-generated voice hung up on me yet again. After awakening in the Doghouse just after seven, I'd tried the number for Thomas Charles Investigations with no luck. After slipping into our suite while Trace was still asleep to shower and change into a teal racerback tank and a short, white denim skirt, I'd tried again. Nada. I'd gone through the motions of eating breakfast, listening to the crew inform us that our next drill was still being set up—which gave us the morning off—and making small talk with the other rehabbers. And at almost ten I'd tried again. No answer. Thomas Charles clearly didn't answer his phone often. Maybe never, if the full voicemail box was any indication.

"Hi, Cam," Bonnie said, coming up behind me in the kitchen as I mumbled a curse word at my phone. She was carrying a large boom mike that tipped awkwardly in her small hands.

"Hey, watch it," Joanie said from the other side of the room as she poured herself a mimosa. "You almost hit me with that thing!"

"Sorry," Bonnie mumbled. Then she turned her shy smile on me. "How are you feeling today?" she asked, her eyes going to my forehead where, last I'd checked, I had a nice purple lump.

How was I feeling? I was about to get fired, my boyfriend hated me, I'd been attacked, and I was stuck in a house with spoiled starlets and murderers. (I was still debating which was worse.) But I went for the short answer. "I'm fine," I lied.

"Any word on the footage from the island yesterday? Any cameras pick up the attack?" I asked hopefully.

But she shook her head. "Sorry. A bunch of us watched it last night, but none of the angles were good enough. Whoever hit you managed to stay just out of view of the cameras. You can't see anything but the rock coming down on your head." She grimaced.

I did the same, the lump suddenly aching. "Thanks for checking."

"Yeah. Actually, most of the footage we shot out there was pretty bad. I guess we didn't account for all the dust the digging would kick up. It's all kinda blurry. I doubt we'll use any of it when the show airs." She paused. "*If* it airs," she said, voicing my same feelings about the fiasco.

"You think Reisner will pull the plug?" I asked.

She shrugged. "Or the network. Reisner just informed the crew this morning that we're ending production a day early. He's moving the big commitment ceremony scene up to tomorrow."

I bit my lip. That wasn't good. As long as our suspects were all stuck in one place, I had a fighting chance of ferreting out the killer. But Ellen shot her news show in DC, Dirk filmed *The Charming & the Reckless* in New York, Antoine had training camp starting soon in Costa Mesa, and Ice was reportedly finishing his album in Detroit. And while Apple, Joanie, and Dr. Georgia were all LA based, if any were the guilty party, it wouldn't be hard to take off for a week or two (or forever) to Mexico. If I wanted to figure out who had offed the doctor, I was on borrowed time.

As I watched Bonnie haul her giant microphone in the direction of the back garden, I turned back to my phone and dialed Thomas Charles again. Again the annoying voicemail lady told me to go to Hades. (Okay, maybe not in those words, but I was learning to read between the lines.)

Out of alternatives, I excused myself to the little girls' room (amidst smirks from Joanie—I didn't think I'd ever be able to go to a bathroom again without someone commenting on it) and turned on the faucet before dialing Tina's number.

Unfortunately, it went straight to voicemail. Dang it. I thought about leaving a message, but I needed help *now*. I hung up and instead dialed my plan B number.

"Hello?" Allie answered on the third ring, her voice thick with sleep.

"Hey. It's Cam."

"Cam? What's going on? I hear running water."

"It's to drown out our conversation on the cameras," I replied. "We're being watched here twenty-four-seven. Sorry to wake you," I added. "But you said to call if I needed anything, and, well…" I bit my lip, hoping Tina didn't hold this against me later. "I need a favor."

"Really?" Allie sounded more alert now.

"Who is it, babe?" asked a man in the background.

"Oh, geez, sorry. I didn't realize you had company." I felt my cheeks heating.

"No, it's just Felix."

I wrinkled my nose. Yeah, like that made me feel better. It was a well-known, ill-kept secret that Allie was dating our boss, but I didn't particularly like being faced with evidence of it.

"Uh, sorry," I mumbled again.

"It's Cam," I heard her tell Felix. "She said she needs my help."

"With what? She bloody well better have something—"

"What do you need?" Allie asked me, cutting off his tirade.

"I need you to meet me here at the estate. As soon as you can get here." A plan was brewing in the back of my mind. Originally I had thought I'd send Tina to go break down the door at Mr. Thomas-Charles-I-don't-answer-my-phone's offices. But with Tina out and Allie in, I had to revise. And while Allie was a few inches shorter than I was, she had a similar build. Almost the same color hair. She could fit into most of my clothes. And since we didn't have any formal drills until later that afternoon… "I need you to be me for a couple of hours. All you'll have to do is hang out by the pool and not talk to anyone."

Allie was quiet on the other end, and I could feel her mulling over my request. "Can I ask why?"

"I need to run an errand."

"One that has to do with William Meriwether's death?"
I could only hope. "It may," I answered.

"And what do I get out of this?" Honestly, it was a fair question, considering I'd already told her the story was Tina's.

"Okay…how about…a photo of Mr. Reisner and his boy toy," I offered.

Allie gasped. "So he *is* having an affair with his assistant? I thought it was just a rumor."

"Saw them with my own two eyes," I told her. "And my camera."

"What? What does she have?" I could hear Felix shouting in the background.

"Shhh." I heard Allie waved him off. "Okay, Cam. You have a deal," she told me. "Without traffic, I'll see you in half an hour."

*   *   *

Exactly forty-two minutes later (This was LA. Of course there was traffic.) I sat at the south gate of the property as a familiar VW Bug pulled up to the curb. A busty blonde stepped out, grinning as she saw me. "Morning, Cam!" Allie chirped, giving me a little wave.

"Right on time," I said. I unlatched the gate and met her on the other side, handing over a tote bag.

Allie peeked inside. "What's this?"

"A disguise." Though we both had long blonde hair, Allie was shorter than I and had a lot more in the chest department. Like at least a couple of cups worth. At a distance, however, I was hoping the crew and other guests might not be able to tell the difference. I'd brought her my voluminous black swimsuit cover-up and a floppy, wide-brimmed hat and huge sunglasses.

Allie lifted out the black cover-up. "Super cute," she said, nodding her approval before she pulled it over her denim short-shorts and sparkly pink tank top.

"The key is going to be avoiding engaging with anyone," I told her. "Your best bet is to act like you're napping. If anyone tries to talk to you, either wave them off or quietly excuse yourself to the little girl's room."

She nodded. "Got it." She paused. "What about Trace?"

I bit my lip. While I'd have liked to include him in our ruse, we weren't exactly on speaking terms that morning. I'd seen him only briefly while he'd gotten coffee, and his only interaction with me had been to stare at the purple lump I was sporting this morning, frown, then grunt and turn away.

"I don't think he'll give you any trouble," I told Allie, glossing over my very real relationship issues. "I left my lapel mike in the pool house, where I'm pretending to be changing right now. So, as soon as you get up to the house, head there and clip it onto yourself ASAP."

She nodded again. Then she grabbed the pair of sunglasses and the floppy hat from the bag and put them on. "How do I look?" she asked, twirling in a circle as she modeled the disguise.

A smile tugged at my lips. "Perfect." Okay, so she still looked like someone had taken about four inches off my height and added them to her chest. But, if she kept a low profile, I doubted anyone would suspect anything. As long as I was quick about this little mission.

I gave Allie directions to the pool and promised I'd be back as soon as humanly possible.

Allie slipped through the gate, latching it behind her, then lowered her sunglasses and winked. "Good luck with your errand." She tossed me her car keys. "And take care of my baby."

"I will," I promised her. I watched Allie disappear into the trees, headed in the direction of the house. Then I climbed into her car and sped toward the Valley.

* * *

Thomas Charles's office was located in a rundown section of Burbank that bordered the seedier section of North Hollywood. That was saying a lot for North Hollywood, which had practically made an industry out of seediness. The building had seen better days—tan stucco crumbled around the edges, and one of the window panes on the first floor was broken. I parked Allie's Bug in the street close to the entrance and locked the doors behind me, praying it would still be there when I came out.

The interior of the building reeked of stale cigarette smoke, and the gray carpet was worn through in places, showing patches of the concrete underneath. Charles's office was at the end of the hallway on the first floor. The black door had a frosted window with his name painted on the glass above the words *Discreet Investigations, open 24 hours.* I lifted my hand to knock, but the door swung open before my knuckles tapped the wood.

A man stood in the doorway and blinked at me, surprised. He was of average height, with thinning black hair and large jowls. His beady brown eyes slid over me, and recognition flashed behind them. "Well, well," he said, offering me a greasy smile. "Good morning, Miss Dakota. Pleasure to meet you in person."

I stared at him for a moment. Then it hit me. He'd researched all of the *Celebrity Relationship Rehab* participants. Of course he'd know what I looked like. I recovered quickly, offering up what I hoped looked like a polite smile. "Nice to meet you too, Mr. Charles."

"Call me Thomas. Come on in." He ambled to the chair behind his desk.

His office looked like a tornado had hit it. Papers were scattered across practically every surface of the room except the two chairs on opposite sides of his desk. He had a big, boxy computer monitor that looked like it had been made in the eighties, and brown coffee mug rings stained several of the folders stacked next to his keyboard. A little hula girl figurine in a grass skirt and coconut bra stood next to his desk phone. Charles caught me looking at her and flicked her backside with his finger, making her hips wiggle from side to side. "To what do I owe this pleasure?" he asked.

"I understand you were employed by William Meriwether?" I asked, eying the chair opposite Charles's desk. My stomach churned as I noted a mysterious filmy residue on the seat. I opted to stand instead.

An amused smile played across Charles's thin lips. "Did you read the door when you came in?" he asked.

"Huh?"

"The door. It says *discreet* inquiries. I wouldn't be very discreet if I gave out the names of my clients, now would I?"

He had me there. "Okay, how about this… You obviously know who I am, so *someone* hired you to investigate me. Correct?"

Charles shrugged, but I could see the concession in his eyes. "It's possible."

"Is it also possible this someone had you dig into the lives of the other couples on *Celebrity Relationship Rehab*?"

"Sure. Maybe."

"Any chance you'd like to share what you found with an interested party?" I asked.

Charles laughed. "That depends on how *interested* you are." He gave me a slow up and down that made my skin crawl.

Sorry, pal, I'd never be *that* interested.

"I'll pay," I tried again, gesturing to the purse dangling from my arm.

He raised one eyebrow at me. "I don't know. It might cost a lot. I mean, I'd hate to breach my trust with my client."

"Your client is dead," I reminded him.

He shrugged. "Which makes our bond all that more sacred."

I barely contained an eye roll. "How much?"

His smile widened. "Twenty grand."

I blinked at him. "You can't be serious."

Charles showed his teeth. "Hey, a man's gotta pay the bills."

"How do I know your info is even worth that? That it's even true?"

He shrugged, leaning back in his chair until it squeaked in protest. "Why else would you be here, sweetheart?"

Why indeed. Just standing in his office was making me want a shower. "Look, I don't have that kind of money," I told him, being 100% honest.

"Then you don't get the goods. No skin off my nose. If you don't buy it, someone else will. Heck, maybe one of the *real* stars will want to keep this info under wraps." He paused, as if an idea had struck him. "In fact, why don't you ask your boyfriend for a loan?" He sneered. "His secret is a real doozy."

I felt the blood drain from my face. While I'd been worried what the PI could possibly have on me, I'd never even considered what he might have on Trace. Did my sorta-hopefully-still-boyfriend actually have some dark, terrible thing from his past that he'd never told me about…or was the sleaze ball bluffing?

Either way, there was no way I'd be able to find twenty grand on short notice. Even Felix wouldn't pay that for a headline.

"Sorry. It's just too rich for my blood." I sighed and walked stiffly toward the door.

"Suit yourself," Charles called after me. "I'll see if your buddies at *Entertainment Daily* are willing to cough up the cash."

I gritted my teeth. "You do that," I said over my shoulder. My hand was on the doorknob when he spoke again.

"Though…I could cut you a little deal, I guess," he said smoothly.

I paused, slowly facing him again. "What sort of deal?"

"I won't part with the secrets Dr. William asked me to dig up for any less than twenty thousand."

I turned back to the door.

"*But* I do know something else that you might find interesting."

Now he had my attention. I turned around to face him again. "What have you got?"

Charles grinned again, showing a row of yellow molars. "I like to call it an insurance policy. See, in my line of work, you can never be too careful. Especially with a big dog like Mr. William Meriwether. I always like to *vet* my clients, if you know what I mean. I like to know everything about the people I'm working for. That way, if they try to stiff me, I have a little leverage."

I felt a thin sliver of hope. "So, you're saying you found out something about Dr. William that he wouldn't want getting out?"

He tapped his nose with his index finger. "Bingo, blondie."

I eyed him skeptically. "Okay, I'll bite. What do you have on him?"

"Ah, ah, ah…not so fast." His smile dropped from his face, and he was suddenly all business. "Three grand."

I stared at him. "Do I look like I carry three grand around on me?"

The shark-like smile came back. "I take personal checks."

This time I didn't even bother trying to hide my eye roll.

I did a little mental math, deciding that if I cleaned out my checking account, dipped into my savings, and ate ramen for the rest of the month, I might be able to scrape the amount together. Of course I would definitely be expensing this to Felix at some point, but getting reimbursement from him was often like getting blood from a stone.

"Fine," I said. "But it had better be good."

Charles's eyes gleamed. "Oh, it is."

Luckily I had one just-in-case check buried in the bottom of my purse, which I made out to Thomas Charles Investigations.

"Just don't cash it for a week," I told him as I handed it over. "I, uh, have to move some funds around."

He nodded and then creased it down the middle and placed it in the top drawer of his desk.

"Okay," I said, my patience wearing as thin as my bank account now was. "Spill it. What do you know about Dr. William?"

"The Meriwethers," he said, pausing for dramatic effect, "have a child."

My brow furrowed. That couldn't be. Dr. Georgia had specifically told me they had no kids.

"Are you sure?" I asked, narrowing my eyes at him.

The man held up his hands. "Hey, I didn't make it up. You paid me, and I told you what I found. The baby was put up for adoption right after she was born."

"Which was when?" I asked.

"Twenty-six years ago."

I did some quick mental math, trying to determine if the couple had been married then. Could that have been their reason for giving her up—having a baby out of wedlock?

"Were they married at the time?" I asked, testing my theory.

"No idea," Charles answered. "In fact, the adoption agency conveniently 'lost' all of the intake forms," he said, doing air quotes. "I imagine some money changed hands to make that paperwork go poof. Seems to me the Meriwethers didn't want anyone finding out about their little bundle of joy."

I studied Charles for a long moment. Nothing in his body language or expression gave any indication that he was making it up. "So how did you find out?"

"Trade secret."

I leaned forward, putting both of my hands on his desk and getting in his face. "Seriously? I just paid you three grand."

Charles laughed. "I like your spunk, blondie. Alright, I'll tell you. In doing some background checks on the good doc, I followed a trail that led to the adoption agency. Turns out, one of the receptionists there was an old-timer, and she remembered Dr. William. Recognized him from TV. Guess she's a fan of his show."

"And she didn't remember Dr. Georgia?" I pressed.

He shrugged. "She said she only dealt with the father. Dr. William said the mother was too distraught, but he got all the release forms signed by her."

"Did you ask her what they said?"

"What am I, an amateur? Of course I asked. The old broad didn't remember. Hey, it's been twenty-six years, and she had no reason to take note of them at the time."

"And what happened to the little girl?"

The PI gave me a blank stare like he hadn't even thought of that. "I dunno."

I straightened up, removing my hands from his desk and blowing out a sigh of frustration. "Great. Thanks," I told him with only the slightest hint of sarcasm as I walked toward the door.

"Don't mention it," Charles called after me. "But this check of yours better be good. One week I'll hold it, but if it bounces after that, I leak what I dug up on you and your boyfriend to that rival paper of yours."

I gritted my teeth. The check wouldn't bounce, but it would be stretching it. I made a mental note to get Allie to help me butter Felix up before asking for the reimbursement.

As soon as I was back in Allie's VW Bug (thankfully still at the curb and still sporting all four wheels), I headed back toward Malibu. Unfortunately, the traffic was terrible, and I found myself in gridlock on the 1. The GPS on my phone estimated that it would take me nearly twice as long to get back to the estate as it had taken to get to Thomas Charles's office.

While I negotiated my way through the traffic, my mind mulled over what I'd learned. While I was still dying to find out what dirt Dr. William had had on all of the contestants and had half a mind to break into the sleazy PI's office myself after dark to get it, the nugget of information he'd given me was interesting. Did the Meriwether's long-lost daughter have anything to do with his death? If the child had been born twenty-six years ago, that was right around when Dr. William had started calling himself a relationship expert. Had they put the baby up for adoption because they'd thought that taking the time to raise her would have hindered their careers? Or was there something darker involved? What if the baby wasn't Dr. Georgia's... What if Dr. William had been having an affair? The missing paperwork, the haste to get rid of the child and cover up any trace of her existence—was it because she was a product of adultery?

The driver of the car behind me angrily honked his horn, and I realized the traffic in our lane had started moving. I waved an apology and pulled off the brakes, my mind still racing.

The more I thought about it, the more it made sense. Dr. William had brought the baby in alone. Then he'd likely paid someone off to lose the paperwork...to cover up her real mother's name? Back then there wouldn't have been any DNA testing to know whose baby it was for sure.

Drs. Georgia and William had built their fortune using the strength of their own marriage as the foundation for their relationship rehab platform—the living evidence that Dr.

William had cheated on his wife would have been devastating to both of their careers. So, they'd hid it.

At least, she'd been hidden until now.

The driver behind me honked in annoyance again as another thought hit me.

Joanie Parker was twenty-six. Goosebumps prickled along my arms and legs. For years, she'd kept quiet about her childhood, never talking publicly about her parents—was it possible that was because she was adopted? If so, and if she'd gone hunting for her birth parents, was it possible that she'd uncovered the same connection that Thomas Charles had found through the adoption agency?

I remembered what Max had told me about Dr. William's lack of will and abundance of family money. At the time that had made for a bang-up motive for his wife. But, if Dr. William had a child—an heir—that suddenly meant a good chunk of his estate could be hers. Which begged the question…was it enough money for the reality starlet to kill over?

CHAPTER FIFTEEN

———

Allie wasn't answering her phone. I'd parked her car on the same grassy shoulder of the road where we'd met up earlier that morning. It was mostly obscured from view of the estate by the shrubs at the edge of the gate. I was dialing her for the third time when rustling in the bushes pulled my attention to the left. I turned my head just as the entire shrub began to move toward me. A chubby hand reached out from the leaves, gripping a camera, and its flash went off in my face.

"Is that our Cammy?" Mike asked, pushing the branches out of his face with his free hand.

"What the—?" I whirled around as another shrub picked itself up and took two steps toward me.

"Morning," came Eddie's voice from inside the bush.

"You have got to be kidding me," I groaned. I glared at the two men and their strange bush costumes. Looking at them more closely, it was obvious that the silky leaves and plastic branches were fake, but I'd been so preoccupied with my discovery about the Meriwethers' daughter that I hadn't been paying close enough attention.

"So, what brings you to this side of the fence?" Mike asked. Then snapped another photo of me.

"Cut it out," I grumbled, turning my face away. I looked from Mike to Eddie. If they weren't the most annoying twins on the planet, their outfits might have been funny. "Look, I'm…busy," I said, eyeing the fence and trying to decide if I could jump it or not. The latch only opened from the inside, and without Allie to unlock it for me, I was stuck with Tweedle Dumb and Tweedle Dumber.

"Come on, girl, we've been sitting in the dirt all morning. Throw us a bone?" Eddie paused. "Wow, what happened to your head?"

My hand instinctively went to the purple lump, and Mike snapped a photo. "I fell," I mumbled.

"You sure you didn't fall into someone's fist?" Mike prodded. "Things getting violent in rehab?"

"No!" Well, at least not the way he was insinuating.

"Oh, Cammy knows something!" Eddie taunted, rustling closer to me.

"I know I'd rather be in there with a potential murderer than out here with you two idiots," I mumbled, trying to get a foothold on the bottom rung in my sandals.

"Murderer?" Eddie piped up. "So, you think one of the celebs offed the doc?"

I pursed my lips together. Dang it. I had let that slip, hadn't I?

"Maybe," I hedged.

"Oh man, my money is on Ice Kreme. That guy's got a temper. Would you believe we snapped pics of him beating up some rollerblader on the Venice boardwalk last month?"

"You don't say?" I responded, testing the hold of the bars.

"So, what do you have on him? Bloody knife? Full confession?"

I shot Eddie a *get real* look. "If I had that, you think I'd be standing here talking to you two morons?"

"Ouch," Mike said. "Your words cut us deep, Cam."

I rolled my eyes and hoisted myself up and over the gate, landing with a thud on the other side.

"Whoa," Eddie said.

Mike did a low whistle. "Dude, that was hot. Who knew you were so athletic?"

"Or that you wore pink underwear," Eddie added.

I looked down at my skirt. Note to self: wear pants next time you go sneaking around the estate.

"Dude, you think we could do that?" I heard Mike asking his brother as I headed toward the house. His response was lost to me, but I put the likelihood of either of those two roly-polies being able to hop the fence at about the same level as Leah Remini joining Scientology again. I put the *ED* boys out of my mind as I dialed Allie's number again.

Straight to voicemail. That did not seem good. Had she blown our cover? I forced down a feeling of panic and set off through the trees in the direction of the pool. It was half past eleven, which meant that lunch would be served soon and PAs would be rounding the rehabbers up for our next drill. I needed to head that off before they rounded up faux me.

I came to the end of the stone path that led to the pool and spotted Allie instantly. Just as I'd instructed, she was lounging in a pool chair, her face covered by big sunglasses and the brim of the floppy hat. I let out a sigh of relief.

One that was short lived as the French doors opened and Trace strolled out onto the patio. I jumped back, shielding myself with some tall shrubbery and thinking a really bad word. There was no way Allie would be able to talk to Trace without blowing our cover. Please don't go near her, please don't go near her, please don't go near her…

Trace spotted Allie and made a beeline right for her.

I cringed, watching as he stopped next to her lounger. "I thought I'd find you here," he told Allie.

She didn't move, thankfully playing "sleeping Cam" to a tee.

"Cam, look. I hate this. I hate fighting. This place is making us both crazy, right?"

Allie didn't move.

"Well, anyway, I just…I just want to go back to being us."

A lump formed in my throat. Honestly? That's all I wanted too. I bit my lip to keep from telling him just that as Allie just shrugged her shoulders from beneath the oversize black cover-up.

"What does that mean?" Trace asked.

She just shrugged again. Really, what else could she do without giving the jig up?

Trace stared at her for a moment, the emotion in his eyes clear even from where I stood. But just that quickly it passed, and he squared his jaw again. "Fine. You don't want to talk, we won't talk."

The lump in my throat formed into a knot that traveled all the way to my stomach. Ugh. What had I done?

Trace turned and stalked back to the house. I could see his reflection heading straight to a bar that looked like the crew had set up overnight in the great hall. (Geez, was there a room in the house that didn't have a bar at this point?")

As soon as he was gone, I hissed at Allie to get her attention. She lowered her sunglasses to peek at me. Then she quickly gathered her tote bag, unclipped her mike and dropped it on the lounger, and met me behind the bushes.

"Oh, thank God," she whispered when she'd joined me. "I thought I was busted for sure when I saw Trace."

"You and me both, girl," I admitted.

"You guys have a fight or something?" she asked, something akin to genuine concern in her eyes.

"It's a long story," I whispered, glancing at the patio door. "Why weren't you answering your phone?"

"Sorry. Battery died." She did a sheepish shrug. "Bad timing, I know, but I couldn't find a charger near the pool and didn't want to risk going inside."

I nodded. I'd have done the same thing.

I told Allie where to find her car and warned her about Mike and Eddie and their plantlike disguises. She gave me the cover up, hat, and sunglasses, and I threw them over my own outfit before re-miking and heading back toward the house.

Once I got inside, Phillip sidelined me and informed me we were all being filmed having a "real moment" eating lunch with our hostess. Nothing about this place was "real," but I nodded, smiled, and generally pretended like I wasn't living in an insane asylum and let him lead me toward the dining room.

As soon as I walked into the room, Joanie looked up and glared at me with a look of pure hatred. I froze, pinned to the spot. Did she somehow know I knew about her secret?

"There you are," she snapped. Her eyes flicked to a point behind me, and I realized she wasn't talking to me. I turned to see Antoine Parker come in behind me. He sat down next to Joanie, and she smacked his arm. "You were supposed to walk

Isabelle this morning. She made a doodie on the carpet in our suite. No one answered when I called the control room, so *I* had to clean it up." She made a disgusted face. "I swear, sometimes I really do think you don't deserve me."

Antoine sat silently next to his whining wife, but I could see the veins tightening in his neck as he clenched his jaw. It seemed even his patience for the bratty socialite was wearing thin.

"Yikes," I muttered under my breath as I took a seat between Trace and Apple.

"No kidding," Apple whispered back. "Poor Antoine."

"You'd better never talk to *me* like that, babe," Ice said from beside her. "Yo, Ice deserves respect, you hear?" he told the cameras.

I covered an unladylike snort with my hand as I dipped a chip in the bowl of guacamole that one of the PAs placed on the table, which was already covered with dishes of black beans and rice, a platter of chicken and spinach enchiladas, and a large bowl of salad. We all fell quiet as we passed the dishes around to serve our plates. Ellen broke the silence with a loud cough as Dirk piled a generous helping of beans onto his plate.

Dirk paused, giving his wife a questioning look.

"You really think that's such a good idea?" she hissed at him.

"What? I like beans. They have fiber."

"And *gas*."

Joanie cackled. Dirk's cheeks flushed, and he loaded his plate with lettuce instead.

"Well, I read that guacamole is super good for you," Apple said, clearly trying to lighten the tension. "It has all these healthy fats in it."

"Fats?" Ice interjected. "Girl, you better go easy on that stuff."

Apple gasped. "*Healthy* fats," she reiterated.

"Still," Ice said. "Girl, your booty is *healthy* enough, you know what I mean?" He laughed loudly at his own joke.

Apple looked down at her napkin, not, I noticed, sampling the guacamole.

"Mr. Brody, would you pass the salad, please?" Dr. Georgia asked loudly.

I glanced at the head of the table to find her wearing an uncomfortable expression. While I knew the hostess and the show thrived on conflict, I could tell she wasn't sure how fart jokes and fat booties would play to the viewing audience.

There was another lull in conversation as everyone tucked into their lunch. I studied Joanie closely as she poured salsa over her salad and then speared a forkful of lettuce. Her eyes were dark, the same color that Dr. William's had been. And if I squinted, her nose and cheekbones did resemble the doc's.

When Dr. Georgia struck up a conversation with Trace about his previous guest role on *Grey's Anatomy*, I leaned closer to Apple. "Do you see any resemblance between Joanie and Dr. William?" I asked, my voice lowered. "I mean, they almost look like they could have been related, don't you think?"

Apple's pencil-thin eyebrows knitted together as she glanced up at Joanie. "I guess so," she said, giving me a confused look. "Why do you ask?"

I shrugged. "I don't know. I just noticed their similarities." I paused, sensing an opportunity as I saw Dr. Georgia's eye flit our way. "I guess I'm noticing things like genetics more now. You know, since my one-on-one with Dr. Georgia got me thinking about our future and children," I said, loudly enough for everyone to hear.

Trace dropped his fork on his plate with a clatter and stared at me.

I sent him a silent apology and plunged forward. "I'm sure the other couples have discussed whether they want to have children. Right?" I looked up again and scanned the table, noting that all eyes were now turned on me.

"Oh, Ice and I definitely want kids," Apple piped up from beside me. "I can't wait to have a little girl to buy dresses for!"

"Oh, hizzle no," Ice said gruffly. "*If* we have kids, we're definitely having a boy."

"You know you can't control the baby's gender," Joanie said in a haughty tone. She reached over and patted Antoine's arm. "We're not having kids," she said. as if she were proud of the decision. "Izzy is the only child we need. Our little fur baby never talks back to us." Below the table, the little dog yapped from Joanie's purse.

"What about you, Dr. Georgia?" I asked, meeting the hostess's gaze. "How did you and Dr. William reach the decision to not have children? Perhaps you have some advice for the rest of us."

Dr. Georgia stared down the length of the table at me, her face placid though I could swear her complexion was a shade paler. She inhaled a slow breath and pushed it back out. Then she set her fork down on her plate and rose from the table. "I'm afraid I can't help you with that, Cameron. I have some matters to attend to before our afternoon drill." Her voice was evenly modulated and businesslike but almost too calm. "I will see you all in the garden at two." Everyone stared after her as she walked stiffly out of the room.

Then all eyes turned back to me.

"Was it something I said?" I asked, going for innocence even though it was clear to all involved it definitely *was* something I'd said. There was no mistaking this time that I'd struck a nerve with the hostess. I glanced at Joanie, gauging her reaction.

She stared back at me with a mixture of annoyance and dislike. "You're such a buzzkill, Cameron," she said angrily. "Someone ought to teach you to butt out of other people's business." Her lips curved in a cruel smirk. "Maybe that's why someone tried to bash your skull in last night."

"Hey," Trace said, standing up suddenly. "That wasn't funny. Cam could have been seriously hurt."

I shot him a grateful look, though he was already up and storming out of the room.

"Wow, touchy crowd today," Dirk said, attempting a smile.

I felt my phone buzz in my pocket. I did my best to discreetly check the readout. Tina.

"Uh, if you could excuse me a moment…" I trailed off, not waiting for an answer before ducking out into the great hall and swiping to accept the call.

"Hey," I said.

"Hey yourself. I saw I had a missed call from you?"

"Um, yeah. It was nothing." I looked up at the cameras mounted in all four corners of the room. "By the way, you're on candid camera," I told Tina, hoping she picked up on my meaning.

"Ah. No hairdryer this time?"

"Bingo."

"Okay, I'll make this quick then. I just wanted to let you know I ran down the information you asked about from James A. Johnson, that divorce attorney."

"And how is Mom?" I asked her, hoping if I made my side of the conversation sound mundane enough no one in the control room would pay attention.

I heard Tina chuckle. "Yeah, anyway. One of my informants has a friend who's an extra on a TV show that uses the same courier service as the attorney. Short story long, for a small fee our courier friend got a peek at the attorney's client list."

"And?"

"I hate to tell you this, but Joanie Parker's name wasn't on it."

I frowned. "Then what was she doing with the—" I looked up at the camera and stopped myself from saying "business card" just in time. "—*Hallmark* card with his name on it?"

"Beats me," Tina said. "But my courier said there were only two people with the last name Parker on their client lists. Both male. A Eustace Parker and an Alfred Parker."

Rats. While it was possible Joanie might've used a pseudonym to avoid the paparazzi—such as the enterprising Tina and myself—from catching wind of divorce proceedings, I didn't see her pulling off a gender switch.

"Sorry to not have better news," Tina told me.

"Not your fault," I told her, meaning it. "I guess it was a long shot anyway."

"True, but you know just because she's not a client yet doesn't mean she wasn't planning to be one," Tina said. "I know it doesn't do much for her motive, but it could still be a nice juicy divorce story."

I grinned. "Thanks for trying to cheer me up, *sis*," I added for the camera's benefit.

"Anytime, *cuz*," she replied with a chuckle before hanging up.

I shoved my phone back into my pocket. Tina was right—the client list had busted my original theory as to why Joanie might want Dr. William dead. Clearly she wasn't violating her contract. It was just possible, though, that a better motive had emerged with my visit to the Valley. One that could mean a whole lot more money in her pocket *and* more publicity than this one season of the show could provide. The only problem was, once again, I was long on theories and short on evidence. And the clock was ticking down. We only had one more day here before all my suspects dispersed and my access disappeared. I bit my lip. Well, as my poker-playing dog friends might say, if you don't have the cards, it's time to bluff.

CHAPTER SIXTEEN

———

I arrived "fashionably" late to the evening drill, after having set up my bluff. The rest of the couples were already assembled. Dirk looked as if he had been drinking all afternoon, swaying heavily on his feet next to his wife, who was wearing a Chanel-inspired suit and a perma-scowl. As usual, Dirk's eyes were on Apple, who I noticed had changed for the evening drill into a short, silver-sequined cocktail dress that looked more like it was going to the club than a therapy session. Ice slung a protective arm around her shoulders, seeming ready to pounce on anyone who looked sideways at her. Joanie twirled her hair, which hung loose tonight, and tapped her heel-clad foot impatiently as if she had somewhere better to be. And Antoine stood a step behind her, his expression as stoic and unreadable as always. Beside them, Trace had his hands shoved into the pockets of his jeans, the expression on his face making it clear that he wanted to be anywhere but there. Part of me longed to confide in him, but I knew if I clued him in to what I was up to today, he would only bring out Angry Protective Boyfriend Trace again. And I couldn't have that character playing into the drama I had planned for tonight.

Instead, I took my place beside him, sending him a tentative smile. He nodded back at me. I took that as some small progress.

A beat later, Dr. Georgia made her way into the garden and commanded our attention. "It's time for our final challenge before you make your decisions about whether you will leave here as a couple—" She paused for emphasis, her eyes slowly roving the group."—or alone." I tried not to take it personally that her eyes rested on me as she said that last part.

"But before you can take that step and be fearless in love, you must be fearless in life," she continued. She gestured for us to follow her across the grass. "That's why tonight, you'll be facing your greatest challenge yet."

At the far edge of the garden, there was a large mound of dirt that hadn't been there previously. Making our way around it, we found a pit had been dug into the ground. It was at least six feet deep, and I estimated it to be around twelve feet wide—it was large enough to hold the whole group, though we would need help climbing out. There were tiki torches posted in each corner of the pit, and in the center burned a path of smoldering coals.

Uh-oh.

I only halfway listened as Dr. Georgia explained how this next fire-walking drill would work, my mind focusing on just one thought—those coals looked hot! Sure I'd seen people do this on TV, and my camera and I had actually been witness, from a well-hidden spot behind a bonsai tree, to Gwenyth Paltrow making a hot-coal trek at a Zen retreat once. But actually doing it myself? *That* I wasn't so keen on.

"Sorry, but that's a hard pass. I can*not* walk on fire," Joanie protested in her nasal voice. She crossed her arms over her chest and scowled down at the pit.

Beside Joanie, Ellen threw her hands up in the air. "Here we go again."

"Oh, come on, Joanie," Apple coaxed. "You'll never know unless you try."

Joanie glared at her. "No. I mean I contractually can't do this. It will *ruin* my feet, and I'm a model for my own footwear line." She lifted her leg to show off her hot pink open-toed pumps. "It's called Fierce Feet by Joanie," she said, flashing a smile at the camera. When she turned back to Dr. Georgia, she was frowning again. "I'm not doing it."

Dr. Georgia gave her a tight smile. "If you refuse to participate in the drills, how can your partner count on you to participate in the relationship outside of rehab?"

"I'll go first," Antoine piped up beside his wife.

Dr. Georgia looked like she was going to protest, but Antoine already had his shoes off and was descending a small ladder into the pit.

"Very well," Dr. Georgia recovered. "Perhaps your willingness to take the first literal step in this drill will inspire your wife to take the necessary steps toward repairing your relationship."

If I had to guess, the only thing Joanie would be taking steps toward would be another footwear endorsement deal. However, we all moved toward the edge of the pit to watch Antoine.

He placed one bare foot on top of the glowing orange coals. Then he took another. He closed his eyes, a serene expression on his face as he continued to walk steadily toward the other end.

As all eyes were on Antoine, I saw it as the golden opportunity that I'd been hoping would present itself that evening. Time to bluff like I knew what I was doing.

I slipped my phone from my pocket and pulled up Joanie's cell number, quickly typing out a text.

I know what you did. Meet me in the confession room after the drill

I hit *Send*, sliding the phone back into my pocket as I watched Joanie's reaction.

As the text buzzed in on her end, she pulled her phone out and scanned the screen. By the way the starlet's eyes went first wide then narrowed into slits as she surveyed our group, I mentally crossed my fingers.

I saw her furiously texting something back—no doubt asking who the heck had sent the threat. I saw Ellen glance over at Joanie on her phone and shoot her a look of disgust, but no one else seemed to notice the diva ignoring her husband and focusing on her flying thumbs instead. Luckily I'd put my phone on silent, and I didn't dare take it out to read her response. Instead, I trained my eyes on Antoine, pretending my heart wasn't going a mile a minute.

When Antoine stepped onto the dirt at the end of the coal pathway, he let out a loud whoop. "Touchdown!" He performed the victory dance he usually reserved for the end zone of a football field.

The group cheered. Everyone except Joanie, that is. She was still frowning. Though whether it was due to the threatening text or the fact that her husband had shown her up, it was hard to tell.

"Well done, Mr. Parker," Dr. Georgia complemented him. She turned to face Joanie. "Are you ready to follow in your husband's steps?"

Joanie crossed her arms over her chest again and gave Dr. Georgia a defiant look that said it all.

"Very well," Dr. Georgia said, turning her back to the spoiled diva. "Let's move on to our next couple. Cameron?"

My head snapped up. "Me?" I asked, my voice coming out in the Minnie Mouse range.

"Let's see how far you would be willing to go for your relationship. Tell me, would you walk across fire for Trace?"

"Uh…" I glanced to my right and caught Trace watching me with an expectant look on his face. I swallowed hard. If ever there was a moment to reverse some of the damage this relationship rehabbing week had done, this was it. "Of course," I said confidently. A lot more confidently than I felt as I stared down at the steam rising off the hot coals in the cool evening.

I didn't dare look at Trace again as I slipped out of my heels. I knew if he gave me one little chance at an out, I would take it. But I didn't want to do that. If this was what it took to show him I was serious about us, this is what I'd do.

A crew member I recognized as the bearded lighting guy helped lower me down into the pit. "Your feet will start to sweat," he told me quietly, "and if you move fast enough, the water vapor should protect your skin from burning."

I nodded, feeling my heart start to pound in my chest. Got it. Move fast.

I gingerly walked over to the edge of the coals. The heat radiated off of them, making beads of perspiration form along my forehead.

"It's easier than you think," Antoine said, giving me an encouraging nod from across the path. "You've got this, girl."

I gave him an attempt at a smile, though it might have been more of a grimace. Then I closed my eyes, sucking in a huge breath. This was for Trace. For us. I could do this.

I slowly took my first step. My left foot came down on the hot orange coals, and I hissed as the heat flared on my skin. "Walk fast," I repeated under my breath. I focused my vision on the dirt just beyond the other end of the coals and began to move quickly, pushing all thoughts of pain out of my mind. I vaguely heard cheers from the other rehabbers (or possibly jeers from Joanie), but I tuned them all out, solely focusing on putting one foot in front of the other. Before I knew it, my feet touched down in the cool dirt on the other side.

A chorus of cheers came from the other contestants as I climbed another ladder out of the pit on the far side. "Go, Cameron!" Apple yelled, jumping up and down so hard her dress threatened a wardrobe malfunction. I sent her a thumbs-up, my eyes going to Trace. For the first time that day, a small smile graced his lips. He was shaking his head at me as if he couldn't believe I'd just done that. Honestly? Neither could I. I sent him a small wave across the pit, which he returned with a full-on dimpled grin. My heart melted just a little, and suddenly my feet weren't the only body parts heating up.

One by one the crew helped each of the other rehabbers down into the pit to do the same ritual. Ice made a big show of strutting across and grabbing his crotch in a victory move at the end. Apple looked like she was doing some sort of yoga breathing and having a full-on spiritual experience. Ellen looked like each step was painful and practically jogged across the coals, complaining at the other end about the entire experience and how idiotic it was. Dirk looked like he didn't even feel the heat, but the alcohol might have helped. Joanie flat-out refused again, leaving Antoine frowning at her, the disappointment palpable.

When everyone had taken their turn or made it clear they weren't going to, Dr. Georgia made a show of giving us each a critique on how our performance in the coal walking was indicative of where our relationships were headed. "I want everyone to think very seriously tonight about their partner's performance and what that says about their level of commitment to their relationship."

Joanie snorted in disgust and rolled her eyes, crossing her arms over her chest again. Antoine just frowned at her.

"Tomorrow, each of you will be making the ultimate decision about the future of your relationships. We will all be meeting in the back garden under the wedding altar, where you will either choose to renew your commitment to each other with a ring ceremony or you will present your partner with an empty ring box, indicating that you have chosen to end your relationship and you will be leaving rehab alone."

Then Dr. Georgia spun on her heels, leaving us all with that last disconcerting thought as the cameras turned off and the lighting crew began to pack up.

The rehabbers dispersed, walking back toward the house. I watched Joanie stomp off on her Fierce Feet in a huff, Antoine trying to catch up to her.

"Hey," Trace said coming up beside me. "That was pretty hot back there." He waggled his eyebrows up and down at me.

"No pun intended?" I asked, matching his playful smile.

He laughed, throwing an arm around my shoulders. "What do you say we go grab a drink by the pool and celebrate this craziness being almost done, huh?"

I paused, biting the inside of my cheek as I watched Joanie wave Antoine off and march purposefully through the great hall. As much as I would love to have a drink and reconnect with Trace, there was a little something I had to take care of in the confession room first.

"Uh, let me just go freshen up first, okay?" I asked. I didn't wait for Trace to answer as I gave him a quick wave and practically jogged toward the house.

Antoine and Dirk were at the bar in the great hall, pouring themselves what looked like double Scotches—Dirk's in celebration of having crossed the coals and Antoine's, if I had to guess, for strength to deal with his wife for the rest of the evening. I spied Apple heading toward the kitchen. Ice and Ellen were nowhere to be seen.

I didn't waste time looking for them, going as quickly as I could without attracting attention to the hallway that held the confession room.

I knew it was a risky move to call Joanie out. But it wasn't like I was going to be alone. I'd made arrangements with Bonnie earlier, strategically choosing the confession booth as the spot to confront the reality starlet. Bonnie would be watching and recording everything from the small control room next door, her finger hovering over the call button for set security the second anything looked sketchy. Plus, I knew for a fact from my earlier search of Joanie's room that she hadn't brought a gun or Taser or other similarly dangerous weapons with her. I felt relatively confident that worst case was that I'd piss her off with my accusations. Best case—I'd be able to wrangle a confession out of her by pretending that I knew everything she'd done…when in reality, all I had were really good guesses.

By the time I reached the confession room, my heartbeat was practically at warp speed. Easing the door open, I cautiously peeked inside. I didn't see anyone lurking in the shadows.

The confession room's light was off, and I slipped my hand up to the dimmer switch. A soft glow illuminated the tiny room, and I breathed a sigh of relief. No Joanie.

Stepping inside, I pulled the door closed behind me.

The first thing I did was check my phone for the reply texts I'd seen Joanie pounding out. Three had come in silently while we'd finished the coal-walking drill.

Predictably the first one read *who is this?*

Then she'd apparently gotten a little feistier with *I don't know who you think you are or what you think you know.*

When no one had answered that one she'd finished with *if you think you're going to blackmail me, you have another thing coming.*

My fingers itched to correct her grammar. "It's 'another think coming,' darling," I mumbled to myself. Though I noticed Joanie had neither confirmed nor rejected the suggestion she meet me in the confession booth. I dimmed the lights again and sat on the low bench. My trap was set, and all I could do now was wait and hope for her to show up.

It seemed like an eternity passed without any sign of Joanie. I sat in silence, listening to the thrumming of my heartbeat in my ears as I waited for her. Doubt inevitably started to creep in. What if Joanie didn't take my bait? Or, worse yet, what if I'd scared her so badly she decided to flee rather than face me? Could she be packing her bags and jumping ship even now? With most of the crew busy cleaning up our fire-walking challenge, it was the perfect opportunity for her to make an escape. She could be halfway back into the city by now. I chewed my lip. What if I was sitting here in the dark like a fool while Dr. William's killer slipped even farther away? Without tricking her into recording a confession in here, I was keenly aware I had no real evidence tying Joanie to his death.

The sound of footsteps coming down the hall snapped me out of my doubt spiral. The unmistakable clicking of women's high heels moved toward the confession room in a quick staccato pattern. I held my breath. The heels stopped just outside the door. I sat in silence, not daring to breathe as I waited for something to happen. I pictured Joanie on the other side of the door, taking a resolute breath as she braced herself for our showdown.

The door opened a crack, and a dark silhouette against the light in the hallway filled the doorway. I blinked, trying to bring her into focus, but the door shut quickly, closing off the light source.

I stood, taking a step backward and coming up against the wall as my heart hammered. "So, you did take my text seriously," I said, amazed at how calm my voice sounded while my insides were dancing with nervous energy.

She didn't answer, instead taking a small step toward me, effectively blocking me in.

While I knew Joanie barely had the strength in her skinny arms to lift her dog, let alone overtake me, I still felt the move as menacing, the entire air in the room changing and making the hairs on the back of my neck stand up.

"Does your husband know you're here?" I asked, switching gears to try to get her to start talking.

She let out a low rumble of a laugh. "No one knows I'm here," she answered.

Only it wasn't Joanie's voice.

The lights suddenly flashed on, and I staggered back, blinded by the sudden brightness. I bumped into the wall and rubbed my eyes, trying to adjust after all that time spent in the dark. I blinked at the woman standing in front of me, my mind trying to play catch-up as it processed what my eyes were seeing.

Ellen Bents stood just a few feet away, aiming a handgun at my chest.

CHAPTER SEVENTEEN

————

I sucked in a breath. "Ellen?"

She laughed again. "Surprised to see me?" she asked, taking a small step forward. "Oh, that's right. Of course you are. You thought you'd be meeting Joanie Parker here, right?"

My confusion must have been clear on my face as she continued with, "Yes, I saw that cryptic text you sent her earlier tonight. I convinced her to ignore it. That it was probably some opportunistic member of the crew trying to make a buck off of her, and if she didn't show, they'd drop it."

I blinked, trying to think fast to save face. And other parts of me in danger of falling victim to that shiny little gun in her hand. "I…was trying to make a buck. I was going to blackmail her with some information I had on her."

Ellen gave me a *get real* look. "Nice try, tabloid girl. We both know this isn't about blackmail but a story. The story of who killed Dr. William Meriwether. You were trying to put Joanie in the role of the star, but I knew as soon as you talked to her you'd realize you were wrong."

I bit my lip, my eyes flitting toward the camera, hoping Bonnie was getting every moment of this. I halfway hoped Bonnie'd hit the security button already, considering the handgun to my chest. But the other half of me hoped she'd wait just a little bit longer in order to record what I hoped Ellen was about to say next.

"And you know that Joanie didn't kill Dr. William because…" I trailed off, waiting for the punchline.

Ellen gave me a tight smile that held zero humor. "Honey, you don't need to bait me. I've conducted enough *real* interviews in my career that I know all of the tactics. We both know there's only one way I could be certain Joanie didn't kill William. And that is because I did it myself."

Bingo! My eyes flitted to the camera again, hoping Bonnie had gotten every last word.

"So that's a confession?" I asked, just to clarify.

Ellen took another small step forward. Her smile vanished, and she shifted her weight while keeping the gun trained on me. "I don't know why you couldn't just stick to reporting gossip like your trashy rag usually does. What made you think you were an investigative journalist? Sneaking off to look at film footage, digging through people's things, trying to stir up trouble. Why couldn't you just leave well enough alone?"

Wow, I guessed I hadn't been as stealthy as I'd hoped if Ellen knew all that. I swallowed hard, my eyes going to the camera again. This would be an excellent time for Bonnie to summon security.

"I don't know what you're talking about," I lied. "I, uh, was just here to repair my relationship with Trace."

"Oh, spare me. We both know what you are really doing here. And we both know that you were already getting a little too close for comfort even before you took to randomly accusing guests like Joanie."

I wanted to reply that it wasn't exactly random, but I had a strict policy of never arguing with a person with a gun. "So you convinced Joanie not to meet me, and your plan was to show up here with a gun yourself and what? Scare me into keeping quiet?"

Ellen shrugged. "That's one scenario." Though I could tell by the look in her eyes another scenario was playing out. One that didn't end with me walking out of this room unharmed.

My eyes flickered to the camera again, and this time Ellen must have caught the movement, as she did that creepy humorless smile again. "Oh, honey, please tell me you didn't think that camera was actually still running."

I froze. It wasn't?

Ellen shook her head. "What kind of amateur do you think I am?" she asked.

I felt a chill run down my spine. "What did you do to Bonnie?"

"That redhead girl in the control room? I'm afraid she's going to wake up with a rather nasty headache and a lump on her head." She paused, tilting her head to the side. "Rather like yours, in fact."

Relief that Bonnie hadn't been a victim of the handgun still pointed at my midsection flooded through me even as her implication sunk in. No one was recording this confession. No one was watching it. And no one was calling security.

"You're the one who hit me over the head on the island?" I said, trying to keep Ellen talking while my mind raced over various escape options. Granted, it was a fast race, as I couldn't come up with any.

"I told you, you were getting a little too close for comfort. I thought maybe if I could put a little fear into you, or that overprotective boyfriend of yours, the two of you would leave."

Wow. She was good. That was exactly what Trace had wanted to do, and I'd been pretty darn tempted for a moment there.

"So, tell me, why did you do it?"

"Are you deaf as well as stupid? I just told you why I hit you over the head."

"I meant why did you kill Dr. William." I'll admit, in addition to stalling for time, I genuinely was curious. While Dirk had been on my radar, I'd never seriously considered Ellen as the killer. The anchorwoman had seemed much too prim and proper to stab someone to death with gardening shears—an opinion I was amending now that her true colors were coming out.

"I should think it would be quite obvious." Ellen raised an eyebrow, as if challenging me to show my cards.

I licked my lips. "Okay, I'd say it was all about the baby."

The smile froze on her face. "Well, you know more than I gave you credit for."

"It was an affair, wasn't it?" Puzzle pieces were falling into place. Dirk and Ellen had been such good friends with the Meriwethers. Who else would've been more natural for Dr. William to have a torrid affair with than Ellen Bents?

Ellen nodded slowly, as if the memory were a painful one. "Correct again. That's two points for you, tabloid girl. It's a shame you won't be leaving this room alive. Perhaps you could have made a good investigative reporter after all."

I glossed over that not-alive thing, trying not to let it make my hands shake as they felt the wall behind me for anything I could use as a weapon. Unfortunately, the walls had been covered in thick velvet curtains to evoke the feeling of a true confessional booth. All I could feel behind them were smooth, stuccoed walls.

"It was the affair that broke up your friendship with the Meriwethers twenty-six years ago."

"Twenty-seven," she spat out. "That tart got pregnant twenty-seven years ago."

I paused. That tart? Then it hit me like a second blow to the head.

"Wait, the baby wasn't Dr. William's at all… it was Dr. Georgia's?"

Ellen shook her head. "Did you think that brat was *mine*?" She made a disgusted face. "The thought of giving birth is horrifying enough, but to a creature like that? You really are a terrible judge of character, Cam."

But I was too busy rearranging my puzzle pieces back into place to even register the insult. "If it was Georgia's daughter…then that means it must be Dirk's." I paused, looking into her eyes, which were dark with memory and emotion. "It was Dirk and Georgia who had the affair. Georgia became pregnant, but she decided to put the child up for adoption."

"Oh, it wasn't her decision," Ellen said forcefully. "That was all William. When he found out his wife had been cheating on him with his best friend, he about lost it. Dirk was actually going to leave me for her." Ellen laughed, a loud, cackling thing that had a maniacal edge to it. "Can you imagine that? *He* was going to leave *me*."

Gee, and here she seemed like such a catch.

But I didn't say anything, instead letting her continue talking as I took a small step to my right, testing out the area behind the curtain in the corner. If only the crew had left a spare boom mike or piece of lighting equipment heavy enough to use as a weapon...

"But William would have none of that," Ellen said, almost lost in her own thoughts now. "If Georgia left him, it would have ruined what was the beginning of his relationship-expert career. Who would pay attention to a relationship expert whose wife became pregnant from an affair and then left him? No one, that's who."

"How did he convince Dr. Georgia to give the baby up?" I asked, remembering the strong reaction the widowed host had every time I'd mentioned children. Now knowing what her history was, I suddenly felt bad for poking at a wound.

"Oh, didn't you know?" Ellen said, her voice dripping with sarcasm. "Dr. Georgia actually believes in love. William laid it on thick for her at the time, promising to forgive her, love her, and be everything he hadn't been that had driven her into the arms of my dear husband. His one condition was that she give the baby up for adoption so they could have a *fresh start*."

"And she agreed?"

"Of course. The woman would do anything William told her."

"So why kill William now?" I pressed, asking the fifty-million-dollar question while my fingers explored the corner behind me. More curtains. More solid wall. Nothing sharp, pointy, or heavy.

The bitter lines tightened around the corners of her mouth. "After twenty-seven years of pretending to have a happy marriage, William was finally ready to throw his wife under the bus for ratings."

"So he didn't care about his image anymore?" I asked, keeping her talking while I tried to formulate a Plan B. And C.

She shrugged. "At this point, he figured he was an established figure in the public eye. His fans would forgive him if he played his cards right."

"And Dr. Georgia?"

"Like he cared." She snorted. "Like that man cared about anything but his own fame."

"So it was his idea to bring Dr. Georgia's daughter on the show, along with Dirk."

She nodded. "One heck of a family reunion, right?"

"And how did you find out about his plan to out them all on national television?"

"I'm not stupid. I recognized the girl the second she came onto the set. It was so obvious she was Georgia's." She rolled her eyes. "Just what the world needed, another one of *her.*"

"And so you confronted Dr. William?"

She nodded. "I did. I even offered to pay him to keep the story quiet. He just laughed at me. It was then I realized he was not only going to drop the bombshell, but he was also going to milk it for all it was worth all over television. He'd make sure we were all laughingstocks. I'm a respected newscaster! My career would be over if a scandal like that hit. Especially considering that girl's...notoriety. She is pure embarrassment."

There I had to agree. Joanie and respected news outlets went together like cashmere sweaters and August in Orlando.

"So you arranged to meet Dr. William to convince him to not air your dirty little secrets?"

She narrowed her eyes at the word *dirty* but nodded. "It was his idea to meet in the garden shed. He said no cameras would be watching us there. So, when Dirk went upstairs to sleep off his lunch martinis, I slipped outside."

"And when you couldn't convince Dr. William to keep quiet, you killed him."

"The way I see it, I was doing everyone involved a favor. I dare you to name one person who cares that man is dead."

I had to admit, none were coming to mind. But that still didn't give her the right to play judge, jury, and executioner. Though, considering the gun, I kept that opinion to myself. "You grabbed the first handy thing you could find, a pair of gardening shears?"

She shrugged. "Crude, yes, but effective. I took the long way back to the house and tossed them in the lake."

"And you deleted the footage that showed you leaving and returning to the house."

She grinned. "Like it was hard. I've been in television longer than you've been alive. I know my way around a control room."

I took another small step to my right, knowing my time was limited. There were only so many questions I could ask her before she ran out of patience. "Does Joanie know she's Dirk and Georgia's daughter?" I asked, switching gears.

Ellen cocked her head to the side. Then she let out a sharp bark of laughter. "Wow, you tabloid trash really are idiots. I take all of that back about you being a good investigator."

I paused. "What you mean?"

"Joanie isn't Dirk's daughter."

I frowned "But then who—"

"It's Apple, you moron."

If I were in a cartoon, my jaw would have hit the floor. Apple! My mind whirled, the puzzle pieces jostling once again to create an entirely different picture. Dirk had been staring at the girl since she'd arrived. Ice had been accusing him of ogling Apple…but as I thought back, Dirk never had looked at her that way. In fact, if anything, he'd seemed to be…studying her.

"Does Dirk know?"

Ellen shook her head. "I imagine he suspects. If I recognize the resemblance, he can't be completely oblivious to it. I've been trying to keep those two apart, but the production staff must have had orders to shove them together at every turn." She rolled her eyes. "William did know how to create a scene."

"He was the ratings king," I said, meaning it as one of his loyal viewers. I took one more small step to the right and felt my fingers come up against something on the wall. It was cold and round. Like a doorknob? I felt my heart lift for the first time since I'd entered the room. I gingerly moved my hand and felt the knob turn in my palm.

"Yes he was, wasn't he?" Then Ellen leveled me with a look, holding the gun straight-armed in front of her. "And now he's dead. And unfortunately, that means you need to be too."

I wrenched my hand farther, unlatching what felt like a door behind me.

"Look, Ellen, you don't have to do this," I said. I needed a few more seconds. Enough time to distract her so I could slip out the door behind me. I only prayed it went somewhere other than a storage closet, where I'd be a sitting duck.

"I'm afraid I actually do, Cameron." She took a step forward.

"You won't get away with this," I told her, feeling frighteningly like I was quoting a line from Scooby-Doo.

"I already have," she said calmly. "When the police come to find your body, they'll find the gun that killed you among Ice Kreme's possessions. And when they look more closely they'll find a pair of Ice's shoes with Dr. William's blood on them."

"You planted the bloody shoe!" I did a mental forehead smack. The shoes hadn't been shoved into the corner of the closet because Ice was hiding them. They had been put there because someone was hiding them *from* Ice. And waiting for the right moment to point the police toward him.

"Oh, you found those too, did you? I knew you were a nosy little thing, but I guess I didn't realize just how nosy. I suppose that means your fingerprints will be all over Ice's room now." Her lips curled. "How convenient for me."

I realized with a sinking feeling just how right she was. I had unwittingly provided perfect evidence of a motive for Ice to kill me. Especially when coupled with Ellen's planted evidence and Ice's near confessions to the cameras all over the house for ratings value. He could try to argue that he'd just been making them up to get camera time, but I had a feeling a jury wouldn't buy it.

"I guess you've thought of everything," I said, trying flattery when all else was failing.

Ellen smiled. "Enough talk, Cameron. It's over." She took a step forward.

It was now or never. I took a deep breath, said a little prayer, and jerked the door behind me fully open as I focused on a point just beyond Ellen's head and yelled, "Look out!"

Yeah, it was the oldest trick in the book. But there was a reason it was still *in* the book—it worked.

On pure instinct, Ellen turned.

That was all the invitation I needed to throw myself backwards through the velvet curtains, out the open door, and into the unknown.

Ellen fired just as I ducked through the doorway, the wild shot embedding itself in the wall mere inches from where my head had just been. My ears rang with a painfully loud buzzing sound. I'd never been so close to a fired gun in such a tiny space, and for a brief moment I worried the sound had busted my eardrums.

Despite the ringing in my ears, I acted fast, running blindly. It took me a moment to realize the door led to the outside, toward the back of the estate. I said a silent thank you that it hadn't been a storage closet and kicked off my heels as I ran. Only my relief was short-lived when I realized this was the deserted side of the property. Even lighting was in short supply here, creating shadows and darkness ahead of me.

Behind me I heard Ellen swearing, her footsteps running toward me. I wasn't sure where I was going, but I ran for all I was worth. The ground was cold and hard beneath my bare feet, but I didn't care. I just had to get as far away from Ellen as possible.

I glanced over my shoulder to see that she was just a few steps behind me. She raised the gun again.

I opened my mouth to call for help, but I wasn't sure if anything actually came out.

Something whizzed past my head and struck one of the trees to my left. Ellen was shooting at me. I zigzagged like I'd seen on a History Channel documentary about Navy SEALs once. I wasn't sure if it was helping, but Ellen's swearing kicked up a notch, so I took that as a good sign.

I spied a large mound of dirt a few yards ahead that I recognized as the site of our fire-walking drill. The sound of Ellen's gun going off again spurred me forward. Maybe I could at least take shelter from her bullets behind the dirt. I all but dove behind the mound. Though I couldn't hear it, I was pretty sure I shrieked when I slammed into someone else already crouched behind the dirt.

I had to wipe my eyes to make sure I wasn't seeing things. Mike and Eddie were kneeling on the ground next to the pit, dressed in nothing but matching Batman boxers. Ellen had actually shot me, and I was in hell.

I didn't have time to ponder that because Ellen appeared above us then, climbing the dirt mound, a wild, desperate look in her eyes. The gun was still gripped in her hand.

"Holy…" Mike's eyes bulged at the sight of the weapon.

Eddie looked from me to the crazed anchorwoman. It was slow in coming, but I saw understanding dawn on his pudgy features. For a moment, I thought he was going to do something extraordinarily brave, like tackle her or wrestle the gun from her hands.

Instead, he raised his camera and began snapping pictures. Mike recovered from his shock and did the same.

At that moment there was nothing I hated more than the paparazzi.

I ducked my head down, thinking this would be my last moment on earth—sandwiched between two half-naked idiots, falling prey to the face of the evening news while lying in the dirt on the grounds of the most famous mansion in all of reality TV. I thought of Trace, Tina, Allie, and even Felix…though in my mind, Felix was yelling at me for letting *ED* publish the photos of my untimely death first. I saw a bright light and knew I was a goner…

Only I wasn't. I blinked, realizing the bright light was coming from the twins' camera flashes. And not only was it blinding me, but it was also blinding my assailant.

Ellen staggered backward, using her free hand to shield her eyes.

Seeing an opportunity, I lunged at her, my hand outstretched toward the gun. My shoulder collided with her midsection at full force. I knocked the handgun from her grasp as the woman staggered backward in a blur of obscenities and fake Chanel. For a brief moment my tackle left her teetering at the edge of the pit. But she couldn't maintain her balance, and her mouth opened in a scream of shock and fear as she fell into the pit of coals.

I decided to amend my last statement on the entertainment media: at the moment I freakin' loved the paparazzi.

CHAPTER EIGHTEEN

———

"So how are you going to thank us for saving your life, Cam?" Eddie's question still sounded slightly like it was coming from underwater as the ringing in my ears subsided and my hearing slowly returned to normal.

I shivered and pulled the blanket I'd been given by the EMTs more tightly around my shoulders. "By convincing Mr. Reisner not to press charges against you two for trespassing?" I offered.

Mike frowned, tugging his own blanket closer to his chest. "Is that the best you can do?"

The gruesome twosome had been inspired by watching me hop the fence earlier that afternoon. While I'd put their chance of succeeding at below zero, they had been more determined. Never underestimate the tantalizing power of a juicy photo op. While it had taken the two the better part of the day to come up with a strategy, apparently by moving their car close enough to the gate to climb on the hood and hoist themselves up, they'd ended up ripping their clothing in the process. All of it. How they'd managed it, I had no idea. But two pairs of size XXL pants were still waving like victory flags atop the south gate.

I was sure Felix would have some pretty choice words for me that the first photos of his star photographer running down a killer were being posted on *ED*'s website and not the *Informer*'s, but at the moment, the only emotion I felt toward my nudist rivals was gratitude. If they hadn't been there with their camera flashes, they might be printing my obituary instead.

"Okay," I conceded. "Let's just say I owe you guys one."

Mike beamed. Eddie did a fist pump in the air, his blanket slipping precariously down his shoulders.

"Oh, you know we'll be collecting on that," Mike told me with a wink.

I sighed. Yeah, I had no doubt.

As soon as Ellen had fallen into the pit, I'd dialed 9-1-1, and in record time, police had swarmed the estate. Set security had already pulled a bruised and slightly singed Ellen from the pit and had her detained by the time they arrived, and the detectives were currently still trying to sort out everyone's statements—from the crew to the confused rehabbers and poor Dirk, who had gone fifty shades of shocked as he'd pieced together what Ellen had done.

Even before the EMTs had arrived, the on-site medic had found Bonnie in the control room, unconscious and bound. She had a nasty gash on her head and the paramedics were treating her for a concussion, but they'd assured us she would be fine. I watched her being wheeled on a stretcher toward a waiting ambulance, and guilt washed through me. I made a mental note to contact her as soon as the mess was over and properly express my apologies and thanks for all she'd done. Possibly even with a new camera. (That I'd expense to Felix, of course.)

As Detective Martinez pulled Mike and Eddie aside to take their statements, I was left alone, sitting on the tailgate of one of the ambulances.

My gaze roved over the rest of the rehabbers. Joanie was clutching Isabella to her chest with one hand, wildly gesturing with the other as she talked the ear off one of the uniformed officers, who looked like he'd rather be anywhere but there. Antoine stood stoically beside her, his arms crossed over his chest like a big statue, though I swear I might've seen him roll his eyes at his wife once. Or twice.

Dirk was crumpled over on a planter ledge, alternating between sobbing and spilling his story to another one of the plainclothes detectives. Apple was hugging her arms around her bare midriff and sniffling, the mascara running down her cheeks an indication that the evening's emotions had gotten the better of her. Ice, on the other hand, looked to be trying to find any cameras that would film him, in the hopes that some of this might still air somewhere.

"Cam!"

I looked up to find Trace jogging toward me. As soon as he reached me, he scooped me in his arms and lifted me off the ground in a tight embrace. My ribs groaned in protest, but my heart melted into him. When he finally let go, he set me down gently and held me at arm's length as he looked me over, concern etched across his brow. "Are you okay?"

I nodded, not trusting my voice as tears suddenly backed up in my throat. The truth was, I was okay. But for a brief few seconds there I'd had my doubts. And the fact that I'd stared down death while Trace and I still hadn't had a chance to properly make up had almost been as disconcerting as the crazed anchorwoman with the gun.

I leaned against his chest, feeling suddenly weak. Until now, I'd been running on pure adrenaline, but it was starting to wear off. I found myself near the brink of exhaustion. "I don't want to fight anymore," I said, totally meaning it.

Trace wound his arms tightly around me again, and I felt him kissing the top of my head. "Me neither. This whole thing has been a huge mistake. I'm so sorry I dragged you into this."

I shook my head against his chest. "No, it's not your fault." I paused. "But the next time we wanna work on our relationship, can we just go to Cabo or something?" I asked, only half joking.

I felt Trace's chest bob up and down as he chuckled. "Deal."

I vaguely became aware of footsteps approaching and tore myself reluctantly out of Trace's embrace to find Apple at our side.

"Hey," she said tentatively. "You okay, Cam?"

I gave her what I hoped was a reassuring smile. "I'm fine." Ish.

"So…is it true what they're saying?" she asked, her voice suddenly sounding very young and small.

"That Ellen killed Dr. William?" I nodded. "Yeah. She confessed everything to me before she tried to shoot me."

Apple swallowed a small sob and reached a hand out to place it over mine. "And it was all over…me?"

I bit my lip, not sure how much the detectives had told her. But they must have clued her in that she was the long-lost

Baby Meriwether/Price. I studied the grieving young woman, noting for the first time how she shared Dr. Georgia's upturned nose and had Dirk's dark, round eyes. How had I not seen the resemblance before?

"Ellen killed Dr. William because of her own vanity," I said, trying to ease the girl's mind. "She was afraid of the scandal that Dr. William would cause for his own gain and what it would do to her career. None of this is your fault." I paused. "Did you know you were given up for adoption?"

She sighed out a shaky breath and nodded. "Yeah, my parents told me when I was probably five or six. So I've almost always known. Honestly, I've always been curious about my birth parents, but I didn't want to upset Mom and Dad by looking for them. I mean, my mom and dad are great, and I was never missing anything." She bit her lip as if just thinking about the couple made her want Mommy and Daddy again.

"That's great to hear," a voice interjected. I looked behind Apple to find Dirk standing there, his shoulders hunched, his posture looking as beaten-down as I'd ever seen the soap star. Beside him stood Dr. Georgia. I had to blink to recognize the woman, as it was the first time I'd seen real emotion shining on her face. Her eyes were wet with tears, her mouth pulled up in a smile as she stared at her daughter. Both of her hands were clenched tightly in front of her, as if she had to keep herself from reaching out to Apple.

"I'm glad to hear you had a good life," Dirk added.

Apple's eyes filled with tears again. "I…I don't know what to say. I mean…I never thought I'd have the opportunity to meet you." Her eyes went to Georgia's. "Either of you." She paused. "Mom?"

Dr. Georgia let out a sob and launched herself at the girl, both arms wrapping her in a tight hug. Dirk joined in, his hands going around Apple's back as she and Georgia clutched each other.

I turned away, feeling like we were maybe intruding on the personal scene.

"Maybe we should give them some privacy," Trace whispered in my ear, mirroring my thoughts.

I nodded and let Trace help me down from the ambulance and toward the main house. Only Ice hailed us down about halfway there.

"Yo, shorty," he said, nodding his chin at me. "Can I talk to you for a second?" He shot a glance at Trace. "Alone."

Trace put a protective hand on my back.

"I'll be fine," I told him with a reassuring nod. Now that it was clear Ice was all bark and not a murderous biter, I wasn't worried.

Trace looked reluctant but finally said, "I'll be right inside." He slipped through the French doors, leaving Ice and me alone on the patio.

Once Trace had gone inside, I turned back to face Ice. "What's up?" I asked, guessing it had something to do with his fiancée and her newfound family.

Ice dropped his gaze to the ground and shifted uncomfortably from one foot to the other. "So, you wanna keep all that 'Morty' stuff on the down low, huh?"

I blinked at him, understanding slow to set in. When it did, I couldn't help the hitch of a smile pulling my lips. "You mean you prefer not to let your fans know you're really Morton Steinberger, chess player from the burbs?"

Ice quickly looked over both shoulders. "Quiet with that stuff, yo!" He leaned in. "How did you even find that out?"

"It's kinda my job to find stuff out," I said simply.

Ice met my gaze. "Well, could you kinda forget it? And, like, not print it?" He looked at me with pleading eyes, for once looking more like the scared middle-class boy he'd really been than some crude punk from a street gang. "Seriously, yo. It would ruin my career."

I took my time in responding, wanting to let him sweat over his dilemma for a little longer. Then I cleared my throat. "I'll make you a deal," I said, looking him square in the eyes. "I'll keep your secret. I'll make sure no one at the *Informer* prints it. I'll carry your true backstory to the grave." I held up a finger. "But I will *only* do this if you get some anger-management counseling *and* promise to lay off Apple. She's a good person and she deserves better."

His shoulders slumped. "I know she does. That's why I get so jealous sometimes, you know? Like, I know she's just gonna leave me when some better guy comes along."

I shook my head at him. "No, she's not. Apple loves you."

His eyes jumped up to meet mine. "For real? She tell you that?"

"She didn't have to tell me. It's obvious to anyone with two eyes that she's devoted to you. I mean, really, who else would put up with your crap?"

Ice smiled. "Good point." He held out a hand to shake. "Okay, you got a deal, shorty. You keep quiet, Apple gets treated like a queen."

I shook on it. But before he walked away, I added, "Just one more thing I have to know."

Ice looked at me expectantly.

"What was with that whole 'if I did it' thing? Where were you really when Dr. William was killed?"

Ice's cheeks colored, and he looked down at the ground. "Dude, I got a rep to maintain. It looked good for my brand to be kinda mysterious about it, you know?"

Figures. It had all been for the cameras after all.

"But I totally cooperated with the police. I told the detectives where I was!" he protested.

"Which was?"

He bit his lip and leaned in again. "You ain't gonna print this, right?"

"Scout's honor." Okay, so I'd never been a Girl Scout, and I had my fingers crossed behind my back, but he didn't need to know that.

"When Apple went to the pool, I was all stressed out about Dirk checking out my girl—at least that's what I thought he was doin' at the time—so I did some yoga and then took a bubble bath. That kind of stuff helps me relax, you know?"

I had to bite my lip to keep the laughter at bay. A gangster rapper who did yoga and took bubble baths? Oh, how I wished I hadn't just promised not to print that.

"Anyway, we good?" he asked, lifting his chin again.

I nodded. "We're good."

He gave me a quick fist bump to seal the deal before heading back toward the police cars, ambulances, and general commotion to find his fiancée again.

I quickly slipped inside before anyone else could waylay me, thankful that this nightmare of a week was finally over.

CHAPTER NINETEEN

———

NASTY NEWSWOMAN NOW NICKED!

I grinned as I read Tina's latest headline. It was accompanied, of course, by an embarrassing photo of Ellen Bents toppling into the pit of fiery coals at the *Celebrity Relationship Rehab* house. As much as I'd like to take credit for it, it had obviously been snapped by Mike or Eddie as they'd blinded the woman with their cameras. I'd had to trade Mike four shots of celebrity baby bumps and a promise to call them the next time I got a hot tip about a new Taylor Swift boy toy for it. Though, I had to admit it was worth it as I read the rest of Tina's article.

Former national news anchor, Ellen Bents, was formally charged yesterday with the murder of reality TV show host, Dr. William Meriwether. While the accused pleaded not guilty, this reporter has it on good authority that the police have a slam-dunk case against her...including a confession to the media!

With police shutting down all further filming on the set of Dr. William's popular Celebrity Relationship Rehab *television show and confiscating all past footage as evidence, the network has made the decision to cancel any further episodes of the show. But have no fear, reality fans! His surviving wife, Dr. Georgia Meriwether, and her long-lost biological daughter and noted adult film star, Apple Pie, will be co-hosting a new show about family counseling. The show is set to start filming this fall with Reisner Productions. If we're lucky, we may even see a few appearances from the star of* The Charming & the Reckless, *Dirk Price, the third member of this long-lost family. Though they may have to work around Dirk's newly busy schedule, as amidst his nomination for his third daytime Emmy, he's just signed on for his twenty-eighth season playing the devilishly handsome Dr. Spencer Carlin on the popular soap opera as well as accepted the role of Tarzan in the upcoming film,* Aging in the Jungle.

"Pretty good, right?" Tina asked, reading over my shoulder from the passenger seat of my Jeep.

I nodded. Once I'd finally made it home to my own bed and blissfully small, cozy apartment, the first person I'd called had been Tina, who had shown up on my doorstep with a bottle of wine and a bucket of fried chicken, ready to hear all the gory details, which, over the next few days as the dust had settled on the scandal, had kept trickling in.

Dirk Price had been all over the news, hitting the morning-show circuit, where I'd learned exactly what Dr. Georgia's ambiguous alibi had been—she'd been with Dirk. Dirk had been unable to sleep, the emotions at seeing Dr. Georgia again too much. He'd waited until Ellen had left him alone in their suite before seeking out his long-lost lover. While he'd promised all the two had done was talk about old times, there was a rumor going around that Dr. Georgia just might be his date to the Emmys. One that didn't seem too farfetched after Dirk's interview with Ellen's former co-anchor on *US Evening News,* where he'd told America he was filing for divorce. And that he was already in talks with a major publishing house to pen his memoir about his life married to a murderer.

Ice Kreme had dropped his latest album a few weeks early to capitalize on the notoriety of being caught up in a murder investigation. He'd even re-titled it "How I'd Have Done It." It had been all I could do to remain true to my word and not leak his less-than-gangster roots, but when Allie printed the tip that Ice and Apple had finally set a date for their wedding—next spring—I couldn't help but be happy for the couple. Of course, I'd been the one to give her the tip, after I'd received my save-the-date invitation from Apple.

Even Trace had been okay after news hit that the reality show was canceled. Just after the story broke, he'd received a call from his agent about a part he'd been waiting on for months. He'd landed a serious role in an upcoming indie drama alongside none other than Sir Anthony Hopkins. While it wasn't his usual action-star fare, it had Oscar potential written all over it. And

Trace couldn't have been happier. The funniest part was that Trace had actually caught the casting director's eye with his performance in *Piranha Man*. Maybe the film had been a blessing in disguise.

He was scheduled to begin filming in London in mid-July—after we finally enjoyed some alone time, of course. Though the show was canceled, we got to keep the prize from the treasure chest Trace had recovered during the island challenge right before I'd been hit on the head. Turns out, it was a weeklong, all-expenses-paid trip for two to a couples' spa and resort in Bermuda.

The only one who hadn't fared so well from our rehabber group was Joanie Parker. In the exclusive interview that Antoine had been so gracious to give the *Informer*, he admitted that he'd actually been planning to give Joanie an empty ring box at our last relationship drill and leave rehab alone. In fact, the business card I'd found in their suite had belonged to Antoine. Joanie had found it in his things and confronted him about it. Antoine had admitted to her then that he wanted a divorce, and that was the secret I'd overheard them arguing about by the pool that day— Joanie had insisted that he keep quiet about it until after the show so she could still get her payday. In fact, she'd even cajoled him into trying to break into the control room to delete the footage of their argument. At first he'd agreed with her plan, going so far as to make sure all the other guests were tucked away in their rooms so as not to get caught, including checking on the occupant of the Doghouse, yours truly. When I hadn't been in the house, he'd gotten nervous. And when Voice Number One had caught him at the control room door, he'd abandoned the idea altogether, opting instead for a very real and heartfelt session in the confession room.

But, true to his word, he had waited until it was announced that the show was canceled, and then Antoine *Eustace* Parker (yeah, turns out he *was* on the attorney's client list after all) had filed for divorce, citing irreconcilable differences. Though, in the interview he'd had some much more colorful language to describe the differences between him and his soon-to-be-ex-wife. Who knew he could be so articulate?

Felix had run the story alongside the incredibly unflattering drunken photos I'd taken of Joanie from her balcony. I had to say, I almost felt sorry for Joanie.

Almost.

"I'm so happy for Apple," I said, focusing on the happy ending to all of this as I finished reading Tina's latest article and swiped my phone off. "It looks like she's about to get the TV career she wanted after all."

"Hey, maybe if she goes mainstream enough, she can even ditch that wanna-be idiot of hers."

I shrugged. "I don't know. Ice isn't all that bad."

Tina looked at me like I'd grown two heads.

I let out a chuckle. "Okay, he's no Don Juan."

"Honey, he's not even a Don Knotts."

We both dissolved into unladylike laughter that was only broken up when Tina pointed out my windshield to a figure on the sidewalk. "There he goes!"

We were parked just down the street from the run-down building that housed Thomas Charles Investigations. Ever since my encounter with the sleazy private investigator, I'd been unable to shake my burning curiosity about what kind of dirt he'd dug up on Trace and me. A curiosity that I'd confessed to Tina, and she'd come up with the bright idea of breaking into Charles's offices to find out. I had a feeling she was hoping to print any juicy tidbits we uncovered about the other *Celebrity Relationship Rehab* guests. I had to admit, the thought had crossed my mind as well.

And as we watched Thomas Charles's ample frame walk out of the building and get into a dented midsized sedan parked at the curb, it looked like we were about to get our chance.

"Let's hit it," Tina said, reaching behind the passenger seat to grab the toolkit she'd placed on the Jeep's floorboard.

Both dressed in fashionable breaking-and-entering black, Tina and I climbed out of the Jeep and stealthily made our way toward the back of Charles's building. I silently pointed to the corner window that belonged to his office. We pressed against the wall, sticking to the shadows, and I kept lookout while Tina removed a miniature crowbar from her toolkit and began prying at the windowsill. Within a minute's time, she had it open and was peeking her head into the office. I thought about asking her how often she did this sort of thing, but then I thought better of it. It was always good for a working relationship to maintain plausible deniability whenever possible.

Tina gave me a thumbs-up to let me know the coast was clear. She hoisted herself through the open window and then helped me climb inside. I fumbled around in the dark for the lamp I remembered seeing on Charles's desk. Switching it on, I saw that nothing had changed in the week since I'd visited the office. Papers were still scattered across every square inch of the desk, and the boxy old computer hummed quietly. I pressed the power button on the monitor, and the screen lit up. A box appeared, asking for a password. Crap.

"Any idea what it might be?" Tina asked, coming to stand beside me.

Frowning, I swept my gaze around the room, looking for something that might spark an idea. My eyes came to rest of the little hula dancer on the opposite corner of the desk. "Let's try *hulagirl*," I said, my fingers moving swiftly over the keyboard. The password was incorrect. "Hmm. How about *hulahottie*?" No luck.

"Try replacing some of the vowels with numbers," Tina suggested. "Replace the *o* with a zero and the *e* with a three."

"Good idea." I typed in *hulah0tti3* and pressed *Enter*. Still nothing. Chewing my lower lip, I changed the *a* for an @ symbol: *hul@h0tti3*. The little box disappeared, and Charles's desktop files began to load. I almost let out a cheer. "You're brilliant," I told Tina, tossing her a smile.

"You're welcome," she said, grinning back at me. "I'll poke around his office while you search his computer files."

I turned back to the monitor and read through the names of the folders on the desktop. Nothing stuck out, so I used the command keys to begin a search for any file name with *William* in it. The search yielded a zipped folder labeled *William Meriwether*. Bingo.

"I've got something," I told Tina as I clicked the file open. In seconds flat, she was beside me, reading over my shoulder as a line of new folders appeared, each one labeled with a rehabber's name. Unable to resist the temptation, I clicked on the files for the other guests.

Apple's secret was that she had been busted for shoplifting once as a teenager. While it was certainly a mistake on her part, the statute of limitations on lifting the pair of legwarmers had long ago run out. Ice's file contained a copy of a lawsuit from another young rapper claiming that Ice had stolen his beats. Ice had filed a countersuit, claiming that the other artist was lying to try to drum up some publicity for his own music. Maybe slightly embarrassing but public record. Nothing earth-shattering.

Antoine's folder had an interview with an old teammate from his high school football team who accused the NFL star of shaving points during one of their playoff games. I clicked on Joanie's file and thought I could have saved myself a lot of grief if Charles had just let me see it when I'd asked. It contained the names of her parents—George and Sandy Smith. He was a sanitation worker, and she had a job in a factory that made tractor parts. They both lived in Wisconsin, where Joanie had been born and raised, according to the files. I smirked. Joanie's big secret was that she was from middle class Middle America?

I shook my head, clicking on the next file, labeled *Dirk Price*. It featured the cover of an adult film from the early eighties called *Young Studs II starring Dirk Bigly*. My nose crinkled. "Ew."

Tina made a gagging sound behind me. "I could have gone my whole life without picturing that," she said. "Gross."

I quickly shut the folder and opened Ellen's. Ironically, hers was empty. Apparently she'd lived her entire life trying to avoid anyone getting any dirt on her. A lot of good that had done her in the end.

Only two files were left. Trace's and mine. I clicked on Trace's folder first, feeling my pulse quicken. I recalled what Charles had said about Trace's secret the day I'd visited his office and steeled myself for a "real doozy."

A photograph filled the screen. It had been taken from nearly a football field's length away and featured Trace walking into a beauty salon in Beverly Hills. A second photo showed him emerging from the same salon with a red-haired woman on his arm. A typed note in the file reader *Cheater?*

"Uh-oh," I heard Tina say beside me. "Who is that?"

I grinned as relief flooded through me. "Trace's cousin, Margaret. She was in town visiting from Minnesota."

"Ha!" Tina said. I could hear the relief in her voice as well.

If Charles had stuck around long enough after taking his photograph, he would have seen my Jeep pull up at the corner to pick up Trace and Margaret outside the salon. Trace had treated his cousin to a little pampering while he'd done an interview for the *L.A. Times*, and I'd met up with one of my sources to follow up on a lead about a certain A-lister's wedding plans. Then we'd all gone to brunch together.

I opened the folder with my name on it, feeling a lot less anxious. It seemed Thomas Charles's definition of bombshell dirt was a lot different than mine. I'd yet to see anything worth the twenty grand he'd tried to extort from me.

Sure enough, I barked out a laugh when I saw the contents of my folder.

One that was echoed by Tina as she dissolved into howls behind me. "Well," she managed between laughs, "Charles was right about one thing. That is certainly scandalous. That hair is a crime of fashion!"

I wiped a tear of laughter from my eye. "I was a rebellious fifteen-year-old. Everyone has their awkward phase." I glanced down at the photograph of teenage me. It was my sophomore year school photo, and it had been taken two days after I'd decided to dye my hair black and then get a perm. My head looked like a giant ball of fuzzy black corkscrews. It was hideous, and my mother had paid a small fortune to get the color stripped and return my hair to normal. The picture also showed off my green army jacket, which I'd worn with army boots religiously for a week before I'd moved on to some other fashion trend.

Granted it was not the most flattering picture, and it would certainly inspire some laughter if it hit the pages of *ED* as Charles had threatened, possibly even at Trace's expense. But after staring down an actual killer from the barrel end of a gun, this hardly registered on my importance meter.

Still... I quickly deleted the photo. In fact, as Tina got her laughter under control, I deleted all eight folders, making sure they were gone from the trash bin as well. Sure, it was possible someone could still recover them from the hard drive, but from the looks of his dinosaur computer equipment, I'd take a chance that it was beyond Charles's technical know-how.

"Come on, let's get out of here," Tina whispered.

I nodded. "Just one more thing..."

I opened the top desk drawer that I'd seen Charles deposit my check into. Still there. I picked it up and promptly shoved it into my pocket.

"Now let's get out of here," I said, feeling a whole lot lighter.

We backtracked through the window again and quietly slid it shut before darting through the shadows to my Jeep.

Tina giggled again as we slid inside and I turned the engine over.

"What?" I asked her.

She shook her head. "Nothing. Just wondering what Trace would say if he saw that photo of you."

I turned on her. "You wouldn't dare."

Tina shot me a wicked grin in the dim interior lighting. "I don't know. Can you ever really trust a *tabloid girl*?" she joked.

I laughed. "Would a margarita from Joe's Taco Casa buy your silence?"

"You're on."

I grinned again. Mostly because I knew we'd both be expensing it to Felix's account in the morning. Hey, how could he complain? He'd gotten the story of the decade, I'd just saved him three grand, and I had it on good authority that Cameron Diaz was vacationing in Bermuda right then with her hottie...conveniently on the same island Trace and I would be staying at. If Felix played his cards right, I might even make it a week-long *working* vacation...

ABOUT THE AUTHORS

Gemma Halliday is the #1 Amazon, *New York Times* & *USA Today* bestselling author of several mystery series. Gemma's books have received numerous awards, including a Golden Heart, two National Reader's Choice awards, three RITA nominations, a RONE award for best mystery, and two Killer Nashville Silver Falchion Awards for best cozy mystery and readers' choice. She currently lives in the San Francisco Bay Area with her large, loud, and loving family.

To learn more about Gemma, visit her online at www.GemmaHalliday.com

USA Today bestselling author Anne Marie Stoddard used to work in radio, and it rocked! After studying Music Business at the University of Georgia, Anne Marie worked for several music venues, radio stations, and large festivals before trading in her backstage pass for a pen and paper (Okay, so she might have kept the pass...). Her debut novel, *Murder at Castle Rock*, was the winner of the 2012 AJC Decatur Book Festival & BookLogix Publishing Services, Inc. Writing Contest, and the 2013 Book Junkie's Choice Award Winner for Best Debut Fiction Novel. It was also a finalist for Best Mystery/Thriller in the 2014 RONE Awards.

Aside from all things music and books, Anne Marie loves college football, Starbucks iced coffee, red wine, and anything pumpkin-flavored. She is a member of Sisters in Crime and the Sisters in Crime Guppies chapter. Anne Marie is currently hard at work on several books.

To learn more about Anne Marie, visit her online at: amstoddardbooks.com

Other Hollywood Headlines novels in print now...

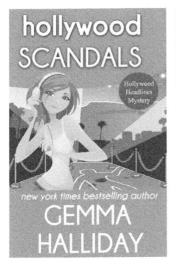

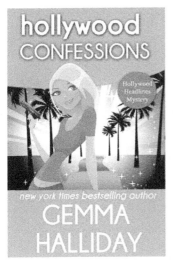
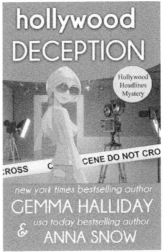

www.GemmaHalliday.com

Made in the USA
Monee, IL
04 August 2021

74739201R00132